Return to Sherwood

Mandi Grace

Chapter 1

IDA

A shriek pierced the air as Ida pulled bread down from the shelf where it was kept, unwrapping the simple cloth that kept it safe from unwanted creatures. Ida glanced toward the door of her home, which was standing wide open to afford her a view of her children while she put supper on the table. William and Edward were wrestling on the ground. They seemed to be enjoying themselves. Ida wasn't sure which of the twins had screamed, but as neither seemed concerned at present, she went back to work. Allen would be coming in from the fields soon and would want to eat. The boys, too, would be starving; they always were.

Ida cut a few slices of bread so it was ready to be eaten and set the slices and the loaf on the table. Then she moved toward the hearth to pull the pottage from the fire. Today's meal consisted of chicken boiled in ale with bread and spices.

As Ida worked to prepare the meal a shadow fell over the room. Ida turned to the man in the doorway, expecting to see her husband Allen. Instead, she saw Robin Hood.

"Smells good," Robin grinned. His blonde hair was askew, as it always was, and his blue eyes were sparkling with mischief.

"What brings you to our farm, Robin? Did you bring Lucy and Marian?"

"No. My wife and daughter are still in Nottingham. Has Allen returned yet?"

"No."

Ida went to the door and called the boys to come inside. They reluctantly set aside the sticks they were using to beat each other and trudged into the house. It was a simple house. The room at the front containing a hearth, a table where Ida had set out supper, a number of shelves on the walls filled with food, pots, and various tools. There were two doors on the wall opposite the front of the house, both leading to bedchambers. Ida and Allen were simple farmers, not wealthy by any means.

Robin helped the boys to sit on chairs around the table and then plopped into one himself. The light in his eyes dimmed a little. "I have news."

"Oh? Of a negative nature it seems?"

"Yes."

"Well?"

"I will wait for Allen and break the news to both of you, if that's alright."

"Of course." Ida helped her boys to a slice of bread each. It was best to keep them occupied until Allen arrived, or they'd likely tear down the house.

Robin tousled William's hair, the sparkle returning to his eyes. "How much trouble have they been causing this week?"

"Probably about as much as Marian," Ida replied. Her boys were rambunctious it was true, and disaster often followed in their wake. Yet Robin's daughter Marian was equally as prone to causing disaster.

It wasn't long before Allen entered the house. "Robin!"

"Allen," Robin stood to shake his friend's hand before returning to his seat.

"What brings you to our humble abode?" Allen asked, seating himself at the table as Ida began to dish up food for everyone.

"None for me, Ida," Robin said. "I have to get back to Nottingham. Allen, I've come with news."

"What news?"

"King Richard is dead."

"Oh my." Ida nearly dropped the ladle on the floor.

Allen sighed. "How?"

"Fighting in France; an arrow wound that festered, apparently. I only just received the news in a letter from Queen Eleanor. Her letter was scarce in detail. I'm bringing the whole gang back to Nottingham, Allen. We need to decide what to do if John is crowned the next King of England."

"You expect him to hold a grudge against us for our part in stopping his rebellion?"

"Of course I do. You don't?"

"I do," Allen sighed. "It's hard to imagine the king gone."

"I know." Robin ran a hand over his face. "It seems only yesterday we were a part of his King's guard."

The King was dead.

Ida had met him only a few times herself, but she knew Robin had been his friend and would grieve his loss. Allen, too, had known him well. Both Robin and Allen had been members of his King's guard during the Third Crusade.

Ida was less consumed with grief and more concerned about what would happen now that Richard the Lion-Heart was no longer the King of England.

What would become of them all if Prince John became King?

Prince John had tried to take power in England while Richard was off on his crusade to retake Jerusalem and Robin had fought him at every turn. Robin had been branded an outlaw and over the years of the rebellion had gathered a small band of friends around him to help fight Prince John.

Ida and her husband Allen had been among the outlaws of Robin's gang. They'd stopped executions, ambushed caravans carrying the spoils of unfair taxes, and in general been a nuisance to Prince John while bringing hope to the suffering people of England. If John became King now that Richard was dead, he would likely want revenge.

"I am inviting everyone to Nottingham," Robin said, interrupting Ida's train of thought. "The whole gang. You will all be staying at Nottingham castle until we know what's going on."

"We'll come tomorrow," Allen said. "We'll need time to pack for an extended stay."

"Of course." Robin stood. "I must get back to Nottingham. I will look forward to your arrival tomorrow."

WILL

Will Scarlett dismounted in the courtyard of Nottingham Castle, surveying the familiar surroundings with a glance. He handed the reins of his white horse, Rebel, to the servant boy who came running over from the stables to his left.

It had been a few weeks since he'd been in Nottingham. Robin didn't often send for him for business purposes any longer and therefore visits to the city were mostly social events that occurred less frequently as the years went on. There had been a time when Nottingham had been his home, but it was no longer. He was only here now because Robin had sent for him.

"Did you expect it to look different?" Dusty asked with a laugh.

Will turned to help his wife dismount her own horse, one they had borrowed from the livery in Middlesborough because they only owned Rebel. She had their eight month old daughter Daniyah in her arms.

"No, I did not expect it to be different. I was simply taking a look around. Robin likes to improve things, I was curious if there had been any alterations."

"Sure," Dusty nodded, unconvinced.

Will then pulled their son John, three years old, down from the horse's back as well. John went running up the stone steps leading to the castle door the moment his feet touched the ground. He loved visiting Nottingham and seeing Robin Hood's daughter Marian.

Dusty passed her horse along to the stable boy and then took Will's hand as they followed John to the door. "I wonder what news Robin will have for us?"

"It seemed urgent, whatever it was," Will replied.

Only yesterday Will had received a cryptic letter from his friend asking him to bring his family to Nottingham because he wished to relate something of importance to them. Robin was rarely mysterious, and Will had therefore set about getting his family ready for a visit to Nottingham the very next day.

Years ago during the rebellion, when Prince John had attempted to wrest power from the King and take control of England, Will had fought with Robin Hood. He'd been living in Sherwood, partaking in daring rescues and clever ambushes for years.

That was where he had met his wife, Dusty. An Arab woman with impressive healing skills whom Robin had befriended during the Crusades and who had come home to England with him to help in the fight against John Lackland. They had been married while the gang were still outlaws living in Sherwood Forest. After King Richard had come home, however, they had moved to Will's hometown of Middlesborough. It was only a few hours ride from Nottingham, but far enough that they didn't make daily or even weekly trips to see their old friends.

When they entered the castle they traversed its halls with ease, having been inside many times before. They found Robin and his wife Lucy in the library.

Robin shook Will's hand and gave Dusty a quick hug before Lucy suggested she take John and Daniyah to where her own daughter, Marian, was playing with her nurse. As the children followed Lucy out of the room, Dusty asked what was at the forefront of Will's mind as well.

"What is your news, Robin? You've been very cryptic."

Robin leaned against a table that was pushed up against one wall, crossing his arms. "King Richard is dead."

"Dead?" Will started. "Are you sure?"

"Yes. He's dead. I'm bringing everyone back to Nottingham, Will. I don't know what Prince John will do once he's crowned the King of England, but you know he's going to want to punish us for all we did during his rebellion."

"Indeed. He's always wanted to. And now he'll have the power to act on that impulse."

"That's why I'm gathering the gang," Robin said. "We'll decide together what we can do, once we know what Prince John is going to do. You'll stay here, won't you?"

"Of course we will," Dusty said.

"I'll head back to Middlesborough today," Will said. "We'll need clothes and other belongings if we're staying for an extended period of time."

"I probably should have explained my intention in more detail," Robin grinned.

"I don't mind a good ride, Robin. I'll be back this evening and we can discuss this further. Is the rest of the gang here, then?"

"Not everyone, yet. But I've sent for them."

Will honestly couldn't remember the last time the entire group had been together after the end of their Sherwood days. They saw each other at least once a year, sometimes more, but in smaller factions. Rarely, if ever, did the entire gang gather together. Robin was clearly worried about Prince John's retribution if he'd gathered the entire gang.

GUY

The cold stone floor echoed with the sound of boots as Guy strode across the corridor. He stopped at the great oak doors leading into the Great Hall and glanced over his shoulder to be sure he hadn't lost his wife. Faith was only a few yards behind him, hurrying up the hallway with their small daughter in her arms. Sunlight streamed through the open casements to her right, making her wheat-colored hair glow.

Guy swung open the heavy doors and marched into the Great Hall. He'd been in this room more times than he could count since coming to Nottingham nearly a decade before, but the furnishings were far different now than they had been when the previous Sheriff held court here. Then the long room had been cold, the stone walls barren of any adornment, with merely a wooden table and the Sheriff's own throne. Now, however, bright tapestries hung along the walls, many candelabra were spaced around the room to bring light to the inhabitants, and there were chairs piled with cushions scattered throughout.

Logs crackled cheerfully in the fireplace at the far end of the room, but the group gathered around the long wooden table in the center of the room were anything but cheerful. Robin Hood, Earl of Locksley and current Sheriff of Nottingham, was there, leaning forward with his hands on the table, speaking solemnly. His blond hair was as unruly as ever, and his blue eyes were piercing as he surveyed the group around the table.

Will Scarlett stood to his right, an arm wrapped around his wife Dusty, both listening to Robin quietly. Allen, Ida, and various other members of the gang were all sitting and standing around the table listening to Robin speak.

"...we have no way of knowing what sort of danger this presents. Arthur may, in fact, prove harmless. John, however, will be far from harmless should he become King. There is the smallest of chances that Arthur would be sympathetic to us..."

As Robin droned on at the head of the table, Guy took in the room; everyone around the table was watching Robin and taking in every word.

Much, Robin's oldest childhood friend and easily the most likely to panic in a crisis had an almost comical look of concern on his face.

Mark, the late Lady Marian's brother, and Little John were paying rapt attention to Robin's speech. Little John's wife Elinor was equally intrigued.

In front of the fireplace, and seemingly less concerned with the serious conversation at the table, sat Robin's wife Lucy, Andrew's wife Jane, and a very pregnant wife of Much whose name was Mary. They were entertaining a flock of children. Every member of the gang, save one, had at least one child after the rebellion and they were a raucous bunch.

Guy glanced around once more. Every member of Robin Hood's gang, still living, was present. He couldn't remember the last time they'd all been in the same room together.

Andrew, Guy's oldest and dearest friend, came to greet him as soon as he noticed him nearing the table. "We've been waiting for you."

"I know. I am sorry to delay you all. But it is difficult at times to get Lucy to sit still long enough to get dressed." He

9

gestured to the small child in Faith's arms as his wife came to stand beside him.

Andrew grinned. "Richard is the same way."

They approached the table and polite greetings were exchanged. Then Robin steered the conversation toward the real reason they were gathered.

"King Richard is dead."

Silence met this announcement. They were all aware of this development and its implications.

"Rumor is that Prince John is returning to England to claim the throne. Arthur of Brittany is also vying for the throne, but I think we can all agree that Prince John is going to win this political fight."

"Let's focus on the facts," Mark said. The brother of the late Lady Marian was seated at the table between Little John and Much.

"Richard is dead," Robin replied. "Prince John has every right to come back to England and he is an heir to the throne. His nephew Arthur is also an heir, and to some minds has the greater claim as he is the son of King Henry's eldest son...but I am convinced Prince John will win out."

"If Prince John becomes King, what will that mean for us?" Much asked.

"Well I think we can all assume he'll remove me from my office," Robin said. There were nods of agreement. Robin had been the Sheriff of Nottingham since the days of living in Sherwood had ended, being appointed by King Richard the Lion-Heart as soon as he had returned to England from his imprisonment in Austria.

"Will he arrest us?" Dusty asked. "Or will he find it more necessary to kill us?"

"He'll probably want you all executed," Guy said. "He is much like our previous Sheriff in that regard."

Though he wished to forget it, memories of working alongside the late Sheriff during Prince John's rebellion while King Richard was in the Holy Land came flooding back. Guy knew perfectly well what atrocities he had committed, and he abhorred the things he had done to gain power and strength.

"Then what do we do?" Ida asked from where she sat at the end of the table, her husband Allen standing behind her. "Go back to Sherwood?"

"Possibly," Robin replied.

"Or we could leave the country," Allen suggested.

"But we'll come back, right?" Much asked. "We won't leave permanently."

"Maybe Prince John won't decide to harm us," Faith said. "Perhaps he'll leave us alone to live in peace."

"That isn't likely," Guy replied. "I'll wager he'll hunt us down and kill us all."

Guy was the only one present who had known Prince John personally, if only briefly. The man didn't strike him as someone who was likely to forget or forgive past grievances. And Robin Hood and his gang had undermined him at every opportunity when he had tried to take over the country in King Richard's absence.

"So what do we do, Robin?" Will asked.

"We'll all have to decide what would be best for our own families," Robin said.

"No, Robin," Much said. "We stick together. All of us."

"Much is right, Robin," Dusty said. "We can hardly go our separate ways now. We're family. Each and every one of us."

"But it may be wiser to separate," Robin insisted. "We'll be less likely to be caught."

"When it is safe once more we can come back together," Mark added.

"I don't like the idea of separating," Much said.

"We can't make a decision today," Dusty said. "We'll never agree. And as of yet, there is no danger. Perhaps we can leave that discussion until the time that it is necessary."

"You're all staying here in Nottingham until then," Robin said. It wasn't a question. Indeed, Robin had summoned them as soon as news of Richard's death had reached him and it had only taken a few days for all of them to travel back to Nottingham with the intention of staying until the crisis was averted.

"We'll all stay in Nottingham until we find out what Prince John is up to," Allen replied.

Everyone agreed.

"Supper should be prepared soon," Robin said. He turned away from the table and toward the group by the fire. "Lucy, shall we take our meal in here or in one of the dining rooms?"

Lucy was sitting on the stone floor, her two-year-old daughter clambering headfirst over her shoulder and Allen's tow-headed twin boys wrestling in her lap.

"Uh," Lucy looked to Robin, confused for a split second. "Supper. Right. Here in the Great Hall, I suppose. There's more room in here. I'll tell Sarah."

"I'll do it," Much said, rising from the table. "You're a bit occupied."

12

Supper was a loud affair, mostly due to the seven children present, all three-years-old and under. Allen and Ida's twin boys, each seated on a parent's lap, were stealing utensils and food and sending them sailing across the table. Cries of "William, don't!" "Edward, put that down!" and the like were a constant refrain throughout the meal. Guy noted with a slight grin that Lucy's daughter Marian was also adding to the chaos, climbing onto the table and into the platter of meat. She was covered in duck and cranberry sauce from head to toe, various bits of food sticking out of her auburn hair.

"I do hope Prince John doesn't do anything to us," Little John's wife Elinor laughed. "If only for the sake of the children. Can you imagine living in Sherwood with this crowd?"

There were groans all around the table from the adults.

Guy looked down at his own daughter, sitting in her mother's lap quiet and content. She squirmed a bit when she wanted a bite to eat, but for the most part his little brown-haired, brown-eyed Lucy was a perfect saint.

"If John does come after us," Mark said, "do you think we could manage to be fugitives with this bunch, or would it be wiser to find them somewhere to stay safe while we go into hiding?"

"You want us to abandon our children?" Jane asked, horrified.

"I don't want you to do anything of the sort, but if we are forced back into Sherwood, or out of the country entirely, in an effort to survive, it would be no life for a child."

"I thought we were saving this discussion for another day," Dusty replied.

"Isn't it better to have a plan in place for when the danger inevitably comes?" Mark asked.

"Not tonight, Mark," Robin said. "We'll make plans for, as you say, the inevitable danger that is coming. But not tonight."

Guy looked around the table again at the other children. Marian knee deep in the pudding now, Robin reaching to pull her out. She dripped pudding all across the table as he pulled her into his lap. Will and Dusty's son John—the oldest of the children—was pulling on his father's ear and shouting across the table at the twins who were still throwing everything they could get their hands on. Allen and Ida could hardly get a bite to eat as their hands were occupied pinning down their sons. Will and Dusty's one-year-old daughter Daniyah—who held a striking resemblance to her Arab mother apart from her bright blue eyes—was trying her hardest to kick her brother, though Dusty was doing her utmost to prevent it. Tiny Richard sat in his father Andrew's arms, chewing on his fist and grinning at the chaos surrounding him as he pounded a spoon on the table with his free hand. And then there was Lucy, sitting so calmly in Faith's lap. Just watching.

Guy felt a weight land on his chest looking at her. Mark had a point. Living as fugitives was no life for a child. But could he ever leave his daughter behind?

***

Guy paused in pulling off his black boots to watch Faith putting their two-year-old daughter to sleep in a small bed across the room. Light flickered from various candles perched on surfaces

14

around the room, and a fire was crackling against one wall. After supper, the conversation had turned toward what they would do if Prince John became King and inevitably came after them. No one had a solution other than running. But run where? That was the question Guy needed to answer.

Some thought leaving the country before John could come for them was the wisest course of action. Some thought returning to Sherwood forest where they'd hidden so expertly during the rebellion was the better option. Guy wasn't sure what he thought would be best. Though Mark's proposed idea of leaving the children behind, whatever they decided otherwise, was one that he could not agree to.

Faith kissed Lucy's forehead and she rolled onto her side and sighed contentedly, nearly asleep already.

"I don't like to separate from everyone," Guy said softly from his perch on the bed, one boot still in his hand. "But if it comes to that, we can go back to my estate where I lived before coming to Nottingham all those years ago."

Faith walked slowly across the room and sat beside Guy on the edge of their bed. "Do you have an army, Guy? Because if not, having an estate won't do us much good."

"The serfs surrounding my estate are bound to me, though their loyalty is doubtful. The number of years I have been away, along with the fact that I was not a just lord when I did live there...still, the estate will at least be defensible."

"If we were going to fight a war, Robin would have us fortify Nottingham. Everyone here is loyal, and we have the castle."

Guy sighed. "I suppose that is true. I just don't like the idea of going into hiding."

"Living in Sherwood really isn't all that bad," Faith said, running a hand through Guy's dark hair. "And maybe it won't come to that after all."

"It will. I know Prince John. The previous Sheriff and I…" Guy sighed. He'd made a lot of mistakes in his life, and siding with Prince John and the previous Sheriff had been one of the worst ones. He knew he would regret the decisions he had made in his youth, and the things he had done then, for the rest of his life. "He'll want us all dead."

"Whatever comes next, you know the Lord will look after us."

"I know." Guy smiled at his wife. "I worry, that is all."

"There is no need for worry," Faith said softly. "He will watch over us."

Her faith was so sure, and had been from the first moment Guy had met her—locked in the dungeon by the previous Sheriff during Prince John's rebellion. Guy had quickly discovered that having complete trust, and therefore peace, was not something that came as easily to him as to his wife.

LUCY

Lucy wrapped her arms around her husband's shoulders, resting her chin on his head. She was worried about him.

Robin leaned back into her embrace. He was seated at a small table tucked in the corner of their bedchamber. Their large bed was across the room, and little Marian was snoring softly tucked into the blankets. The only light in the room came from the slowly dying fire in the grate behind them. Robin was reading the last letter he ever received from Richard before the late King's death.

"When are you going to have a son, my friend? I want a young Hood by the name of Richard to grace the world. You must convince Lucy to call him that. I won't allow for anything less. I wish I could see Marian. I'm sure she does her mother justice, and her namesake as well."

Most of the letter was amusing condolences in regard to some small complaint of a villager in the shire that Robin had expressed annoyance about to the King. Richard felt that his job was harder than Robin's, but at least he could understand the sentiment of being annoyed by the many complaints of those underneath him. It was the end of the letter, however, that Robin kept rereading. The desire for a son of Robin's to be called Richard, and then a short paragraph expressing his warmest friendship.

Robin had met the King on the Third Crusade and had soon gained his trust, becoming one of his four personal guards. It was during that time that they became friends. Their life experiences were vastly different as was their age, but somehow they had become close friends, relying on each other in battle and over the years leaning on each other when in need of advice for political or personal matters.

Other letters from Richard lay scattered on the small table, becoming less and less visible as the red fire behind them died down.

"Rest in the knowledge that he is safe with our Lord."

"I'm trying," Robin sighed.

Lucy hadn't known the king as well as Robin. She hadn't met him until after his return from imprisonment in Austria and had only known him a few short days before he left Nottingham, leaving Robin as Sheriff. In the years following she had read many of his letters to Robin but hadn't written to him herself. Her grief was for England losing their king, and for her husband losing a friend, but not for herself.

Robin's pain, however, was something that she would carry. Lucy tightened her embrace and Robin chuckled.

"Don't strangle me."

Lucy kissed the top of his head. "Sorry."

"Come on," Robin tossed aside the letter and stood, pulling her toward their sleeping daughter. "It's time to rest. I cannot remain melancholy forever. When John becomes King, there will be much to occupy my mind, I am sure."

Chapter 2

GUY

Guy stepped into the library, intent on finding the maps and charts of Nottingham castle and the surrounding city. He'd studied them extensively when he first came to Nottingham years ago, under the service of the worst Sheriff the shire had ever seen. He'd been searching for various things back then; the quickest routes his men could take to get away from angry mobs or ambushes from the outlaws, the secret ways those outlaws traveled stealthily through the city. He never had figured out the latter.

Though, years later, when he was a changed man and working with Robin Hood instead of against him, Robin had admitted that more often than not, they weren't stealthy at all. The people of Nottingham simply loved Robin of Locksley and would do their utmost to protect him—distracting any soldiers who happened to be on the same street if Robin came to town. Guy often wondered what it would be like to be so well loved and respected.

He had inspired fear and awe in the common people in his youth. Disgust and anger had been the usual emotions felt toward him during the rebellion of Prince John. Even after Guy had switched sides and begun to help Robin and the others, no one ever truly forgave him; at least, not among the people. Most of the gang had moved past his mistakes.

Guy moved toward the nearest shelf. Every wall had one, from floor to ceiling. There were several tables stacked with parchments in the center of the room, and a handful of carved wooden chairs as well.

Today Guy was after those charts he'd once known so well so that he could study the defensibility of Nottingham. Robin insisted they weren't going to put up a fight, but Guy wanted to be prepared for a siege or an all-out war with King John.

As he searched the shelves for the parchments he wanted, the door opened and Ida strode in. She paused in the doorway and glared at him.

Guy continued his mission, pulling first this book then that scroll off the shelves in a methodical search for what he wanted.

"What are you doing?" The clear accusation and suspicion in her voice caused Guy to sigh heavily before he looked up from his search.

"Well?" Ida demanded, arms crossed and eyes glowering.

"Looking for a few old parchments I know are here somewhere. I'd like to reassess the defensibility of this city in the event that King John comes for us."

Ida looked entirely unconvinced.

"Were you looking for anything in particular?" Guy asked.

Ida hesitated. "I had a similar idea—though having not served our hideous sheriff myself, I didn't know for certain I would find what I needed."

"Feel free to help me search. They should be in here. Robin doesn't want to fight the King, and I understand the sentiment, but we should be prepared for all eventualities."

Ida huffed and moved to a different shelf.

Her remembrance of Guy's service to the previous Sheriff and John put a sour taste in Guy's mouth. It was a part of his life he certainly took responsibility for, and yet he was past it. He was a different man.

He could never be a new man in Ida's eyes, however. He would forever be the man who tortured innocents and served the wrong side of the rebellion. Never mind that Ida's own husband Allen had betrayed Robin Hood and spent his own time serving the previous Sheriff and Prince John. No, Allen could be forgiven but Guy was a living breathing horror to be hated forever.

Ida soon gave up searching and left the room with a sneer. Guy did his best to ignore her and continued on about his business.

JANE

Jane smiled at her six-month-old son, softly snoring in her arms. Richard was perfect. Of course, every mother thought so of her own children, but Jane was convinced Richard truly was.

"We might be able to rebuild the wall to make it defensible," Guy said, seated across the table from Jane.

"Guy, if Robin wanted a fight, he would stay here, in Nottingham castle."

Jane stopped admiring her son long enough to glance toward her husband, Andrew. They were all three seated at the table in the small room adjoining Guy's bedchambers. It was a simple room, with just the table and a handful of chairs, and one tapestry hanging on the wall to her left. A fireplace on one wall lit the room, as well as a single candelabra standing in the opposite corner.

Guy's wife Faith was seated near the fireplace, humming softly to her daughter Lucy. Andrew and Guy were discussing the possibility of taking their families to the Gisbourne estate to avoid a confrontation with King John.

Jane hadn't known King Richard personally, but of course the death of the King was a solemn affair. And she knew how much it was affecting Robin. Her own husband wasn't grieving personally for the King either, but he was concerned about the safety of everyone connected to Robin Hood now that John was King.

"I don't want to take us from the rest of our family," Guy said, "but to be honest, we might be safer separated. As a large group we're easily tracked. And more than that, Robin doesn't have a plan yet, other than simply waiting to see what happens. I need to know my family will be safe in the event King John decides to punish us for our involvement in the rebellion. I can't just...wait."

"I understand that, Guy. And I share your concern. But Robin has never yet led us astray. I don't think we need to break off from the rest of the gang in order to remain safe. Robin will have a plan, and if not, Will or Lucy will have one that they'll convince him to use. Either way, he will lead us well, all of us. He always has."

"He led the gang well when it was a handful of young men and women living as fugitives in a forest. Now we're families; married, with children. It's entirely different. We can't plan on living in a forest forever, there's more at stake here."

"More as individuals, I agree." Andrew glanced to Jane and Richard. "I don't want my family forced to live in the forest either.

22

But politically, there's so much less at stake. We aren't fighting a war between the King and his usurper this time."

"Now, we'll just be trying to avoid an execution by the King who was once the usurper. Our very lives are at stake, Andrew. And I know they were before as well, but again...it was only us. We all only had to think of our lives, our own skin to save. Now I've got Faith to think of, and little Lucy."

"I know."

"And I can't abide by the suggestion that we leave our children with some respected family and go on the run alone. I can't abandon them."

"I know, Guy. I wouldn't leave Jane and Richard either."

Jane wasn't too concerned about Robin's lack of a plan, or about King John coming after them. It had been years ago when John had tried to take over the country while King Richard was away. Time had passed, Richard and John had reconciled to a point. It was entirely possible that he wouldn't try to punish the people who'd opposed him. And assuming he did try to kill them, Jane agreed with her husband. Robin would lead everyone well and safely. They were in good hands.

GUY

They had all been living in Nottingham castle for less than three weeks when Mary went into labor. Lucy and Dusty acted as her midwives. They had both been known for their skill in healing during the years in Sherwood, so Guy wasn't at all surprised. Guy knew Dusty had trained as a healer in Palestine before her move to

23

England, though where Lucy had acquired that particular set of skills, he couldn't say. He assumed it had something to do with her being raised by the monk Friar Tuck, and learning from him until his death.

Much had melted into a chair in a state of shock the moment his wife had started having contractions and now, hours later, he was in that chair still, staring into space. Guy and the rest of the men were there too, presumably to support Much although some of them were in a worse state than the father-to-be. Robin entered the room bearing a tray filled with mugs of ale.

"Anyone need cheering up?" he asked.

He set the tray on a small wooden table near the door, grabbed a mug, and walked over to his friend, still sitting dazed in his chair.

"Much? Ale?"

Much didn't respond.

Robin shrugged, grinning, and sat at his friend's feet. Mark was leaning against the back of Much's chair, also grinning.

Allen perched himself on the edge of a second table after grabbing one of the mugs of ale Robin had brought and taking a long draft. "Do you suppose Much is ever going to come out of that stupor?"

No one responded, but several chuckled.

Little John retreated to the window after retrieving a mug of ale, though what he was watching out there Guy couldn't say. Will was pacing the far wall, back and forth, back and forth.

"You would think it was Will's child, not Much's," Andrew laughed, watching Will's endless trail. Back and forth. Back and forth.

Guy leaned against the wall, enjoying the banter that was tossed around the room. None of the ladies were present. Guy assumed they were either with Mary or with the horde of children the gang had acquired over the years. They were more than a handful when all together.

Guy studied Much's blank expression for a time, and then turned slightly to watch Will's pacing. When Faith had given birth to little Lucy, Guy had acted more like Will than Much. He hadn't been able to sit still.

Guy turned back to Much. He was just staring into the fire. Robin elbowed his legs every now and then but got no response.

"Mary will be fine," Little John commented at one point. Much didn't seem to hear him.

An hour dragged by. Elinor and Faith brought food to them at one point and then disappeared again.

The chattering slowly quieted until there was dead silence in the room. The shadows were growing longer outside as well as in the room. Guy could see the sun beginning to set through the window. It was shining in his eyes.

Guy winced, and turned away. And there was Will to his right, still pacing.

"Will. You've already had two children," Allen laughed. "You should be used to this."

"And this one isn't even yours," Guy added.

Will glanced toward them with a grin, but kept pacing.

There was a knock on the door. Several "come in"s were followed by Lucy sticking her head in the door.

"Much? Do you want to come and meet your daughter?"

Much stirred. He looked at Lucy, thoroughly confused.

25

Robin grabbed his arms and pulled him out of the chair, turning him by the shoulders and pushing him toward Lucy. "Go on, Much."

Much walked toward Lucy slowly. When she stepped into the room, grabbed his arm, and dragged him out the door, the rest of the men burst into laughter.

"You can stop pacing now," Robin pointed out, cuffing Will on the shoulder.

"Lucy said it was a girl, right?" Will asked no one in particular.

"Yeah," Robin replied.

"Another girl," Little John said. "The boys will be outnumbered yet."

Guy sank into the chair Much had vacated. "It's probably better that way. Allen's rowdy boys count for about fifty, I should think."

Allen grinned. "Perhaps, but let's not forget the wildest one of the bunch is little Marian."

LUCY

Lucy could not contain her joy as she pulled Much along toward the chamber where Mary had given birth only a short while ago. Dusty was still there, with a handful of servant girls, cleaning the new babe and making sure Mary was comfortable. It had been an easy labor, as far as most labors went. Lucy was glad. Too many women died in childbirth for her comfort, and too many babes didn't survive the ordeal. So far both Mary and the baby appeared to be healthy.

Lucy opened the door to the chamber and pulled Much, still clearly dazed and confused, into the room. A servant girl named Martha was piling the dirty towels in a basket and another, Poppy was wiping Mary's brow with a wet cloth. Dusty was just placing a newly swaddled baby girl back into Mary's arms as they entered.

Lucy pushed Much toward the bed and he walked over and sank down next to his wife without a word.

"Oh, Much!" Mary looked up at him briefly but then turned back to her child. Her eyes were filled with wonder and tears.

Lucy grinned. She remembered the first moment Marian had been placed in her arms. She'd forgotten the rest of the world even existed. Nothing mattered except the tiny bundle in her arms, and it was clear that Mary now felt the same way.

Lucy moved to help Martha clearing away the mess left from the birth. She was glad for everyone's sake for the reprieve in solemnity. The threat of King John's possible retribution had been hanging over Nottingham Castle for three weeks, though no word had yet reached them of any real danger. Much and Mary's new daughter would give them all something pleasant to occupy their thoughts, at least for a day.

GUY

Nearly a week after baby Mary was born, Guy made his way to Robin's personal study and soon found himself sifting through the letters on Robin's desk.

As the Sheriff of the shire, Robin received plenty of them; letters from nobles in his shire with complaints or helpful suggestions as to how to deal with their complaints, letters from other Sheriffs and nobles around the country—politics were a delightful thing. There were even, at times, letters from other countries. The late King Richard had kept up a correspondence with Robin as well, and his widow Berengaria still did.

As Guy shuffled the letters, he caught sight of one with the seal of the Queen Mother, Eleanor of Aquitaine, who was currently retired to an abbey on the continent.

Any correspondence the members of the gang hoped to receive was now brought to Nottingham castle as well, which is why Guy was rifling through Robin's letters. He was looking for one from his own steward.

He'd written to Gisbourne estate hoping to ascertain from his steward the state of affairs there. He hadn't been back in years, though the revenue he earned from the estate was still collected and he received a letter every few months detailing his affairs. The letter was purely business, however. Hardly a greeting from the steward, let alone any knowledge of how things on the estate were going aside from monetarily.

Guy hadn't cared that the letters were such in the past because he'd built a life for himself in Nottingham. Now that Guy was considering returning, assuming King John decided to come after them, he wanted to know in what state he would find his childhood home when he returned. Thus far, he had received no reply to his inquiry.

"Still nothing?" Robin asked, entering the room and moving toward the table. He, too, began sifting through the letters.

"There's one from the Queen Mother," Guy said, "but none from my steward."

"Sorry about that. I hope it won't come to us abandoning each other, however."

"I have no plan to abandon anyone," Guy replied. "I am willing to remain with the rest of you as long as it is safe for my family to do so."

"You keep saying that," Robin replied, "but you are clearly making plans to leave."

"I am making a plan, Robin, which is more than you have done thus far. I am not accusing you. I simply cannot wait and do nothing."

"I understand. And I am formulating plans for our safety, Guy. I simply do not like our options. I have no desire to put the people of Nottingham, who have already suffered much, through a siege. And living as outlaws once again will be difficult with our children. But abandoning our children is not any more delightful of a prospect. Every option appears terrible."

"You'll have to settle on one eventually."

WILL

"Do you think it is wise to go to Sherwood?"

Will studied his friend, letting his question hang in the air for a moment. Robin seemed uninclined to reply.

"Our 'plan' thus far is as follows—and correct me if I leave anything out, Robin: wait for John to be crowned King. Wait to see if John tries to kill us. If he does, flee to Sherwood Forest. And

29

then...live there for the rest of our lives or until John is dead? It's not a plan, Robin."

"I don't want to uproot anyone...it's possible John will leave us alone."

"And when he doesn't leave us alone? Are we living in Sherwood forever?"

"I hope not, but I don't have a plan beyond that, yet."

"Shouldn't we be making one?"

"I'm considering it, Will, I really am. I just haven't come up with anything yet."

Will and Robin were sitting on the steps of the castle that led down into the courtyard. To their right were the stables that housed Robin's many horses as well as those of other nobles living in the castle.

It was a courtyard full of memory. How many executions had they stopped in this courtyard? Even Lady Marian herself was almost hung here once, saved in a daring rescue by Allen, Guy, and Andrew.

There were a lot of memories everywhere; at the castle where Marian's father had once been Sheriff and Robin had grown up exploring, in the courtyard and the secret passageways inside the castle where Robin and the gang had stopped executions and spied on the Sheriff—and Sir Guy, while he was still working for Prince John. In Nottingham, where so much of their lives had transpired. In Wetherby, where Mark lived, and Robin had spent so much of his childhood. In Locksley, where Robin grew up. In Sherwood Forest, where Robin and the gang had lived for years, and fallen in love.

Robin had always been a sentimental man; Will understood why he was reluctant to leave England. But hiding in Sherwood for an undetermined amount of time seemed absurd.

"What's the alternative to living in Sherwood till John is dead?" Robin asked. "Living in France or Spain or somewhere abroad? I don't want us so far from home. If it comes to that...I'll deal with it. But I'd rather not plan on it."

"Personally, as a father of two very young children, living as fugitives in a forest does not sound more inviting than being uprooted from England and living abroad."

"I know. I can't imagine all of us in Sherwood for an extended amount of time. I'm giving it thought, Will. I just don't have an answer yet."

"You need to find an answer. Guy is going to take his family elsewhere if you don't have a plan. I know Ida is considering the same. If the plan is 'hide in Sherwood for the rest of our lives' then I might have to take my family my own way, too, Robin."

"It won't come to that," Robin said. "I'll find a solution."

MARK

Mark stroked his horse's neck, enjoying the feel of Lumpy's soft skin and hair beneath his fingers.

"Hey, boy. Should we go for a ride?"

Lumpy nuzzled Mark's shoulder.

"Is that a yes?" Mark chuckled. He set to work saddling his horse, though his mind wasn't on the task.

John Lackland was going to be the King of England. His coronation day had been set. There were still some nobles vying for his nephew Arthur to be king instead, but most of those were on the continent. At any rate, Robin wasn't concerned about Arthur; he firmly believed John would be King. Robin was rarely wrong.

And how would John being King affect them? The questions had been asked a hundred times by everyone in the gang. Would John try and punish them or have them killed? Or would he forgive the past? And if he did come for them, what would they do? Where would they run?

Robin didn't have a plan beyond waiting to see what happened. He had mentioned Sherwood many times in the weeks since everyone had gathered in Nottingham. Hiding in Sherwood had worked well for them once before. Yet living in Sherwood now, with all the children in tow, seemed far less than desirable.

Mark led Lumpy out of the castle stable and into the courtyard. There he mounted and set off out the gate, nodding to the guards as he passed. He followed the street south toward the other end of town, where he would exit the city gate and then ride through the open fields. Lumpy loved a good gallop. And Mark loved the time alone with his thoughts.

What were they going to do with John as King of England?

In Mark's mind, the easiest solution was leaving England altogether. They could live almost anywhere in the world, as long as they weren't within John's reach. Robin was opposed to that idea, however. He was far too sentimental.

They could move to Austria, perhaps. John didn't have many ties there. The King would not be able to harm them, and they could build new lives for themselves. Get employment, raise their families. Of course, Mark had no intention of raising a family. He alone of the gang hadn't married thus far, and he intended to keep it that way. It wasn't that he didn't like women, he just had no desire to be a husband or father.

Austria was definitely a better plan than Sherwood Forest, at any rate.

Mark was sentimental, too, though he wouldn't admit it.

His beloved sister Marian had died in Austria and was buried there still.

Chapter 3

GUY

It was the day of the coronation. Robin had been right in his prediction. Prince John, and not Arthur of Brittany, was being crowned King. Robin and his friends had chosen not to attend the coronation. They had stayed in Nottingham castle, wondering whether King John would be coming for their heads.

The adults were gathered around the fireplace in the Great Hall, the children being entertained by Sarah—the castle cook and the woman who'd raised Robin Hood—in another part of the castle.

Guy absent-mindedly swirled the ale in his mug in slow circles while he watched the flames eat up the logs in front of him. His life was so different now than it had been only a few years ago. He'd been considered a close friend to Prince John once upon a time, and now he wasn't even attending the coronation. Now, they were mortal enemies. Assuming John came for their heads, as he was sure to do.

"I think we made the right decision not going to the coronation," Mark said.

"Best to keep our heads low for now," Will agreed. "No need to draw attention to ourselves. Perhaps we've all been worried for nothing."

"I doubt it." Allen said. "King John is likely to notice us soon enough. After all, we're one of the biggest reasons his regime failed while King Richard was away."

"We'll simply have to be on our guard," Robin said.

Guy was only half listening to the conversation around him. His mind was working through everything that would have to be done in order to make a quick escape from Nottingham should King John come calling. They all hoped that day wouldn't come, but they were all equally aware that it was only a matter of time. And the one thing Guy was sure of right now was that no one, *no one*, was going to hurt his family.

He was also fairly certain Robin was going to take them to Sherwood and John would track them down and kill them there. The old camp, after all, was now a beloved spot to many in England whom Robin had saved. Its whereabouts, though perhaps not widely spread, were not a secret any longer.

Sherwood was not the option Guy had in mind.

***

Later that night as Guy tucked his daughter into bed, Faith gently demanded to know what he was thinking.

"I know you don't want to leave the group, but I also know you don't like Robin's plan, or lack of a plan…" Faith shrugged. "So what are you thinking?"

"We stay with everyone for now. If trouble comes, and Robin's only plan is to hide in Sherwood, I may take you and little Lucy somewhere else."

"Where?"

"Gisbourne estate. I'd like to go home."

"Won't King John simply find us there? Will that really be different than hiding in Sherwood or staying in Nottingham?"

"Perhaps not. But Robin won't prepare Nottingham for a siege, he'd rather hide in Sherwood. I don't plan on hiding forever. I don't have the influence here to use Nottingham or the castle as a defense against the King, but I do have that influence at Gisbourne. I can make our estate defensible should King John come calling."

"I will go wherever you go, my husband." Faith kissed his cheek. "But we should carefully pray over every available option. God will direct our steps to the safest path, I'm sure."

IDA

Ida shifted closer to her husband, laying her head on his shoulder. They were seated outside the castle on the steps leading down to the courtyard, watching the stars. Today John Lackland had been crowned the King of England.

Would he come for them?

It was the same question still, the one they were all asking. There was not an answer yet.

"Have you ever thought about going back to Scotland?" Ida asked. Her husband was a Scotsman, born and raised, but had come to England after the Crusades.

"No. I've never considered it. There is nothing for me there, you know that."

"I know. Your family is here. But with King John possibly considering killing us, or imprisoning us, or whatever he decides to do, we might be safer outside of England. I know Robin wants to wait and see what happens, and then move us to Sherwood in case of an emergency, but we have to consider we might be safer elsewhere."

"I have considered that, but I hadn't pictured us returning to Scotland." Allen sighed heavily. "I don't imagine I would want to see that place again, my home...I'm not eager to relive the memories that made me join King Richard's Crusade in the first place."

"I know."

Allen had grown up in Scotland and had married at a young age. He'd even had a son. But a terrible accident had killed his entire family and that was why he'd gone to war. To forget. To die.

But he'd lived. He'd met Robin and become his friend during the Third Crusade and had chosen to follow him to Nottingham afterward. And through Robin, he'd found a new purpose. Saving England from Prince John and the Sheriff of Nottingham.

He'd also found Ida.

Ida's own family had died in a similar method, a fire, but theirs had been set by the Sheriff of Nottingham. They were both of them broken and bitter back in those days, but had found solace in one another.

"I still feel, Allen, that we should remove ourselves from England. We can take everyone with us, or just ourselves—just us and the boys."

"Guy has been considering a similar removal," Allen said. "And I know Will is trying to convince Robin he needs a better plan than simply removing to Sherwood. But until Robin himself has a different idea, we follow Robin. I trust him. And after my betrayal, however many years ago it may have been, I cannot abandon him."

Ida couldn't argue with her husband on that point.

Allen had fought beside Robin during the Crusades and later followed him to England to help stop John's rebellion. But in the height of that rebellion, he had chosen to betray the gang's secrets to the Sheriff of Nottingham. His reasoning had been to protect Mark and Lady Marian's father, but the reason did not lessen the sting of his betrayal. He had come back to the gang, however, and done his best over the years to prove his loyalty to them. No one held it against him still, as far as Ida was aware, but she understood why her husband would be eager not to give the appearance of abandoning Robin a second time.

ANDREW

In another part of the castle, Andrew and his wife Jane were settled in bed, contemplating the day's events before they slept. Their son Richard was nestled in Jane's arms as she laid against Andrew, resting her head on his shoulder.

"John is King," Jane said softly.

"He is."

"Has Guy decided what he's going to do?"

"No. For now, we're staying with everyone."

"But if Guy goes elsewhere, you plan on following him?"

Andrew shifted, trying to see his wife's face. This was difficult not only because of their position on the bed, but also because the only light in the room was the moon filtering through the window.

"I do plan on following Guy. I've been his constant companion since he was a child, I wouldn't wish it any other way."

"Rather like Much and Robin," Jane said, laughing softly. "I do understand, Andrew, and I am willing to follow you anywhere."

"For now, that means simply staying in Nottingham."

"Robin isn't going to call on the people of Nottingham to fight if King John comes to harm us, is he?"

"No. He's spent so many years in hiding, I don't think he remembers there are other ways to fight."

"And Guy spent his whole life trying to be stronger than he is able to be, and therefore doesn't know how to run and hide."

Andrew didn't respond.

Jane wasn't wrong; Guy had been abused as a child, his father always demanding he show no weakness and then beating him when he perceived that weakness. Andrew had been there, had watched it all growing up.

Guy had learned to be impenetrable so that no one could accuse him of weakness. He had become more open in recent years and was trying to change the thought patterns and behaviors that carried over from his troubled childhood, but no one could erase the scars his father had imprinted in his mind and heart. Guy was always going to balk at the idea of anything remotely weak, and hiding was certainly one of those things.

"Whatever happens, I am sure we will be okay," Jane said. "Robin always led the gang well. And I trust you and Guy to make whatever decision is best for our family."

Andrew kissed her forehead. "Thank you. I do hope you're right and all will be well."

Andrew wasn't convinced Robin would come up with a better plan than hiding in Sherwood. It had worked too well for him last time; he was unlikely to see a better alternative. That meant Guy was going to take his family to Gisbourne estate instead. The prospect of returning after so many years away wasn't exactly pleasnt.

Andrew had as many dark memories of that wretched place as Guy himself did.

GUY

It was dark outside, the stars shining brightly in the sky. Robin stood by the fireplace in the Great Hall, a frown upon his face. In his hand was a parchment bearing the seal of the King. He was reading silently.

It had been two weeks since the coronation and so far there had been no word from the new King. But perhaps now John was finally coming for their heads.

Robin had received the letter only a few minutes before, and in that time all of the gang seemed to have got wind of it and gathered in the Great Hall.

Guy sat at the long wooden table where they had taken so many meals together since learning of Richard's death. Meals filled with laughter, meals filled with serious conversation.

There were memories here in this room, and they didn't just pertain to recent months. This room had been where the late

Sheriff and Guy had done much of their scheming against the residents of Nottingham when they worked for Prince John while Richard was on his Crusade.

A past Guy wished he knew how to forget. He knew he was forgiven, and yet he couldn't seem to let it go.

"What news, Robin?" Lucy asked, coming up behind her husband and placing her hand on his shoulder. She'd asked the question that Guy, and indeed everyone else in the room, was wondering.

Robin sighed, glancing around the room at everyone assembled.

"I am being removed from office, as we suspected I would be. Prince John—or rather, King John—has appointed a Sir Ralf to replace me as Sheriff of Nottinghamshire."

"Do we know a Sir Ralf?" Dusty asked.

Robin shook his head. "I don't."

"So what do we do?" Guy asked. "If you're no longer the Sheriff, we cannot stay in the castle."

Was it time to leave? Guy slipped his arm around his wife Faith. Whatever happened, his only priority was to keep his family safe.

"We can stay until Sir Ralf arrives," Robin said. "If he is friendly, he may let us stay and even shelter us from King John. It is more likely he is an enemy, considering who has appointed him. So when he arrives, we may be forced to leave. We can go to Locksley. It is large enough to house all of us, even if it will be a bit cramped for quarters."

"Will living in Locksley accomplish anything?" Guy asked. "If Sir Ralf is loyal to King John, then he will likely want our heads on spikes."

"If trouble ensues, we can move back to Sherwood," Robin said. "No one knows that forest better than we do." Robin linked hands with his wife. "Let's hope, for the children's sake, it doesn't come to that."

"What about staying here?" Guy asked. "Fortifying the city? We have the people's support, thanks to you."

"But I don't think we could hold them off indefinitely," Robin sighed. "Besides, I have no interest in subjecting the people of Nottingham to a siege. Us against, what? All of England? We couldn't win that fight, Guy."

Guy reluctantly agreed. But hiding in Sherwood wasn't sounding particularly inviting either. And Robin's insistence on waiting until Sir Ralf arrived was irksome; by then it might be too late to run.

"The King offers no threat in this letter," Robin said. "It is only business. I've been replaced as Sheriff and the new Sheriff will be arriving soon. The fact that he doesn't make any threats is promising. We may yet get through this without any trouble."

Guy thought Robin was being annoyingly naive about their new King, but he kept his opinion to himself.

ROBIN

The streets were crowded with the residents of Nottingham and the surrounding villages. Voices calling out to one another, the smell of sweat, bodies bouncing off each other as people jostled into the best positions. Nottingham Square, too, was packed with people trying to catch a glimpse of the new Sheriff as he rode toward Nottingham castle.

It was a bright summer day; hot, clear, and with fat white clouds floating across the sky.

Robin was waiting on the steps leading down into the castle courtyard—which was empty but for the guards at the gate—Lucy by his side. Lucy was in a dark blue dress that happened to be one of Robin's favorites, her hair pulled back in an ornate braid that Robin couldn't begin to comprehend. Robin himself was wearing a forest green tunic, reminiscent of his days in Sherwood, covered by a thin chainmail shirt. His sword was at his side, but he had elected not to have his bow and quiver. There was no need to be threatening or immediately hostile with this new Sheriff.

The rest of the gang were scattered about the castle. They had all gathered that morning to discuss what to do when Sir Ralf arrived, and had decided that should he be hostile they would leave immediately for Sherwood Forest. And if he wasn't hostile, they would prepare to move to Locksley within a few days time.

Sir Ralf rode into the castle courtyard on a tan horse, wearing chainmail and a flowing crimson cape. He stopped before the steps and sized up Robin.

"Good morning!" Robin said cheerfully, though he kept his hand on his sword hilt just in case. "I trust you had a safe journey?"

"So this is the famous Robin Hood," Sir Ralf grinned, but he didn't look particularly happy. "I'm going to give you a piece of advice. Scram."

43

"Excuse me?"

"King John has appointed Sir Hugh, a mercenary from Scotland, as the commander of a small army tasked with one purpose. Killing Robin Hood and his gang. He is on his way to Nottingham. I have no personal quarrel with you, Robin Hood therefore, I won't kill you myself. So I'll say it again; scram."

There was a moment of silence, and then Robin smiled politely. "The castle is yours. I've called the head of the servants, the captain of the guard, and the chief cook to the Great Hall to await your orders."

Robin was worried about leaving Sarah—the chief cook, and the woman who had been the only mother he'd ever known when she was the household cook on the Locksley estate while he was growing up—alone in Nottingham castle, but she refused to leave. She insisted she was getting too old to be running about the country.

"I was going to ask if your hospitality would allow my family and friends to remain as guests under this roof," Robin continued, "but I take it you'd prefer we 'scram' so I will simply thank you for your warning and be on my way." Robin turned on his heel and entered the castle. Lucy jogged to keep up with him.

"What now, Robin?"

"We gather the gang and we head straight for the camp. We won't go to Locksley."

"How long do you think it will take this Sir Hugh to get to Nottingham?"

"There's no way to know."

Robin led the way to Will and Dusty's quarters. He knocked briefly on the thick wooden door, and then immediately entered the room.

Dusty was sitting by the window, the early morning sunlight streaming in around her. Her one-year-old daughter Daniyah was sitting in her lap and she was singing softly to her. Will stood by the large bed, folding three-year-old John's clothes and stuffing them in a bag. There were several cloth bags, a few of them silk, on the bed, all bulging with various contents. John was holding one in his lap that was open; cloth wrapped bread and a few apples could be seen through the opening.

Will turned as Robin and Lucy entered the room. "Judging by your expressions, packing was not such a bad idea on my part."

Robin sighed. "Meet by the stables, now. I'm going to fetch everyone else."

"I'll head to the kitchen and make sure we have enough provisions to take with us," Lucy said.

"I'll get Little John and Elinor," Will said.

Robin nodded. "I'll go find Ida and Allen, first. Send everyone to the stables, Will. We are going to Sherwood immediately."

Robin went to the apartments where Allen and Ida had been staying since coming to the castle two months earlier. After a swift rap on the door, he entered.

Allen was stuffing some clothes in a bag when Robin walked in the room, and Ida was on the floor trying to separate her boys. The latter were both screaming rather loudly, though Robin couldn't make out what was being said.

"Sir Ralf has arrived," Robin said calmly. "He has informed me that King John has hired a mercenary, Sir Hugh of Scotland, to kill us. Sir Hugh is on his way to Nottingham now. We leave for Sherwood immediately. Meet at the stables as soon as you can."

Robin left again before Allen or Ida could respond and made his way toward Much's rooms. When he arrived Much and Mary were both curled up in bed with their newborn daughter, simply watching her sleep.

"I'm sorry to interrupt," Robin said, entering the room without ceremony.

Much sat up grinning. "No need to apologize, Robin. Has the new Sheriff arrived?"

"He has. And he has advised us to leave because a mercenary hired to kill us is on his way to Nottingham."

"Oh dear!" Mary sat up, her eyes wide. "What are we going to do?"

"For now, we're going to Sherwood. Pack quickly, and meet us at the stables."

His next stop was Mark's quarters, but Mark was not within his rooms. Robin began a methodical search of the castle to find his friend. It was slow progress. Everywhere he went were nobles and merchants of the city, those living in Nottingham castle and those visiting the city, and they all wanted a word with their Sheriff. Most wanted to know if the new Sheriff had arrived and what Robin thought of him. Robin didn't have time to sit and talk to every noble who wished it, and had to rather rudely push past a few of them in order to continue his search for Mark.

He ran into his wife near the Great Hall.

"Will and Dusty are at the stables," Lucy said. "I've packed provisions, with Sarah's help. Little John and Elinor are headed to the stables now, and I saw Allen and Ida dragging the twins that direction."

"I can't find Mark," Robin said.

"Oh! I found Mark; he was in the library. I sent him to his room to pack."

"Much and Mary are packing and will join us shortly."

"Has anyone told Guy and Faith yet?"

"I haven't."

"I'll go fetch them."

"And I'll find Andrew and Jane."

FAITH

Faith watched little Lucy wobble across the floor toward her father. Faith was standing by their bed, carefully folding Guy's tunics and putting them into a satchel.

Lucy toddled forward, and then paused. Her balance wavered, her arms went out to the side for a moment. Then she caught herself and kept walking forward with her little steps to her father.

Guy was sitting at a small desk near the window looking over parchments; letters from Gisbourne estate and other nobles, maps and charts, and other such things. Faith wasn't sure what he intended to do with the information contained in those parchments, but it was clear he was keeping some of them because as he sifted through them he would place some in a stack of papers and scrolls on the desk, and he would place others in the satchel at his feet.

When Lucy reached her father, she lost her balance and fell forward into his leg. Guy caught her up and placed her on his lap, kissing her cheek.

Faith smiled as she watched her little family. Wherever they ended up in the end, she was truly blessed.

Guy had decided to start preparing to leave Nottingham the night that Robin received official notice from the King that he was no longer the Sheriff. In the two weeks since that time, Guy had done much thinking and planning and searching for information in the library—some of which Faith did not understand, but she trusted her husband in all things.

Packing, however, had not actually occurred until more recently, in the last few days. And now they were nearing the end of their exertion. They had two trunks packed, and several satchels and were nearly ready for removal should that day arrive.

Faith finished putting the last shirt into the satchel on the bed, and then turned to survey the room. She wanted to be sure she hadn't forgotten anything in her previous sweep of the environment. Nothing jumped out at her screaming to be packed.

A knock sounded on the door and then it opened, revealing Lucy.

"Faith, Guy, we have to leave."

Guy turned in his chair to face Lucy. "Leave?"

"Sir Ralf has arrived. He informed Robin that King John has hired a mercenary to kill us."

"What?" Faith gasped.

"Are we leaving via the secret passages?" Guy stood up, still holding little Lucy.

"No. The mercenary isn't here, but he's on his way to Nottingham. We're going to Sherwood tonight and will regroup from there. I think Robin intends for us to stay there for a time."

"I don't think that's wise," Guy said.

"I know." Lucy crossed her arms and shrugged. "But he's never led us astray yet."

Faith grabbed the satchel she'd just finished packing. "Let's get our things and head to Sherwood. We can further discuss other options later."

Guy grabbed a couple bags and Lucy helped as well. Between the three of them they carried most of their belongings to the stable.

As they walked through the familiar halls of the castle Faith considered their current situation.

She had been a member of Robin's gang, albeit a passive one, during the rebellion. She and her father had been imprisoned in the dungeon of Nottingham castle. They were going to be executed, but Guy—who at that time was in the Sheriff's employ and yet working with Robin Hood—had helped to secure her release. The gang had stolen her and her father away from the previous Sheriff and they had lived in Sherwood with the gang.

Faith had never used any weapons or helped in any of the raids on the caravans carrying taxes or the rescues of innocents being executed. She simply lived with the gang and provided a different sort of role. A friend. She cooked with Much and Ida, she prayed with Dusty and Lucy, she encouraged the gang in any way that she could.

Robin had been her leader as much as Lucy's, and yet she hadn't had to follow his orders or learn to trust his instincts in the same way. Therefore, when faced with the question of whether to trust Robin now, in regard to living in Sherwood, or trust her own husband, she relied on her husband's wisdom.

Faith was sure Lucy was likely partially relying on her own husband in the same way, however there was also the fact that Lucy had been under his command. She had learned to trust him in all things on a different level than as a wife; to follow him into battle and trust him to lead her out again. Robin had led his followers well during the rebellion. Of course, as one of those followers, Lucy would trust his plans. Faith simply didn't have that pull of allegiance.

ROBIN

When they were all finally gathered in the stables, Robin gave out his instructions. "Get your horses, and if you don't have one take any from my stables. We're going straight to the camp in Sherwood. I have been informed by the new Sheriff that a Sir Hugh has been tasked with killing us, so we're going into hiding immediately."

The group began tying their packs onto their mounts and figuring out who would transport the children and so forth. As soon as each was ready, without waiting for any of the rest of the gang, they began to gallop out of the stables and out of Nottingham.

Robin made sure he had his sword, a few daggers, and his bow and quiver, and then mounted his most prized horse—an expensive bay war-horse named Arrow. "Lucy."

Lucy was just swinging into Scamper's saddle, her chestnut horse, with their daughter Marian in her arms. "Yes?"

"I'm going to Marcus' home to explain what we're doing." Marcus was a dear friend; a blacksmith who had helped them on many occasions during the days of Sherwood and fighting against Prince John by providing weapons or horses to them, and sheltering them in his home when need be.

"Alright. I'll see you in Sherwood." Lucy leaned forward across her horse's head and kissed her husband. "Be safe, Robin."

"There's no immediate danger yet," Robin replied, before trotting away on Arrow. They had time to settle in Sherwood before Sir Hugh made an appearance, so Robin wasn't too worried on that front.

Hiding in Sherwood was their specialty. It would be different, of course, with the children along. But Robin was confident they could manage. At least until they could come up with a solution to their problem.

Chapter 4

LUCY

A flood of emotions enveloped Lucy as she rode into the clearing in the heart of Sherwood Forest. In the four years since this had been her home, small trees had shot up in bright greens around the more stately ones that surrounded the clearing. The grass had grown tall and proud, except in square patches of dirt and short clumps of grass where huts had once stood and in the circle where their fire ring had been. The rough logs still sat around the ring, with weeds sprouting around them and vines crawling over them.

Everyone had already arrived, except for Robin, and were gathering at the old fire ring. Their horses were tethered to various trees around the clearing. Several of the children were already exploring through the tall grass.

Lucy slipped to the ground with little Marian in her arms. As she reached for the reins to secure Scamper to a nearby tree, Marian struggled from her grasp and fell with a thud onto the ground. Lucy paused to see if Marian was hurt, but the two-year-old scrambled to her feet and ran through the grass toward the sound of the other children laughing.

"Where's Robin?" Will asked as Lucy joined the group by the empty fire ring.

"Explaining the situation to Marcus," Lucy replied.

"Do you think we'll need Marcus' help as we have previously?" Much asked.

"Robin does seem intent on making us live in this forest for the rest of our days," Guy replied.

Lucy glanced around the clearing. She could still picture it as it had once been, not so long ago. She could hear the laughter of the children that had lived here—children they had rescued from the Sheriff's malicious schemes—or the clanging of swords as Mark, Will, or Allen sparred.

She remembered sitting just over there when Mark said the first words he'd spoken after Marian's death, or standing on the other side of the clearing when Robin had argued with her about the merits of Sir Guy of Gisbourne.

So many memories permeated from every surface around her.

"I know," Mark said, elbowing Lucy out of her reverie. "There's a lot to remember here, isn't there?"

Lucy smiled and nodded, soaking in the vision of the overgrown clearing and remembering it as it had once been.

"How long will we stay?" Much asked. "Do you think we'll have to build our huts again?"

"It depends on how big of a threat this Sir Hugh turns out to be," Will said. "If he sticks around, terrorizes the neighborhood, searches Sherwood, then yes, we will have to make this our permanent home."

"What happens if he finds the camp?" Ida asked. "That is a very real possibility. So what are we going to do then?"

"No one found the camp the first time," Little John replied gruffly.

"But that's because our dearly departed old Sheriff was…" Ida shrugged. "You know...dumb."

"We searched the forest fairly systematically," Guy said. "And I and many others in his employ were not dumb. It would have taken a miracle for anyone to find the camp."

"I agree," Andrew said. "And now the forest is even more overgrown than it was then. We should be safe here."

"But how many people know where the camp is?" Elinor asked. "After Richard returned, this place became sacred to England's subjects. You know that. A lot of people came just to see where Robin Hood had lived as an outlaw."

"That is true," Lucy said. "Many people have visited."

"How long before one of them tells Sir Hugh?" Ida demanded.

"Most of those who visited were Nottingham residents, loyal to Robin," Dusty said. "And those who were not from Nottingham were equally indebted to him for saving their lives. That's why they came to visit this place; because Robin Hood saved them. I don't think they will betray the whereabouts of the camp to our enemies."

"It's only a matter of time before someone passes that information along," Guy said. "It's not a secret anymore. Too many people know. Now it is simply valuable knowledge that will eventually spread."

"Then we find a new location," Will said. "It wouldn't be difficult to do. It's a large forest. And we are experienced in the art of hiding out in the woods. We wouldn't be found."

The laughter of the children nearby was interrupted by someone wailing.

"That's mine," Ida sighed as she got up to investigate.

"Hiding with our horde of youngsters…" Little John shook his head. "I do not think this will work out quite as well as we hope."

"We had children in the camp before," Will said.

"They were older children," Guy replied. "And they were not in your camp very long."

Robin came riding into camp then, and quickly dismounted Arrow and tethered him to a tree by the other horses. He then strode across the clearing to join the group by the empty fire ring.

"What's our plan, Robin?" Guy asked.

"We live here for now. We wait and we watch. We don't know yet how much of a threat this Sir Hugh will turn out to be. Nor do we know whether Sheriff Ralf is a true threat or not. He did warn us about Sir Hugh…" Robin sighed. "For now, we simply wait."

Lucy slipped her hand into her husband's and received a half smile in return. She could tell he was worried, immensely so. Lucy, however, was not. Robin had led them through such trials before, he could easily do it again.

MARK

Word soon reached Nottingham that King John was traveling abroad. He had gone to his lands on the continent to settle disputes with his nephew, Arthur.

"It seems so odd that Arthur has been crowned the King of England by his own supporters," Faith said. They were gathered around the fire ring in the clearing in Sherwood Forest. No fire was lit, but it was where they enjoyed gathering. The well placed logs for seating perhaps added to its charm. The children were in various states throughout the camp. Some playing, some sleeping.

"Politics," Little John grumbled. "There will always be someone else vying for power."

"Arthur, and Philip of France as well, have been confiscating John's lands," Lucy said. "I imagine that's why he rushed off in that direction. He needs to convince Arthur to renounce his claim on England, and to win his land back."

"And thus England falls into another war," Mark groaned.

"He does have a lot of disputes to settle," Guy said.

"'Settle' being, perhaps, a more polite term than the King would use," Lucy laughed. "This could turn into a full-scale war with France."

"As long as he doesn't force me into his army," Mark shrugged. "I have no desire to fight another war."

"You didn't fight the last one," Robin said. "You weren't on the Crusades."

"I know. Because you wouldn't let me go. You and my father...and Marian." Mark sighed. "But I did fight against Prince John, which was more than enough for me." The thought of his sister brought a familiar ache to Mark's heart, but he did his best to ignore it.

"Are we safe then?" Much asked. "The King is off in France and while he's on the continent and distracted by Arthur and Philip...are we safe?"

"Just because the King isn't in England doesn't mean we're safe," Ida rolled her eyes. "Sir Hugh is still headed for Nottingham intent on killing us all, is he not?"

Mark silently agreed with Ida. It would be foolish indeed to assume their troubles were so easily avoided.

Laughter drifted across the clearing from the children.

"I don't think hiding will be much of an option, we're too conspicuous," Little John sighed.

Mark followed his gaze toward the opposite side of the clearing. William and Edward were wrestling in the grass and, as Mark watched, Marian ran over and dove on top of them. The three of them rolled along the grassy ground, a jumble of arms, legs, and brown and blonde hair.

"I'm not sure we have a choice," Robin said. He had his sword in his lap and was calmly sharpening it. "Even in France the King is out for our heads. If we want to live, then hiding here is our safest option. Either that, or running and hiding somewhere else. But traveling with our group of children will be no easier than hiding in Sherwood with them."

No one argued with him. None of their options were particularly easy.

Mark glanced around him, at his friends, and at the camp. Over the last week, the camp had begun to take shape, much as it had years before. Instead of wooden huts this time, however, they had merely put up lean-tos and tents. They had decided not to build a permanent home due to the fact that they would likely have to run at any time. Robin had been to Locksley a few times to gather more supplies, but otherwise they'd simply stayed in the camp discussing their options and entertaining the children.

"For now we just stay here," Mark said. "We're safer here than on the move—we can all agree that traveling with the children would be slow and obvious. We're safer here than in Nottingham or anywhere else, where someone can inform the King where we are. And until Sir Hugh arrives we won't know how much of a threat he is."

"I agree," Robin said. "We stay."

"Waiting and watching are not the most fun things to do," Allen sighed.

"We've little else to do," Mary said.

"Will we give Sir Hugh a fight when he comes?" Little John asked.

"That will entirely depend on the size of his army," Robin replied. "As I said, we can only wait and see. There's nothing else to be done."

Mark doubted very much that Robin would have them fight Sir Hugh and his army, no matter what the size of it turned out to be. If he'd been planning on fighting off their enemies, he would have stayed in Nottingham castle and fortified the city rather than give it immediately over to Sir Ralf. What his friend's plan was, he wasn't sure, and he wasn't convinced Robin even had a distinct plan at all. Yet whatever happened, he had confidence that he would lead them well. He always did.

LUCY

Lucy ran her hand along the cool stone wall beside her to keep her bearings. The hidden hallway she was currently in was no more than two feet across at its widest points, though often thinner even than that. And it was dark. That was the hardest part to get used to. The absolute blackness.

The secret passageways inside Nottingham castle were legend among England's residents these days. Yet few had ever been inside them and hardly anyone knew where they were located, or where the entrances were. After Richard had returned and Robin had been appointed Sheriff of Nottingham, he'd reopened the secret entrances that the previous Sheriff had closed up. Then the late Sheriff, along with most of his cronies, had been executed for treason once King Richard returned. So the passages themselves, though their existence was known, remained secret.

It had been Andrew who had suggested they not remain in the dark about what was happening and instead go to Nottingham so they would know when Sir Hugh arrived, and pick up any other news that might be of interest to them. Lucy's husband had immediately agreed.

Robin had made the decision that they would go in shifts, three people at a time spending a day in Nottingham, and then a new group of three the next day. Getting through Nottingham to the castle was hardly a problem. The residents of Nottingham, down to the last child, loved Robin and his extended family. They were more than willing to assist if need be to hide the gang from Sir Ralf's soldiers now patrolling Nottingham's streets.

So far Sir Ralf had not turned out to be a tyrannical Sheriff as had Sir John while Richard was on his Holy Crusade. He might not be exactly kind or compassionate, but he seemed fair and just. His only real fault was that he was loyal to King John. That, and he disliked Robin Hood and his gang. Whatever the reason for that was—a love for King John, a jealousy of their popularity—Lucy wasn't sure. Not that it truly mattered. It was enough that he did dislike them and wasn't about to shelter them from Sir Hugh or his coming army. His reasons were irrelevant.

Lucy concentrated on the sensation of the smooth stone under her hand as she tentatively walked along the dark corridor. Will was in front of her—his voice the only thing assuring her he really was still with her—instructing her on how to find the doors that led into the castle's rooms. Lucy had never ventured to explore the secret passageways after her husband became Sheriff as she had never had a need to do so, and during the adventures in Sherwood, Lucy had been a guest in the castle allowed to move about freely. That left her as one of a very small group among the gang who didn't know the secret passageways as well as they knew their own names. The secret passageways had, after all, been Robin Hood's main source of information for much of Prince John's rebellion—up until the late Sheriff found them and closed them.

Robin had assigned them into groups with someone acquainted with the passageways given at least one person to teach, or more if necessary. Will had only Lucy to instruct because the other member of their group was Mark. His father had been the Sheriff of Nottingham when he was a child and he knew the passageways better than anyone, save for Robin himself.

Will was speaking softly as he told Lucy how to locate the cracks in the smooth stone that indicated a doorway. The passageway might be secret, but voices carried. And in these tight spaces, surrounded by stone, they echoed quite beautifully.

"The key," Robin had told her with a smile that morning before she'd set out, "is to keep your ears wide open for any sounds and to hush up the minute you hear something. Once you know the passageways, avoid talking unless absolutely necessary because they will hear you."

Lucy was trying hard to take in everything Will was explaining. She knew he was risking both their lives using his voice right now. But until she knew what she was doing, it could hardly be helped.

GUY

Guy leaned against the cool stone, pressing his ear to the invisible crack in the wall. The crack was only invisible because he was in complete darkness. There were no torches lit in the secret passageway. Guy listened for a moment for sounds, which would travel muffled through the stone, and yet heard nothing.

Taking a chance, he pressed gently and let the stone door slide forward an inch. Enough that the light of the room beyond spilled in and he could see inside, if only through a vertical opening an inch wide. It was an odd view of the room, and he had to turn his head to get a view of the whole thing, one vertical-inch-slice at a time.

The room was empty. Guy pulled the door shut again and continued on his walk, keeping his left hand pressed against the cold stone.

Guy had been working for Sheriff John during the rebellion and had therefore been on the receiving end of such spying antics. And once the passageways were discovered, when Allen betrayed Robin and the gang and disclosed their whereabouts, they had simply been closed off. Guy had never had occasion to travel inside them.

Little John and his wife Elinor were the two people Robin had assigned to work with Guy. Little John had patiently taught his wife the secrets of the passages, and had mostly left Guy to fend for himself. Probably hoping that Guy would get lost and never be seen again.

During the rebellion Guy had switched sides, mostly due to Lucy's gentle wisdom showing him the error of his ways. He had helped Robin as only a member of Sheriff John's most inner circle could. And yet, it had taken many years for most of the gang to forgive him.

Not only for working on the wrong side of the rebellion for the first half of it, but also for his role in killing the late Lady Marian, Robin's first wife. It was his greatest regret.

Now, years after the rebellion, most of the gang considered him part of the family. Ida still despised him and Little John as well, but even Mark—Marian's own brother—had learned to be civil with him so Guy had hoped the others would follow his example.

The only reason Guy could attribute to the fact that they lived in peace together despite what he'd done in his past, was the grace of God. He alone could have granted Robin and the others the ability to forgive him for his wrongs, and had helped him forgive himself as well.

But it was clear that Little John and Ida had no intention of following the rest of the gang in that forgiveness.

So Guy had spent his days traveling the secret passageways alone, learning where they went in the castle and to which rooms they opened without help from the others.

LUCY

Lucy hummed slightly as she leaned against a tree across the camp from the assortment of tents. Everyone had gone to bed, and she was on watch. As Sir Hugh had yet to make an appearance, she wasn't worried about staying quiet. She hadn't been there long when her solitude was intruded upon.

Elinor came out of the tent she shared with her husband, Little John, and walked across the clearing by the light of the moon that filtered through the branches above them.

When she reached Lucy, she carefully eased herself to the ground beside her.

"Couldn't sleep?"

"I need advice."

"Oh?" Lucy turned to get a better look at her friend. The seriousness in her voice concerned Lucy. "What's wrong?"

"Little John led the group that spied in Nottingham today."

"I know. He reported that nothing of importance happened."

"Nothing of importance regarding the new Sheriff or Sir Hugh…" Elinor sighed.

"What is it, Elinor?"

Elinor shifted her weight to lean back against the trunk of the tree as Lucy was. "My husband, whom I adore, was being rather rude to your friend all day. He has been every time we spy in Nottingham together. And I can reasonably understand why," Elinor shrugged. "I was one of the subjects who suffered at Guy of Gisbourne's hand before he joined our side."

"I know. But he's sorry, and has been sorry, for that time of his life for a long time now."

"I know! It has been years now and he's proven himself to all of us again and again. But my husband just can't forget the fact that he was an enemy."

"I know. It isn't just Little John. Ida has trouble adjusting to Guy and Andrew being part of our gang as well."

"Ida should know better," Elinor said. "After all, her own husband Allen was with the late Sheriff for a time."

"A short time," Lucy agreed.

"What am I supposed to do with Little John? He's so good, and generous, and kind. But he can't let go of this, he can't forgive Guy."

"Have you talked to him?"

"Multiple times."

"Give it time, Elinor."

"How much time? It's been years. I hate to see my good and kind man reduced to such petty anger."

"Well, as you've pointed out, it isn't petty. He has just grounds for his anger. Guy wasn't always the man he is today. And as you said, Little John is good, through and through. He'll see the truth sooner or later, that Guy is a good man now and one worthy of being trusted. He'll learn to forgive Guy."

"I want to believe that."

"Just be gentle with him, Elinor. Don't force him to forgive Guy. It won't work. I tried that with Robin many years ago, and it was a disaster. He has to come to that conclusion on his own."

Elinor sighed heavily.

"And he will," Lucy added in response to Elinor's gloom. "He will figure it out, Elinor."

Lucy could easily sympathize with Elinor's predicament. It had taken Robin a long time to forgive Guy for killing Marian, and unlike Little John who expressed his anger quietly, Robin had often times been a raging fire that Lucy felt quite unable to put out. The arguments they had had, some in this very clearing, had been anything but quiet. Yet he had come around eventually, as had most of the rest of the gang. Little John would too. He was a fellow believer; however hard it might be, he would follow Christ's example of forgiveness eventually.

Elinor soon struggled to her feet and headed back toward her tent for the night. As Lucy watched her friend walking away, a suspicion began to take root in her mind. One that shot a glimmer of excitement through her.

ANDREW

Andrew felt the reverberation of his blade striking Guy's all the way down his arm. He grunted and stepped back, preparing for another strike.

Guy grinned. "You've never yet beat me in a sparring match, Andrew. I don't know why you keep trying."

"It's a matter of pride."

Andrew darted forward again with a sharp twist of his wrist. Guy easily blocked his sword and knocked it to the left. It was all Andrew could do not to lose his grip and send the sword flying.

"Keep trying, old friend," Guy laughed.

Andrew knew it was hopeless, but he struck again and again regardless. Guy had been one of the greatest swordsmen in England since his youth.

Andrew and Guy had removed themselves from the camp clearing and wandered the woods to find their own small spot to spar. Within a few minutes of beginning, every bird and woodland creature within their hearing had fled the noise of metal striking metal that rang out again and again.

"How are you enjoying your days of spying in Nottingham?" Andrew grinned.

"They are remarkably pleasant," Guy replied with a grimace.

Andrew winced as Guy's blade poked his chest. "Try not to actually kill me."

"I didn't even break your tunic, let alone draw blood," Guy replied.

"Little John seems more fond of you than ever," Andrew said.

"I know. When we lived in our separate cities and only met a few times a year he could pretend to be civil, which is more than Ida ever bothered to do. But now that we live under the same roof…" Guy paused, grinning. "under the same trees, I should say, the facade of civility has melted away."

"Are you okay?"

"Perfectly fine. Mistrust is a normal part of my day; that's what I get for working for Prince John in the past, and being the cruel man that I was. The hatred is justified, I will not blame it."

Andrew tried to get the better of Guy as he talked, but Guy flicked his blade away like he was waving off a fly of no importance.

"It doesn't make my days pleasant, being paired with Little John for spying duties, but it could be worse. How are you finding the mistrust these days?"

Andrew shrugged. "It has never been as bad for me as for you. Ida has her suspicions, always, but most of the gang don't bother me."

Guy stepped back, sheathing his sword. "There is still an underlying feeling of mistrust, though, with all of them."

"I suppose there is. But they hide it well."

"For most of them, I don't think it's a matter of hiding it. Little John always tried to hide it and be civil in spite of it, but Robin, Lucy, Mark and the rest try to fight it, not hide it. They are trying to move past it and see us as trustworthy."

"I know." Andrew sheathed his own sword and he and Guy moved to sit, their backs against a tree.

"Have you decided what to do, Guy?"

"About what?"

"Staying with the gang or not? I know you don't like hiding in Sherwood. You think it is inevitable that we will be found. So what are you going to do?"

"I want to go to Gisbourne estate. Yet I'm not sure when to break away from the gang, or if we will need to at all..."

"Whatever you decide, you must tell me. I intend to follow you."

"I never thought you would do anything else."

FAITH

It was an overcast day; dark clouds broiling overhead, the wind shaking the trees surrounding their camp. Faith was sitting off to one side of the camp, baby Mary in her arms, with her mother Mary sitting beside her. They were watching Faith's daughter little Lucy playing with small rocks.

The two-month old infant was fast asleep in Faith's arms, snoring softly into her shoulder. Faith loved the feel of the small body breathing against her.

"I think perhaps little Lucy needs a sister or brother."

Mary laughed. "She has all the children to fill that role," Mary gestured around the clearing. The twins were violently playing a game with Marian with Lucy watching over them. Will was sitting with his two children and little Richard near the fire ring, telling them stories.

"It's true. They are all one family. But perhaps I just want another baby to claim as my own."

"How has it been, spying in Nottingham? I know you didn't participate in that much the last time you lived in Sherwood forest."

"It's been...a different sort of experience than any I've had before. I'm not sorry I missed out on it the first time around. What about you? You were living in Nottingham back in those days, but

68

didn't know your husband yet. You weren't participating in any such shenanigans."

"Oh, I participated in shenanigans, alright," Mary laughed. "During many of the interrupted executions in Nottingham Square there were a handful of us who would assist the outlaws in their efforts by forming mobs to tackle soldiers and various other tactics to ensure Robin Hood got away with whomever he was rescuing."

"I can picture you doing such things," Faith said. "Though I'm not sure I ever could have."

"Spying in the castle is quite different," Mary replied. "There's no excitement, no immediate obstacles to overcome. Just the silence, the darkness, and the occasional noises inside the castle to listen to. I preferred pouncing on soldiers during ambushes and rescues. If I could have found the camp back in those days I would have joined the gang whole-heartedly."

"I believe it."

"How has Guy been handling spying in Nottingham? Or living in Sherwood, for that matter. He was, after all, on the other side of things back in those days."

"Living in Sherwood hasn't been too much of an adjustment. That is, not any more than for the rest of the gang as well. And as for spying in Nottingham, the hardest part is that he is paired with Little John. The only person here who likes my husband less than Little John is Ida."

"Have they fought?"

"Not exactly, no. But I know it troubles my husband that Little John doesn't trust him after all these years."

"It is still hard to imagine him not being the brutal, violent, cruel man that we knew him to be during John's rebellion. He's a completely different man. It's...remarkable."

"A living testament to God's grace."

Mary nodded. "But you can see why it is hard for us to accept his change. He wasn't good, Faith. You met him after he had already joined our cause, but before that he was truly a terrible person."

"I know. But so are we all without Christ."

"We don't all run around murdering people or burning down homes for no reason. I know he's a different person now, and I can accept that. But I'm not surprised other people find it difficult. You shouldn't be either."

"I'll just keep praying for Little John and Ida. Eventually they'll see the worth of my husband, I'm sure."

Chapter 5

LUCY

The air was warm, despite how early in the morning it was. Lucy turned her attention away from the rowdy bunch of children she was keeping an eye on as she felt Robin's hands settle on her shoulders. She leaned her head back to rest against his chest.

"I'm heading out," Robin said. "Ida and Much are coming with me. If we learn anything, we'll report it when we get back to camp this evening."

Lucy turned to face her husband and wrapped her arms around his waist. "Be safe, Robin."

"Always." Robin kissed her forehead. "Don't let Marian cause too much trouble today."

Lucy laughed, turning to watch their daughter wrestle with Edward. "No promises there."

She released Robin and watched as he joined Much and Ida and they left the camp. They'd been taking shifts spying on the new Sheriff for over a week now. Lucy had had two days in Nottingham in that time, and was still learning the secret passages. Mark had sat her down only yesterday and drawn a map of the castle and its secret corridors in the dirt around the fire ring to give her a visual to memorize.

Turning back to the children, Lucy couldn't help but smile. The twins, along with Marian and John, were fully occupied wrestling; Richard and Daniyah were sitting together drawing in the dirt, supervised by Much's wife Mary, who was sitting beside them with her infant daughter in her arms; little Lucy, however, was sitting all alone.

Lucy went and sat down beside her, still keeping the twins and Marian in her line of sight.

"What are you doing, Lu?"

The little girl looked up, her huge brown eyes alight. Whatever was putting that smile on the one year old's face, Lucy had no idea. She pulled little Lucy into her lap. The little girl kicked her legs and giggled.

Lucy noticed Elinor moving across the clearing towards them. As she knelt beside Lucy, she placed a hand on her stomach.

Lucy gave her friend an appraising look and Elinor merely arched her eyebrows in response.

"Something going on in there?" Lucy asked, indicating Elinor's hand which was still resting on her stomach.

Elinor smiled. "You can't tell a soul. I haven't even told Little John yet."

Lucy tried to conceal a squeal by hiding her face in little Lucy's hair. "How long have you known? I suspected a few days ago when we had our late night chat."

"A couple months."

"Months!?"

"It's so easy to lose babies before their time," Elinor sighed. "I wanted to wait to tell Little John and the rest of you until I was sure I wouldn't lose it. I'm still not sure."

"You worry too much. How far along do you think you are?"

"Not sure; I'd say around 4 months. I'm hoping to feel the little one moving soon."

"That's so exciting! You have to tell Little John. Right now."

"Now?"

"Yes, now!"

Elinor laughed. "I suppose it's about time I did. But I'm still wary."

"Of course it is time! And then tell everyone else...as soon as Robin, Ida, and Much get back from Nottingham we'll have a celebration."

Elinor laughed. "We don't need a whole fuss and bother about it."

"Yes, we do. Don't we, little Lucy?"

Little Lucy merely giggled in response to her question, but that was no deterrent. Lucy got to her feet, settling little Lucy on her hip, and reached down to pull Elinor up. "Come on, let's go tell your husband the news!"

Elinor laughed and allowed herself to be pulled to her feet and dragged across the clearing to share her news.

"Lucy, you are incorrigible!" Elinor laughed.

Lucy pushed Elinor toward her husband. "I am and I'm proud of it. Little John, be a dear and listen to your wife for a moment. She has something to tell you."

JANE

Jane was kneeling behind her son, holding his waist gently, ready to let go at any moment. Lucy was a few feet away, kneeling

73

as well, her arms outstretched as she eagerly begged Richard to walk toward her.

Richard took one tiny step forward.

"That's it!" Lucy encouraged. "Come on…"

Jane grinned. The whole gang was one family, that much was true. Yet within that family there were clear factions.

Robin, Mark, and Much shared a bond none of the others could, having been raised together.

Even more so, Robin, Allen, Much, and Dusty had an unbreakable friendship born in the battles they fought together during the Crusades.

Guy and Andrew were the outsiders even still. And besides these factions, there were also the individual family units that broke them up into smaller portions.

But through every small family and every division within the group, there was Lucy.

Every child preferred Aunt Lucy to any of their other aunts and uncles. Every adult could confide in her and rely on her. She was, somehow, everyone's best friend. Jane didn't know how she did it, but she was convinced the wife of Robin Hood could be no one better. She was the perfect leader's wife. At times, Jane even thought Lucy might have done better leading without her husband's impulsive nature guiding the gang.

Richard tottled forward and then paused, glancing back toward Jane.

"Go on, sweetheart! You're almost there."

As Richard took a wavering step toward Lucy again, Jane said, "Can you believe we're going to have another baby in the gang? It feels like yesterday little Mary was born."

"What I can't believe, is how long Elinor kept it a secret from us!" Lucy laughed.

"Do you think we'll get another girl, or a boy?"

Richard finally reached Lucy and she scooped him up, kissing his cheek. "I don't know."

"We'll probably still be in Sherwood…" Jane looked around the clearing. The trees, the grass, the make-shift tents. "I wouldn't want to give birth here...or raise a child here."

Lucy set Richard down and pointed toward Jane. "Go get your mother! Give her a big, wet kiss."

Richard giggled and started walking carefully toward Jane.

"I don't want to raise our children here either," Lucy said. "Sherwood is a good place for now to stay safe from the mercenary King John has hired to kill us. Yet I don't intend to stay here forever."

"Does Robin have a plan yet? Where will we go when we leave Sherwood?"

"He is thinking Scotland, for a while at least," Lucy said. "But even though he is considering it, it will take a while to convince him to actually leave this place. You know my husband, Jane...he's sentimental to a fault."

"It's sweet."

"At times. It's also unwise in the current situation." Lucy sighed. "I do trust him, though. He's always led us through every disaster and war."

"I know." Jane hadn't been a part of any of those disasters or wars, not as a member of the gang at any rate, so living in Sherwood and following Robin into battle were rather new concepts. She had met Andrew after King Richard had returned to England and Prince John's coup had been overthrown.

"I'm not opposed to staying in Sherwood for a while longer, but I don't want Richard to be raised here."

"Well, if I can convince my husband to let go of the past in favor of protecting his family in the present, your son will be raised in Scotland."

GUY

Guy lifted the mug of ale to his lips, eyeing the occupants of the tavern common room. Guy had been spying in Nottingham with Little John and Elinor, wandering the dark passageways hoping to hear anything of importance, for some hours. They had now removed themselves from Nottingham castle and were eating a much deserved meal before they subjected themselves to the dark once more.

Little John and Elinor had sat at a table near the door, Little John making it clear Guy wasn't welcome. So Guy had taken a seat in the corner of the room, where he could see everyone and no one could sneak up on him.

The sound of yelling in the street caught Guy's attention. He watched through the open door as a crowd began to form. Some people from within the tavern spewed out as other buildings along the street emptied of their inhabitants. The sound of many horses hooves clip-clopping along the street reached Guy's ear.

Guy leaned forward. That was a lot of horses.

Sure enough, in another moment mounted soldiers, three abreast, went trotting past the tavern door led by a noble looking man with bright red hair. Guy counted the soldiers silently as more trotted past the tavern. This went on for several minutes.

When the army had passed by to a different part of Nottingham, presumably headed for the castle, and the people of Nottingham had once more retreated from the streets to their various homes and businesses, Guy moved to join Little John and Elinor at their table.

"Sir Hugh, I presume," Guy said, sitting down.

Little John grunted.

"Do you think it is Sir Hugh?" Elinor asked. "The man in front? With the red hair?"

"I'll slip into the castle to confirm it," Guy said. "But I'm certain it is. He's come for us at last. With an army, no less."

"I'll go confirm it," Little John said, glaring at Guy.

Guy shrugged. If Little John didn't trust him enough to secure credible information, there was nothing he could do about it.

"Elinor, come with me." Little John stood. "We'll be back."

Guy crossed his arms, leaning back in his chair. "Am I allowed to tag along?"

"I'd rather you didn't."

"I know."

"Just wait here," Little John growled.

LUCY

Lucy was sparring with Mark when Little John burst into camp with Guy on his heels. Elinor came along much more slowly behind them.

"Robin!" Little John came to an abrupt halt and tried to catch his breath.

"What is it?" Robin asked.

Most of the gang began to gather around Little John and Guy. Lucy studied her friend with concern. He looked sick. Little John caught his breath and then said slowly, "Sir Hugh has arrived in Nottingham."

A brief silence met his words.

"How many soldiers did he bring with him?" Mark asked. "I'd like to know just how big is this group that is under orders to kill us all?"

"There were at least 300 of them," Guy said. "But maybe more."

"What do we do, Robin?" Mary asked, hugging her baby girl close to her chest.

"We wait," Robin said firmly. "And we prepare to take flight. We don't know if that will be necessary, but we need to be ready at a moment's notice. Will," Robin turned to his friend.

"Yes, Robin?"

"You and I will draw up a route of escape should Sir Hugh come calling. Lucy," Robin turned to her and placed a hand on her shoulder. "Figure out the best way to remove the children in the event of an escape. Who carries whom and so forth."

Lucy nodded. The gathering began to disperse. Robin and Will went off to one corner of the clearing to figure out the best way to leave once Sir Hugh found them. Ida and Mary went to keep an eye on the children. Little John wrapped his wife Elinor in a bear hug and tried not to cry. Lucy was worried about him. He'd just found out he had a baby on the way, and now it was likely they'd be on the run.

Lucy studied the group of rowdy children tumbling over each other, counting heads and deciding which of the adults would be the best to guard the group while everyone else carried a child or two.

ROBIN

Robin studied the arrows Will was drawing in the dirt. "That could work. What if Sir Hugh comes from the north, however."

Will, who was kneeling beside Robin, sat back on his heels. "Robin...we need to think about more than just getting out of the camp if Sir Hugh finds us."

"I know. We can't go to Nottingham or Locksley as Sir Hugh will look for us both places. Wetherby, Mark's home, will probably also be watched closely. I say we gather in Middlesborough. It's some distance from Nottingham...we could be safe there."

"For a time, but not long. Sir Hugh will follow us, Robin. Perhaps we should go somewhere we won't be suspected and looked for."

"Where would you suggest, Will?"

"Gathering in Middlesborough if the camp is compromised will work as a starting point. But we can't *stay* in my home. Ida and I were speaking the other day, and she suggested we go to Scotland, to Allen's old home."

"Lucy has suggested the same idea to me," Robin said. "But Sir Hugh is from Scotland."

"Hardly anyone knows that Allen is Scottish," Will replied. "He hides it well. He has lost his accent over the years...No one will suspect us to go there."

"If the camp is found we go to Middlesborough," Robin said. "But if Middlesborough is compromised, I like Ida's idea. Let's go to Scotland. Will, go fetch Allen. I'd like to know what he thinks of this plan, and where exactly in Scotland we should be going."

Will brought Allen over and apprised him of their plan.

"That could work," Allen said. "We'd be away from England, and perhaps Sir Hugh would not know to look there at all, considering no one knows where I am from. Ida has mentioned this to me multiple times, but I have never fully agreed to the idea."

"Why?" Will asked.

"I've never been back. I'm afraid of the memories," Allen shrugged. "But it would be safer for us than staying in England. Robin, we should do it."

"Where should we go?" Robin asked.

"Just go to Edinburgh," Allen said. "I grew up a few miles from there, but if you go there, and to Holyrood Abbey, we can find shelter and find a place to gather as a group."

Robin nodded. "Edinburgh, Holyrood Abbey. I think we can manage that.

LUCY

That evening they gathered around the fire so Robin and Will could present the multiple escape plans that they had decided on, which everyone was charged to memorize.

"Maybe we should practice them instead," Faith suggested. "That way we'll really know what we're supposed to be doing if Sir Hugh shows up at our camp with an army."

"That's a good idea," Mark said. "That way, we can also practice wrangling up the kids. It may take some getting used to, running to fetch a child and get on a horse before Sir Hugh manages to kill us."

"Did you formulate a plan for that?" Robin asked Lucy.

"I did." Lucy leaned forward, placing her elbows on her knees and eyeing her friends gathered around her. "Since Robin and Will's escape plans involve Robin, Will, Mark, and Little John to stay in the rear to fend off soldiers, they won't be required to carry children. And since Dusty is leading our charge out of the camp, she won't have to transport a child either. As for the rest of you...Mary—you take your daughter Mary. Much—you carry John. Jane—you take your son Richard. Andrew—you'll carry Edward. Elinor, as you are with child, I won't make you carry the other children. Ida—you'll take William. Allen—you carry Daniyah. I'll carry Marian. Faith, you take Lucy. That will leave Guy as the only person free to protect us from being flanked or from a head-on attack. But Robin, Will, Mark, and Little John can move about wherever they're most needed."

"All of you need to remember who your charge is," Will said. "We need to be always packed and ready to flee at a moment's notice. You need to know exactly where the child you're carrying is at all times so you're ready when Sir Hugh comes for us."

"Which means," Robin added, "that for the remainder of the time we live here in the camp, only myself, Will, Mark, Little John, Guy, and Dusty will be spying in Nottingham."

Everyone nodded their agreement.

"If the camp is compromised and we have to put this escape in action, go to Middlesborough. Once we've gathered there, we go to Scotland. The abbey at Edinburgh, in particular."

Ida nodded. "I'm glad you agreed with that idea, Robin."

"It's a good one," Robin replied. "Now get some rest, everyone."

Chapter 6

IDA

As wonderful as it felt to be wrapped in her husband's embrace, Ida bolted upright the minute she heard Edward roll over in his sleep. Two seconds later, William squeaked and sat up, and then the chaos broke loose. It started with William realizing his brother was still sleeping and deciding to jump on his blonde head, and then they immediately began to wrestle. In their enthusiasm they rolled right out of the tent. Ida hurriedly slipped on her brown dress and chased after them.

The sun had barely risen outside of the forest, and within the cover of the trees darkness still clung to every corner of the world under the leaves. The clearing itself was wrapped in early morning greyness. Ida breathed in the fresh, clean air. She placed her hands on her hips and watched her boys wrestle.

Much and Faith were both up, working over the fire making enough sausage and eggs for the entire gang. The sizzling sausage, and Faith's soft voice, were accompanied by one or two chirruping birds. Otherwise the world was quiet, except when a grunt or groan from one of the wrestling boys punctuated the air.

Ida enjoyed the relative stillness of the morning, watching her boys tumble across the dirt. She had missed this place. She loved her home; working the farm with her husband, raising her boys where she herself had been raised. But this clearing? This was her truest home.

It hadn't been long after she had joined Robin Hood's band of outlaws that the previous Sheriff had retaliated and burned her farm, killing her mother and brother, and imprisoning her father. He had tried to execute her father, but Robin had stopped it and brought him to live in the camp. Her father had only stayed for a week, and then he had vanished. Ida had never heard from him again.

In the midst of their wrestling match the boys got lost in a fit of giggles. Ida couldn't help but smile at their infectious laughter. They were often a pain, but they were her greatest joy as well. And she knew full well that she only had them in her life because of the gang. She never would have met Allen anywhere else.

After losing her family in such a tragic way, the gang had become her family and living with them in this clearing had meant the world to her. Yet after King Richard had come home, they had all moved to various places in England to go about their lives as ordinary people and her family unit had shrunk to only Allen.

She loved her husband and wouldn't trade her life with him for anything. And of course now she had her rambunctious boys as well. But being back in Sherwood meant more to her than she could easily explain.

Allen soon emerged from their shared tent and came to stand beside Ida. He slipped his arm around her waist and kissed her cheek. "The boys…"

"The boys," Ida agreed with a roll of her eyes.

"You know they take after you."

"Is that a fact?" Ida laughed. She knew it was partially true. She had been a rambunctious child; she was still impulsive and energetic. But it was also true that the same could be said of Allen. Her children hardly had a chance to be well-behaved and polite, their parents were too alike in their faults.

The boys finally rolled to a stop and sat panting for thirty seconds. Then they darted across the clearing to the fire and demanded Much and Faith give them food.

"I'm hungry!"

"I want sausage!"

"And eggs!"

Much and Faith obliged, letting the boys sample a sausage. They seemed to forget they'd also asked for eggs, because they plopped onto the ground in front of one of the log benches and contentedly chewed on their respective halves of the sausage without saying another word.

The other members of the extended family began to emerge, and soon everyone was gathered around the fire enjoying their breakfast. If hiding in Sherwood looked like this for the remainder of their time here, Ida thought it might not be so bad.

***

A few days later, Dusty and Will were both spying in Nottingham with Robin, despite the fact that it was their daughter's birthday. Robin, Dusty, and Will had left for Nottingham as soon as they'd eaten that morning.

The children were scattered about the clearing, filling the air with shrieks of laughter and a few cries of anguish now and again. Most of the adults were scattered as well, keeping an eye on the children, sharpening swords, sparring, running through the escape routes in their minds. Ida approached Much as he was washing up the mammoth pile of dishes from the breakfast meal.

"Need some help?"

Much smiled at Ida. He had his sleeves rolled back to the elbow, and his arms were covered in soapy water. He'd somehow managed to get a splash of soap on his chin as well. "I'd be grateful to you. This job is never ending." He said it with a sigh, but his grey eyes were sparkling.

Ida sat on the log beside him, grabbed a wooden plate, and plunged it into the bucket of soapy water at Much's feet.

"I wish I had my kitchen, like last time," Much sighed.

"You make do," Ida said. She had shared cooking duties with Much during the years of hiding in Sherwood Forest, so she could readily agree that having the kitchen the gang had built on the previous stay in this clearing had indeed been nicer than what they had to deal with now. Yet, as she told Much, they made do.

"I do have a reason for helping this morning, other than being kind."

"Oh?"

"Do we have the supplies necessary to make a special meal for Daniyah? Not that she'll remember it when she grows up, but I think it would be nice to do something for her. Her parents will appreciate it at the very least."

"Hmm. I'll see what we can put together."

"Great. Tell me how I can help."

"I will. I know how you cook. You nearly lost me my job as the official cook of Robin Hood's gang."

Ida laughed. "I did no such thing. I merely helped."

"We both know everyone enjoys your cooking more."

"Much…"

Much grinned. "No hard feelings. I love your cooking, too."

Ida had never celebrated her own birth growing up; her family had been far too busy working the farm and trying to survive another year to celebrate something so simple. But Robin had grown up the son of an Earl and had celebrated every birthday. He had then passed that tradition on to the children of the gang, all of whom he claimed in some way as his own. He was in Nottingham today with Will and Dusty, but Ida knew he'd want Daniyah to have a special day. This was, after all, her first birthday celebration.

***

Ida and Much managed to make several vegetable pies, chicken turnovers, and a batch of biscuits. Lucy made a covert trip to Locksley manor to secure wine for the adults to drink, and sugar for the biscuits. She also brought back garlands of summer blossoms that the villagers in Locksley had woven when they heard the reason for her visit.

Ida helped Lucy hang the garlands around the clearing on trees and tents. Ida even put one of the larger garlands around her black horse Midnight. The purples, pinks, and oranges of the blossoms stood out starkly against his dark coat. Ida kissed his velvet nose, grinning.

Little John and Mark chopped some wood and made a make-shift table. They made several rough, long planks, and placed these over half a dozen thick stumps of wood, creating the table, and then spent an hour or two smoothing down the surface.

Jane and Faith used various blankets as a tablecloth, and Mary picked some flowers to set on the table. By the time Robin, Will, and Dusty returned, the clearing had been transformed into a banquet hall of sorts, and everyone was bustling about making last minute touches to the table, the food, and the decorations. Guy and Andrew, meanwhile, had been keeping an eye on the herd of children.

Dusty clasped her hands to her heart when she saw what had been prepared. "Oh! Is this for Daniyah?"

"It is," Ida said. "We wanted today to be special."

Dusty hugged Ida, and then everyone else by turn. The group gathered around the table and the usual chaos that accompanied a family dinner ensued. The twins contributed to most of that chaos, although young Marian was equally responsible. It was a birthday celebration the adults would never forget, although the likelihood of the children, and Daniyah in particular, remembering any of it was slim.

***

Ida rolled her wrist, watching the sun glint off of the blade in her hand as she twisted it in slow circles. She took a deep breath. "Ready."

Mark's sword cut through the air in front of her in a downward motion. Ida quickly crossed the two daggers in her hands and caught Mark's blade between them. He pulled his sword free and she darted forward, one dagger extended and one resting by her waist.

Mark used his sword to deflect the dagger in front, and in the split second his side was exposed Ida brought her second dagger forward and lightly tapped him under the arm. "Gotcha."

Mark huffed, and bounced backwards two paces. "Again."

The laughter of the children echoed across the clearing and the grunts of Andrew and Lucy sparring nearby punctuated the air. It was nearing midday and it was hot. Ida tightened her grip on her daggers, trying to compensate for her sweaty palms. It wouldn't do to have her blade go flying out of her hand and seriously injure Mark, or even simply lose the sparring match due to losing her grip on her blade.

Ida felt hot and Mark looked equally so. His hair was damp and appeared permanently attached to his forehead, which in turn was shining as the sun reflected off of the gathering sweat.

Ida darted forward again with her left arm extended and right hand by her waist, exactly as before. Mark once again blocked her first blade, but this time he knocked it to his left—her right—so his side wasn't exposed as it had been before. Ida, however, followed the direction he'd knocked her arm and did a tight spin leaving her in her original position.

Because his blade was already to his left, Mark was forced to parry her second attack to his right, once again leaving his side exposed. Ida grinned as she brought her second dagger up and tapped him under the arm once more.

Mark groaned. "Why does this keep happening to me?"

"You should take a step back," Ida said. "You know I've got more blades than you do, so if you expose yourself, jump backward out of my reach. I've only got daggers, I can't reach you if you take a step back, unless I throw them. And you should also make more use of your sword. You've got a lot more range than I do. Quit sparring like I've got an equal blade."

"Can you teach me?" Jane asked, coming to stand beside Ida and sweeping her curly black hair behind her and tying it with a red ribbon at the base of her neck. "I've not used a weapon before, but considering how dangerous our lives are likely to become because of Sir Hugh, I'd like to know how."

"What weapon would you like to learn?" Mark asked. "Sword, daggers, bow and arrow?"

"What do you think would be best?" Jane asked. "In the event one of you more experienced warriors isn't able to defend me against Sir Hugh or his soldiers...what would be best in that situation?"

"Probably not the bow and arrows," Ida said. "If you get separated from someone who can protect you in a fight, it'll be close combat. I'd suggest a sword, as learning to fight a sword with only short blades like my daggers is a bit more advanced."

Ida walked over to where she'd left her sword a few feet away from the sparring match. She brought it back to Mark and Jane. "You can use my sword for now, and I'll teach you how to use it. Mark, you can help by demonstrating different motions while I guide her in doing them."

As Ida began to patiently instruct Jane, she wondered why she hadn't thought to teach her before. Jane hadn't been a member of the gang during the years in Sherwood Forest. She'd married Andrew after King Richard had come home and they'd been living in peace. Yet since they'd come to Sherwood again, someone ought to have thought to train her.

Jane was an eager student, listening intently to everything Ida said and trying to mimic the motions Mark was demonstrating.

Ida's mind drifted as she guided Jane's hand with her own. Elinor and Faith didn't use weapons either, and ought to be taught as well. Faith had been part of the gang, but hadn't chosen to learn to defend herself, while Elinor—like Jane—had married a member of the gang rather than being one herself. Although, being pregnant, it might prove hard to teach Elinor the use of weapons at present.

Ida glanced across the clearing to where Faith was sitting with the children, braiding flowers into a squirming Marian's hair. It would be nigh on impossible to teach that weak girl to use any weapons. Not because she wasn't capable, but because she insisted on being meek and afraid. Ida rolled her eyes, and concentrated on Jane. Faith's ridiculous ideas about life were best left alone. She wasn't likely to change her mind.

ANDREW

"If you had ever asked me, my love, I would have taught you myself."

Andrew and Jane were preparing for bed. They'd just entered their tent and Jane was settling Richard down on his small blanket. Andrew had spent much of his afternoon sparring with

Lucy. She had impressive skill with a blade, but wasn't difficult for Andrew to beat. He'd spent his entire life training with Guy, who was arguably one of the most skilled swordsmen in all of England. When he and Lucy had taken a break from their sparring match, he'd watched as Jane had gone to Ida and Mark to learn how to use a sword.

"You were busy this afternoon," Jane said. "You and Lucy had plenty to occupy your minds, and someone had to save Mark from humiliation."

"But Ida, of all the members of the gang…"

"Just because she doesn't like you, doesn't mean she doesn't like me. Besides, a stronger friendship with me might mean a better relationship with you."

"You think her hostilities toward me will stop because she is training my wife how to use a sword?"

Jane laughed. "You are jealous, aren't you? Well, if it makes you feel better, I will gladly take your instruction as well."

Andrew grinned. "That's all I wanted to hear."

"I thought so."

"But seriously, Jane...why Ida?"

"She's one of the best."

"You're living with Robin Hood and his entire gang of outlaws...they're all the best."

Jane laughed. "Perhaps. If I wanted to use a bow I'd ask Robin or Lucy, but Ida and Mark agreed that learning to use a sword will likely be the most useful for me."

"I agree...but if you wanted the best in terms of swordplay, Guy would have been the best choice."

"You really don't want me training with Ida, do you?"

"She isn't kind to me or Guy."

"I know, but that's not an excuse to treat her with the same attitude. You're only going to exacerbate the problem. If you want Ida to trust you then you have to trust her, too."

IDA

One evening, Ida sat by the fire ring with various members of the gang, waiting for Dusty and Guy to return from Nottingham and report what they had learned. Mary and Elinor were watching the children who were still awake, though several of them had already been put to bed.

Robin was calmly fletching arrows across the fire. Ida watched Robin's progress, not because it was particularly interesting but because nothing else was interesting enough to catch her eye.

When Dusty and Guy entered the camp, they both looked grim.

"What news?" Robin asked as the two of them joined the circle by the fire.

"Sir Hugh has begun searching Sherwood," Guy replied. "He and Sir Ralf were devising plans to search the woods systematically."

"And Sir Hugh commissioned fifty soldiers to interrogate the locals," Dusty added, "to find out where the camp is should searching the woods fail."

"In the event that he does find us," Robin said, "we go through with our escape plans. When you get free of any soldiers, head for Middlesborough to the tavern on the western edge of the town. When we've assembled there, we'll discuss further plans. Most likely we'll go to Scotland."

"And if we're followed to Middlesborough and aren't able to gather long enough to make plans?" Andrew asked.

"If we're followed to Middlesborough, then we scatter. Go wherever necessary to get free of the soldiers following you. When we've all found relative safety again, no matter how long it takes, we'll meet in Edinburgh at the abbey Allen spoke of. Tomorrow morning as soon as breakfast is over and before anyone goes to spy in Nottingham we'll practice all of the variations of our escape plan. We need to know we can easily get out of this clearing if we're found. I want everyone confidant in their roles within our plans. Now go get some rest, all of you."

Ida watched as the gang slowly dispersed from the gathering and collected their children to go to their tents and do as Robin had said.

It was the beginning.

Sir Hugh was interrogating locals to find their camp. It was a good strategy. Most of the residents of Nottingham had been among those who visited the camp after King Richard's return. Eventually one of them was going to give in and share the desired information.

Ida resigned herself to moving to Scotland.

ROBIN

Robin leaned against the rough wood of the side of the butcher's shop overlooking Nottingham Square. With his hood low over his eyes, Robin surveyed the square. It was market day, and there were various booths with merchants hawking their wares; cloth, breads, meats, baskets, weaponry, etc. It was a typical market day, but Robin could already see changes. There was still a month or more until the Nottingham Fair, but unknown faces were already appearing in Nottingham as people began to arrive in anticipation of the Fair, and merchants came bringing their wares in readiness to sell. Some of those merchants were already doing business on this average market day, while others were waiting until the Fair to unveil their goods. More people would continue to flock to Nottingham over the coming month. Nottingham Fair was renowned, not just in England, but across the world.

It was a hot day and the crowded square didn't help Robin's growing discomfort.

A man moved through the crowds that filled the square—weaving around women with baskets over their arms, children chasing dogs, and men testing new swords—and made his way to Robin's side. He leaned casually against the wall a few feet away, as though he were bored and had nothing better to do.

"Robin."

"Marcus."

They both spoke softly, so as not to draw attention to themselves. Robin wasn't too worried; after all, Nottingham was his home and these were his people. If trouble started, they'd back him without question. But Robin preferred not to start a fight with Sir Ralf or Sir Hugh's men and get innocents killed in the scuffle. It was best if Sir Hugh's soldiers, some of whom were milling the crowds even now, didn't notice Robin.

"Sir Hugh came to interrogate me last night," Marcus said. "It's well known I was your safe haven in Nottingham during Prince John's rebellion. He thought he could get useful information from me. You can rest assured he got nothing out of me."

"I had no fear of that," Robin replied.

"He's going to find the camp, Robin," Marcus said firmly. "And not by searching Sherwood."

Marcus slowly rolled up his sleeve to reveal four incisions from his wrist to his elbow, all roughly parallel to his wrist. The scabs were a bright red, and the skin around them a deeper shade of scarlet. The skin was inflamed, and a few areas looked like they were beginning to fester. Marcus rolled back his other sleeve to reveal five similar marks on his other arm.

"I fainted on the last incision. And you should see the bloodstain on my table. My wife Lillian is beside herself; she can't wash it out."

Robin clenched his fists. Anger coursed through him, fast and hot. "I'm sorry, Marcus. This won't go unanswered."

"I know, Robin. I'll be fine. But someone in Nottingham with knowledge of the camp is going to cave. Not everyone can bear this kind of pain silently. The first few cuts aren't so bad, but it soon becomes unbearable, believe me." Marcus pulled his sleeves down again.

"Thank you, Marcus. For keeping our secrets, spilling blood for us. And for the warning. I'll have us move camp tonight."

"That would be wise. I need to go. Sir Hugh's soldiers have been watching me most of the day. I'm surprised they haven't come over here yet."

"I'll leave before they become too suspicious of our conversation. I'm headed into the castle to see if I can learn anything more."

"Be safe, Robin."

"You too, my friend. I am sorry for what you have suffered. I'll make it up to you eventually. And tell Lillian I'm sorry about your table."

"Just don't die, Robin. And don't worry. Other than Sir Hugh's antics, Sir Ralf has been a decent Sheriff. Your people are not suffering."

Robin only half believed Marcus as he slipped through Nottingham towards the castle. Perhaps Sir Ralf wasn't as cruel as the late Sheriff had been, but Sir Hugh obviously was. Even if they weren't all being oppressed, some of his people were indeed suffering. They were being tortured.

Robin wished he could protect them all. Maybe he should have called upon Nottingham to back him when Sir Ralf first arrived, fought off the new Sheriff and King John's men…

But that would have eventually led to a siege of Nottingham which might have left them all starving to death or worse. Robin felt he had made the right choice in running, as much as he hated it.

IDA

Ida was tending to a scrape on Edward's arm—which he'd acquired when his brother threw a jagged edged rock at him—when Robin returned from Nottingham that evening.

"I have urgent news," were the first words out of Robin's mouth. The grimness of his voice and face made Ida's stomach turn. She'd rarely seen his blue eyes so steely. "Everyone gather around, please."

The whole gang gathered around Robin, mothers holding onto their squirming children, everyone waiting with bated breath.

"Sir Hugh is not questioning people for information about us. He's torturing them for it," Robin said. "Marcus was tortured last night. To his credit, he didn't betray us. But it is more than likely someone will give in. And I will not shame them for it. Torture is not something any of our friends asked for, nor do I wish it upon them."

"What can we do for them?" Dusty asked. Ida was sure she was probably already running through a list of supplies she'd need to heal people. Dusty had been invaluable in that regard during the years they lived in Sherwood Forest during Prince John's rebellion.

"You can come to Nottingham tomorrow, Dusty," Robin said. "We'll find anyone who has been tortured and do what we can for them, whatever you're able to do."

Dusty nodded.

"And in the meantime, we're moving camp. Someone will crack, and Sir Hugh will find this camp. We move tonight. Gather your things. We leave within the hour."

"Where, exactly, are we going?" Andrew asked.

"Further into Sherwood," was Robin's only response.

Ida carried Edward over to her tent and Allen soon joined her with William. "You fill our packs," Allen said. "I'll get our horses and then take down the tent."

Ida began stuffing blankets and clothes into packs at random, trying to elicit help from the boys. At first they eagerly brought her things to pack, but they soon got bored with that activity. Ida was then forced to point out specific items for them to grab for her, else they wouldn't have helped at all.

Allen soon returned with the horses—Ida's horse Midnight, and Allen's dappled grey horse he'd ironically named Outlaw—and Ida began to strap their packs to them as Allen pulled down their tent. The other members of the gang were busy packing their own meager belongings.

"Quiet!" Robin bellowed above the general noise and bustle.

Everyone went completely still, other than the children.

The first thing Ida heard was baby Mary gurgling in her mother's arms. And then young Marian's tiny voice, saying,"Mama?"

Finally she heard what must have caught Robin's attention. Hoofbeats.

Everyone looked to Robin.

"Looks like we're doing our escape plan for real this time, gang." Robin grabbed his bow and moved toward the sound of the horses, calling over his soldier, "Dusty, get them to safety!"

Ida scooped up William and mounted Midnight, urging him to follow Dusty who had already mounted her own horse and was preparing to leave the camp.

Ida glanced over her shoulder to make sure Allen had his charge, Daniyah, and that Andrew had picked up her son Edward.

Ida wished Lucy had chosen someone else, anyone else, to care for her eldest son. Ida didn't trust Andrew, or Guy, and she certainly wasn't comfortable leaving her children in their care. Voicing such a concern to Lucy had only earned her a pitying look and a sigh of resignation from Robin's wife. Lucy refused to change the escape plan. She, at least, trusted everyone present.

The clash of metal on metal soon rang out behind those running on horseback and Ida risked a glance over her shoulder again. Robin, Will, Mark, and Little John were in the heat of battle, and sorely outnumbered. Ida lost sight of them almost immediately, however, as the fleeing group plunged deeper into the woods and the trees obscured her view of what transpired behind.

A moment later, a group of Sir Hugh's soldiers came charging at them on horseback from the left. Guy swerved his mount in their direction and unsheathed his sword, but Ida knew he couldn't take down fifteen or more men on his own.

Ida looked around to see who was closest to her. "Elinor!"

Elinor turned to her, eyes wide.

"Take William!" Ida kissed her son's head and then briefly let go of Midnight's reins to take William in both hands and toss him across the foot of space between her horse and Elinor's. Elinor looked completely taken aback, but luckily was able to catch William instinctively.

"Mama!"

Ida ignored her son's terrified scream, though her heart constricted at the sound, and charged after Guy.

She decapitated the first soldier before the group seemed aware Guy wasn't alone. Then it was strike, parry, block, in successive blows—opponent after opponent—and Ida soon lost track of how many she killed or wounded. Her only thought was survival. She had to get back to her sons. To his credit, Midnight behaved magnificently in spite of being surrounded by swords, screaming men, and the smell of blood. Ida's horse hadn't seen combat before, at least not since she'd owned him, so she was pleasantly surprised by this, though she had little time to dwell on it.

"There're too many!" Guy's voice called out as another wave of Sir Hugh's soldiers came charging into the fray. "Follow me!"

Ida wanted to refuse, but Guy was right. They'd die if they stayed. She ducked under a soldier's sword swinging towards her head and galloped after Guy as he darted away from the soldiers on his impressive black stallion, Shadow.

The pounding hoofbeats behind them had Ida glancing over her shoulder every few seconds to see if their enemies were gaining on them. Her heart was racing, her palms sweaty, and she had a cut in her left shoulder from the fighting that stung with every step of her horse.

Guy was ahead of her, leading the retreat. Ida realized Faith, with her daughter Lucy, had somehow ended up with them. Ida supposed she probably didn't wish to be separated from her husband and had followed for that reason. She certainly wasn't there to fight or be helpful in any way. Andrew was also with them, but Ida noticed with some terror that Edward was not with him.

"Andrew! My son!"

Andrew glanced her direction. He was sweaty and tired, and had a cut on his cheek that was bleeding profusely. "I gave him to Jane!"

Ida told her heart to be calm, but it refused to listen. She would have turned around and gone in search of her sons if not for the forty or more soldiers that were chasing them. That number continued to grow as more and more of Sir Hugh's soldiers took up the chase.

Chapter 7

MARK

Mark quickly deflected an incoming sword, trying to remember the things Ida had taught him about not exposing himself and opening up to get himself killed. Sir Hugh had brought more soldiers than seemed possible. They'd swamped the camp. Robin, Will, Little John, and Mark were in a tight little knot in the center of the clearing, trying to fend off the overwhelming amount of soldiers.

Sir Hugh himself was simply sitting on his grey horse at the edge of the clearing, watching. The sneer on his face was more than a little unpleasant. He had fiery red hair that made him stand out among the soldiers, even more so because most of them were wearing their silver helmets and their hair wasn't to be seen. He just sat there, enjoying the spectacle of Robin and his band about to be brutally murdered. The soldiers on horseback had gone after the fleeing gang members, and the infantry, which seemed never ending, was left to deal with those in the camp.

Mark danced backwards half a step, out of reach of another blade, and bumped into Will's shoulder. He muttered a quick apology and got a noncommittal grunt in return.

Two more soldiers advanced on Mark, and swung their swords in opposite arcs. Mark winced as he raised his sword to block their blows. He couldn't stand much more of this; he was going to die.

Mark raised his sword horizontally to block the incoming blades. One sword crashed into his own with enough force Mark's arm felt the reverberation from his wrist to his shoulder. The second sword, however, fell from the soldier's hand as an arrow sprouted in his wrist.

Mark risked a glance in the direction the arrow had come from and saw Lucy at the far end of the clearing, on her horse Scamper, with little Marian still in her lap, shooting arrows at the soldiers. Allen was beside her on Outlaw, Daniyah in his lap still, his own bow in his hands as he shot down as many soldiers as he could.

"They need to get out of here," Will grunted behind him. He'd obviously caught sight of Lucy and Allen as well. From the tone of his voice, Mark could tell Will wasn't at all happy his daughter was in the midst of this. Robin had his back to that side of the clearing, and Mark wondered if he was aware his wife and child weren't fleeing to safety.

The pile of bodies in front of Mark's feet was up to his knees. There were only half a dozen or so fallen soldiers there, but they were piling up. Mark felt a twinge of guilt at being grateful for that pile of corpses. It made it harder for the attacking soldiers to get close to him; they had to step on or over soldiers to do so, either action leaving them vulnerable to losing their balance.

"We can't beat them," Robin grunted. "Little John, get ready to clear a path for us. We've got to get out of here."

"Our horses are gone," Little John huffed back. Mark felt a twinge of worry at that, both because it would be difficult to get out of the clearing without them and also because he was worried about where his horse, a bay named Lumpy, would go. He'd owned Lumpy for half a dozen years, and he was quite proud of owning his own horse.

"Lucy and Allen have horses," Will called over his shoulder.

"What?!" Robin twisted his head around. "Why are they still here?"

"They saw we needed help," Mark said.

"My daughter needs to be miles from here," Robin hissed.

"My daughter doesn't need to see this either," Will bit out, "But I won't say I'm not grateful for those arrows."

Mark caught sight of a group of soldiers coming out of the forest behind their mounted comrades and his heart sank.

"Allen!" Will bellowed. "Behind you!"

Allen and Lucy both swung around to face their new opponents, and then Mark lost sight of them as two more soldiers advanced on him, scrambling over the pile of corpses. One of them lost his balance and in that split second Mark's sword sliced through his chest. And then he was locked in combat with the second soldier.

"We need to go and we need to do it now!" Robin ordered.

Little John let out a roar so fierce and loud the soldiers in front of him paused. That was all he needed to charge through them, knocking them left and right out of his path. Will, Robin, and Mark took off after him.

Robin and Mark both stopped in their tracks when they heard Lucy cry out and then the wail of young Marian pierced the clearing.

"Mama!"

Robin spun around, eyes wild as he searched for his wife and child. Mark was almost more afraid of the expression on his face than the soldiers coming towards them.

"Where are they?" Robin hissed.

"There," Mark pointed. Sir Hugh had Marian tucked under his arm, though she was writhing and shrieking, and his horse had just kicked Lucy to the ground. How she'd lost her own horse, Mark had no idea.

Robin rushed through the oncoming soldiers, seemingly unaware of their presence. He was throwing them out of the way in an even more maniac-like way than Little John had. Mark ran after him, aware that Will was beside him now, and Little John thundering behind him.

So much for escaping.

When they reached Lucy, she was desperately fighting off three soldiers with one arm, the other one hanging limply, and at odd angles, by her side. Mark and Robin took up position on either side of her.

Will ran toward Allen, still on his horse. "Trade me! I'll get my daughter out of here, you help Robin get Marian back!"

Allen immediately leaped off Outlaw, handing Daniyah to her father, and then Will galloped out of the clearing.

Mark, Robin, Lucy, Little John, and Allen stood shoulder to shoulder now, fending off soldier after soldier.

Sir Hugh was nowhere to be seen.

"We have to get out and regroup, Robin," Little John roared over the din of swords clanging.

"Lead the charge, Little John," Robin yelled back.

With another fierce yell that left the soldiers trembling, Little John spun to his left and ran for the cover of the trees, clearing a path through the army. Mark, Robin, Lucy, and Allen followed close at his heels.

Mark's arms were tired from swinging his sword, and the initial adrenaline from the battle was wearing thin. "How far do we run?" he asked.

"Until the soldiers stop chasing us," Robin panted in reply. Mark gritted his teeth and prepared to run the longest race of his life.

DUSTY

When the initial chaos started, Dusty had gotten to her horse, a chestnut mare named Fiddle that she'd borrowed from Robin's stables, and waited at the edge of the clearing until everyone was mounted and following before she took off through the woods. She'd only gone a few dozen yards when she heard Lucy shout, "Robin and the others are overwhelmed. I'm turning back to help!"

Allen's voice had come a moment later, "I'm with you, Lucy!"

Dusty spun around in Fiddle's saddle and watched the two of them turn around at the tail of the group and head back for the clearing. She sent up a quick prayer for their safety, and then turned her attention to leading the rest of the group out of danger. She was in charge of seven adults and as many children and she needed to get them clear of all the fighting.

"Follow me, and keep up!"

It wasn't long before soldiers on horseback flanked them and Dusty heard Ida pass her son off to Elinor and then veer off to help Guy.

Dusty swung around in her saddle to count heads after that.

"Stay with me!" she ordered.

It was pointless. Not two minutes later Faith had gone tearing after her husband and Andrew had followed her. At least he'd had the good grace to give the child in his care, Edward, to Jane before he'd taken off. Faith still had little Lucy in her arms. Faith, the one member of the gang with no training and no weapons, and a child no more than a year old, had just gone into the thick of the fighting. And on her bay mare Promise, no less, who could hardly claim to be faster than any average horse.

Dusty sighed. This wasn't going as planned.

But now most of the soldiers on horseback were chasing after Guy and his ever-growing crew, which left Dusty free with the few who were still with her. They only had three soldiers still chasing after them.

Dusty reined in Fiddle slightly. "Much, Jane, deal with those soldiers!"

Much and Jane dropped to the back of the group, leaving Elinor, carrying William, and Mary with her namesake daughter in the middle of the group. They continued their race forward, but Dusty kept an eye on Much and Jane to make sure they successfully dealt with the soldiers.

A moment later Much had disarmed and maimed two soldiers and Jane the other one.

Jane's first battle, and with children in her arms, no less. Dusty made a mental note to talk to her when she first got a chance. Jane wasn't used to combat, she would need comfort and advice to deal with the emotions of today. The children, too, would be traumatized by everything they were witnessing.

Elinor was also unused to the ways of being an outlaw and being hunted, so she'd need a talk as well. Dusty sighed. She was going to have her work cut out for her in the coming days.

The children, of which Dusty now had five to look after, would be her priority as soon as they were safe enough to make camp. Most of them were already crying, or screaming for their missing parents.

With no soldiers following them, Dusty had her group slow their pace so they could be more careful about the tracks they left behind. It was crucial they weren't going to be followed.

They made their way along with the utmost care, making sure their horses didn't snap any loose branches lying on the ground. Dusty had Much get off his horse and clear any hoof prints they left in the dirt. And in the meantime, they all crooned softly to the children in their care, trying to quiet them so they wouldn't attract the attention of the soldiers.

They hadn't been traveling for very long when Dusty heard pounding hoofbeats behind them. She swung around in her saddle again, looking behind to find the source of the sound. It wasn't a soldier who came galloping through the trees though; it was Will.

And he had Daniyah.

But he wasn't riding their white horse Rebel; where their horse had run off to Dusty didn't know, but Will was riding Allen's horse Outlaw. Allen himself was nowhere to be seen.

Will had multiple cuts on his arms, as evidenced by the rips in his blue tunic and the darkened splotches where the blood was drying on his clothes.

"Will! What happened?"

"You need to change direction," Will replied, riding up beside her. "You aren't leaving tracks, but you're still going in roughly the same direction as when you left camp. We need to zig and zag more to lose anyone who tries to follow. And let's find a stream or two to pass through while we're at it. And whatever camp we set up needs to be farther from the first one. And as deep into the woods as we can get."

"Where's Allen? And Lucy? And everyone else?"

"Lucy's wounded, but Robin and the others are with her still. I traded places with Allen because I needed to get our daughter to safety. Lucy and Allen were in the thick of things like we were; that was no place for children. Marian's been captured by Sir Hugh."

"Captured!"

"Should we go back?" Much asked.

"Absolutely not," Will replied. "We get to safety and then we head to Middlesborough, or Scotland if need be, as planned."

"But Marian!" Jane cried.

"Robin will do everything in his power to save his daughter. My concern is saving the rest of you," Will replied.

"Let's get moving," Dusty said. "We can discuss everything once we've found a place to make camp."

Dusty was worried about her friends; the group with Robin, the group with Guy, and poor little Marian being kidnapped. It was awful and terrifying. Yet at the same time, she felt an overwhelming sense of relief that Will was with her, and that both her children were safe with them as well.

***

It was well into the night, the forest nearly pitch black, when they finally chose a spot to make camp. Will refused to let them light a fire, so they huddled close together to keep warm, for the night was chilly. Dusty mixed together a drink, water and certain herbs, which she gave to everyone to help ward off the cold.

"Do you think everyone made it out?" Much asked.

"I'm sure they did," Will replied. "We've all gotten very good at surviving over the years."

Dusty had her three-year-old son in her lap, holding him close to her heart. Will still held Daniyah and seemed unlikely to ever let her go. They could have lost their children today, and Dusty was immensely grateful that they had not.

Still, Marian was missing.. There was no telling what Sir Hugh would do to her, or how he would treat her. Would he be gentle because she was a child or would he treat her as he had the residents of Nottingham that he'd been torturing? Dusty didn't want to think about that.

"Papa?" little Richard asked from Jane's arms, looking up at his mother expectantly.

"Papa's busy," Jane whispered. "But he'll come back. I promise."

111

"Where's Mama?" Edward asked. He and William were, for once, sitting still. They were huddled together at Elinor's feet, looking as forlorn as Dusty had ever seen them.

"Your mama and papa are taking care of the bad men," Elinor said. "They want to keep you safe."

"Are we going back to camp?" William asked.

"No," Dusty said. "But we're going to make a new camp, won't that be fun?"

"Mama will be there?" Edward asked.

Dusty sighed, trying not to give in to the tears that threatened. "Eventually, yes, all the mamas and papas will be together again, I promise."

When that might be, Dusty had no idea. But she knew they would eventually find each other and at some point the world would be a safe place for them to live in. This wasn't the first time they'd been forced into hiding. They'd survived before and then had several years of peace. That peace would come again, and in the meantime God would take care of them. He always did.

MARK

His legs ached. His arms ached. His teeth hurt with every jarring step as he ran. Breathing had become nigh on impossible an hour ago.

And yet Mark kept running.

He had no choice.

The soldiers were still running behind them.

The light had long since disappeared. Both Mark and his friends, as well as the soldiers, were simply stumbling through the darkness, tripping over fallen logs and large stones or plunging unexpectedly into streams of cold water. It was not a pleasant trip.

Little John had dropped to the back of the pack so that whenever a soldier happened to overtake them a single hit to the head with his fist would knock them out. They were more than safe from being captured with Little John watching their backs.

As long as they kept running.

If all the soldiers caught up to them at once, they'd be overwhelmed. Thankfully none of them were on horseback.

Mark wondered what had happened to everyone else. Had they gotten away safely? Were they even now headed for Middlesborough? And what of poor little Marian?

Lucy stumbled in front of him, and Mark ran into her, sending them both sprawling to the ground. Robin groped through the darkness to pull his wife to her feet and Mark scrambled up on his own.

"Keep running," Robin said hoarsely. Shouting orders had left his voice ragged, running had left him short of breath, and losing his daughter had left him emotional. It was little wonder he sounded as bad as he did.

They continued on, stumbling blindly through the forest, hoping the soldiers would tire out before they did. The fact that the soldiers were in full armor was to the gang's favor. The heavy armor would assist in exhausting them before Mark and his friends collapsed.

The forest began to slowly lighten. Mark could see the vague form of his friends' bodies now. He could tell Lucy's arm was still hanging limply at her side in odd angles. He could see the ground in front of him, which made running slightly less difficult than it had been in the darkness.

Yet their pace slowed even as the forest brightened. They all knew it, but there was nothing to be done about it. They were tired. Beyond tired.

Yet they had to keep running.

The crunch of their feet in the dried leaves and twigs on the ground, the loud huffing of Little John behind him, and clinking chainmail of the soldiers behind them. These were the only sounds that filled Mark's ears as he ran. Little John's huffing became louder and louder by the minute.

"Don't...stop..." Mark called faintly over his shoulder.

Little John merely grunted in response.

How long had they been running? Twelves hours? More? It didn't matter. All that mattered was that they kept moving.

One foot forward. And the next. And the next.

The trees were thinning in front of them. They were either drawing close to a clearing or meadow, or they'd reached the edge of the forest.

Mark suddenly realized he was very hungry. Famished, in fact.

His stomach ached and seemed to be gnawing on his insides as if it was trying to eat him from the inside out. Mark was almost too exhausted to form a coherent thought, but he did vaguely wonder if his stomach had become a cannibal.

A loud crash behind them had the group turning as one to see what had happened.

One of the soldiers was laying on the ground, face in the dirt; the others continued to run on, leaving him there.

"I think...one...fainted..." Robin panted.

"Good," Mark responded. "Now...they...all..need..to..."

It was difficult to talk when running, exhausted, and having trouble breathing, so Mark stopped.

His lungs burned. He could barely draw a breath. His legs felt like lead and ached from his toes to his waist. There was a pounding in his head that made him feel like his whole head was about to explode.

The group moved onward in silence, on and on and on through the forest. Their movement could hardly be described as running anymore, but they kept moving regardless. More soldiers began to collapse behind them.

They broke free of the trees half an hour later. Robin paused for a mere second to get his bearings and see where in the world they'd come out of Sherwood before leading the group onward across the open plain. Mark kept his eyes on the back of Robin's head, focusing on his friend so he wouldn't faint, forcing his feet to follow wherever Robin might lead.

Of the hundreds of soldiers that had been following them, about fifty remained. Mark reluctantly admired their determination.

As they ran across the open plain, passing one farm house and several clumps of trees, Little John lagged further behind Mark unable to keep up their already slowed pace. Lucy nearly fainted, tripping over her own two feet, so Robin attempted to carry her which slowed him down as well until he was running beside Mark rather than in front. This left Allen to lead the charge.

And all the while, the soldiers followed along behind. Yet with every passing hour, more and more of them collapsed to the ground, exhausted, gasping for air, their legs unwilling to move another inch, and often even unconscious.

Mark couldn't breathe. Every time his foot hit the ground it sent a jarring vibration up his leg, through his torso, and to his throbbing head which compounded his headache and caused him to gasp for air. Which was unfortunate, because he couldn't breathe. His lungs were burning. He was fairly certain he was going to pass out from his inability to draw a breath.

Mark focused on his breathing, trying to get air to his desperate lungs. He'd never imagined breathing would be such a difficult thing to do. He finally managed to get a small amount of air to his starved lungs.

Unfortunately, being so focused on breathing, he'd lost his concentration on his surroundings and tripped over a log in his path. He stumbled for a moment, trying to keep his balance. He knew if he hit the ground he wasn't getting back up again.

He managed to stay upright, and then to his dismay he realized the log he'd tripped over was in fact a small branch from a nearby tree, no bigger than an inch thick.

He was losing his ability to function. Mark was now also convinced, due to that log that turned into a tiny stick, that he was losing his mind.

After several more hours of running, the small town of Ilkeston came into view.

Mark glanced over his shoulder. Only eight soldiers were still keeping up the chase.

Mark was desperate to reach that town. If they could just reach Ilkeston, perhaps the villagers would assist them. Then again, maybe they would side with King John and then Mark and his friends would be doomed.

It wasn't long before they reached the town. As they trotted passed the first few houses, people watched with curious eyes from gardens and windows, those in the street stepping off to the side to give the straggling group space.

Allen slowed as a nobleman approached them.

"You look like weary travelers, and wounded too," he said. "I am Sir Henry, Baron of Ilkeston. What business do you have here?"

"Robin...of...Locksley..." Robin panted, kneeling—not out of respect, but to lower Lucy to the ground because he could no longer hold her weight.

"Robin Hood? The Sheriff of Nottingham?"

"Ex-Sheriff," Allen huffed, struggling to breathe, and bending at the waist, hands on his knees.

Sir Henry noticed the soldiers now entering the town behind them. "Ah. Ran into some trouble, did we? Gilbert!"

Sir Henry called to another man nearby, armed with two swords, with the hilt of a dagger visible over the top of his boot. "Dispatch those soldiers of King John's."

"With pleasure," Gilbert responded, moving toward the soldiers and drawing one of his swords.

"Come with me," Sir Henry said. "You can take shelter at my home. You need sleep, food, and to get off those feet." He scooped up the barely conscious Lucy into his arms, and walked up the street. Mark and the others scrambled to follow him. Now that the immediate danger was over, Mark could hardly force his legs to keep moving. He just wanted to lie down and never move again.

Unfortunately for Mark, and the rest of his friends, Sir Henry's manor was located outside of Ilkeston and they had quite a walk.

Mark was only vaguely aware of entering a house and being led to a room. He saw a bed and collapsed into it without a second thought. His legs were burning, his lungs on fire, and he had a pounding headache. He thought he might die from exhaustion, right there in that bed.

Instead of dying, however, Mark simply drifted off into sleep.

***

It was several hours before he woke again. When he did, the first thing he noticed was that his legs still hurt, and not only his legs but the rest of his body as well. His lungs still felt like a fire had been lit inside them, his ribs felt like they'd been trampled by fifty horses, his head still hurt.

The second thing he noticed was a platter of food sitting on the small table by his bed. Mark sat up immediately and tore into the piece of chicken first, then devoured the thick slice of bread next. He washed this down with the entire mug of ale that had been set out for him before he dove back into the food.

After a few minutes he lay back down on the bed, feeling nauseous. Maybe eating so much food so quickly hadn't been such a good idea.

After a few minutes, during which his stomach continued to rebel, Mark drifted back to sleep.

***

The next time Mark awoke, there was a fresh platter of food by his bed. This time, however, he merely grabbed a slice of bread and some cheese and then left the room. His room opened into a large square room that was empty save for one bookshelf against the wall to his right, underneath the window. Outside, the sun seemed to be getting ready to set, although the brilliant array of colors that would accompany such an event had yet to appear in the sky. There were several doors scattered about the open room. Most of them were open and revealed spacious sleeping chambers such as the one Mark had just exited.

Mark left the square room and the sleeping chambers behind and wandered down the hall toward the sound of voices. He passed several closed doors before he came to an open one. Inside was a large room filled with chairs, with tapestries on the walls, and a long table at the far end of the room. The chairs were occupied by Robin, Lucy—with her arm in a splint—Allen, Sir Henry, and Gilbert.

"Mark," Robin said as he entered. "I'm glad you're up. We were beginning to think you'd sleep for another day."

"Day?" Mark asked, taking a seat beside Allen.

"We arrived here early yesterday morning," Robin replied. "And most of us slept till the middle of the night before we ate the food Sir Henry had his cook prepare for us. And now it's almost evening again."

"How do you feel?" Lucy asked, concern evident on her face.

"I ache," Mark said, "but I feel better. Much better. And you?"

"Now that my arm has been dealt with, I feel physically better. However, I won't feel truly well until I have my daughter back." Lucy's voice trembled as she spoke, and tears glistened in her eyes.

Mark looked toward Robin and saw that he, too, was fighting tears.

"We'll get her back," Sir Henry promised.

"We?" Mark asked.

"Oh, I intend to help," Sir Henry replied. "I am no friend of King John's. And I know many of the people who were saved from death by Robin Hood and his gang, you that is, during King Richard's absence. I will do whatever I can to help you all, for the sake of all the people you have helped over the years."

"Do we head back to Nottingham then?" Allen asked.

"First you rest and regroup," Gilbert said. "Then you can make plans."

"What of the rest of the gang?" Mark asked.

"They'll hopefully follow the plan," Robin said bitterly. "Middlesborough, and if that isn't safe, Scotland."

"Will we visit Middlesborough to see if they made it, or go to Nottingham and get Marian first?"

"Rest first," Gilbert interjected before Mark could ask more questions or suggest other possible plans they could make.

"Rest, eat, gather your strength," Sir Henry agreed. "Then make plans."

"We make plans tomorrow," Robin said firmly. "As soon as everyone is awake."

"That isn't much of a rest," Sir Henry said. "You had quite the run."

"My daughter is currently in the clutches of a man who has already tortured a good friend of mine. I'm not going to *rest* any longer than necessary," Robin said angrily.

Sir Henry raised his hands, gesturing for Robin to calm down. "My mistake. Getting your daughter back is of the utmost importance. However, it will be easier to do so, and likely more effective, when you are fully rested and not still exhausted."

Mark agreed with that assessment, but he was just as anxious to get Marian back as Robin was.

SIR HUGH

Sir Hugh strode through Nottingham castle, headed for his own room. It had been a busy and disappointing day. He'd expected to catch an outlaw. It hadn't happened.

The entirety of Robin Hood's gang seemed to have escaped in the last two days. Over a hundred of the men that Sir Hugh had brought with him from Scotland had been killed; some in battle with the outlaws, some from exhaustion from chasing Robin Hood across England on foot. Those left alive had come straggling back into Nottingham that very morning and Sir Hugh had been furious.

He'd ordered some hanged and some tortured, and had even decapitated one the minute he set foot in the castle.

Sir Hugh hated incompetence, and he hated losing. His job was to kill Robin Hood and the rest of his band of outlaws. Sir Hugh intended to do just that, and if his soldiers were going to fail him they didn't deserve to live.

Sir Hugh paused when he reached the door to his room. He took a slow deep breath, releasing the frustration from the day, and rolled his shoulders to help himself relax. Then he opened the door and went in.

The sun had set, but there were logs crackling in the fireplace to his left, and a lantern hung from a wooden post in the ceiling near the middle of the room which emitted enough light for him to see. A table in the center of the room was covered in various papers, maps, and books. On the bed against the wall opposite the fireplace sat a young servant girl Sir Hugh had hired.

"Are they sleeping?" Sir Hugh asked softly, so as not to wake his young charges.

"Yes, sir," the girl responded timidly. "They've been asleep for nearly an hour." She kept her head lowered, her dark hair hiding most of her face, but kept sending furtive glances toward his face.

"You can go now."

"Yes, sir." She jumped up immediately and darted to the door.

When the servant girl was gone, Sir Hugh approached the bed and gently sat on the edge of it. Two tiny forms were blissfully ignorant of the woes of the world, sleeping soundly. Sir Hugh gently brushed red curls out of the sweet face of the child closest to him before he bent and kissed her forehead.

A gentle and good feeling, the only goodness Sir Hugh believed he possessed, filled his being. He loved his daughter more than anything in the world. He'd never felt this overwhelming, pure emotion for her mother, and was not distressed when she died, merely inconvenienced.

Sir Hugh turned his attention to the second child, brushing hair out of her face in equal tenderness. He was sorry he'd terrified the girl in Sherwood, but he'd make it up to her. His intention had been to wound Robin Hood and the outlaws, not this sweet child.

Sweet was, perhaps, not the word best used to describe the little girl Sir Hugh had picked up in Sherwood. She had bitten his arm three times in the last two days, and spent most of her time wailing for her mother and kicking and scratching the servant girl Sir Hugh employed to look after his daughter, and now this little girl as well.

The servant girl's shock when he'd brought the little girl to her to watch over alongside his daughter, along with her involuntary cry of "Marian!", had made Sir Hugh realize just how fortunate he'd been. There were many children among the outlaws, and Sir Hugh hadn't had the least idea which one he'd taken. It soon became apparent, however, that he'd managed to collect Robin Hood's own daughter. Sir Hugh was delighted. It would be a crushing blow to the outlaw and would leave him vulnerable.

But the child wasn't responsible for who her parents happened to be, and Sir Hugh wasn't going to hold it against her. He'd decided he would keep her. She was feisty, which he loved, and she was also alone in the world now that her parents were going to be killed. Sir Hugh didn't want her to have to make her way in the world as an orphan. That was a cruel fate for a child. So he was going to adopt her. When she grew up, she would hardly remember these first two years of her life. She wouldn't know who Robin Hood was, or care.

Chapter 8

ANDREW

Andrew leaned back in his chair, lifting the spindly front legs up off the floor to rest his head against the wooden wall behind him, closing his eyes. Faith was across the room on the bed, crooning to little Lucy. She'd drawn the canopy back so that she could see the rest of the room and engage in the conversation. Guy and Ida were arguing over what the next course of action should be.

They'd managed to kill or evade all of Sir Hugh's soldiers that had been chasing them. The moment they were clear of any opponents, Guy had led them straight to Middlesborough. The four of them, plus little Lucy, had been here at a tavern on the edge of town, for two days. There was no sign of any of the others. Thankfully there was no sign of Sir Hugh either.

"We wait as long as we have to!" Ida hissed. "We're not giving up on them."

"I'm not giving up on them," Guy replied angrily. "I'm thinking of the safety of my family, and you, and Andrew. We are a group now, and you're going to have to trust me."

"And why would I do a thing like that? You're one of the worst men of the century."

"I was, but I'm not anymore. And right now, we have bigger problems than your trust issues with me."

"You think I don't know that? I don't care how many soldiers Sir Hugh sends to Middlesborough, we wait for Robin and Allen and everyone else."

"We don't have time to wait," Guy insisted. "When Sir Hugh brings his army here, how do we escape? We barely escaped in the forest."

"Then we go to Scotland," Ida said reluctantly. "That's where everyone will eventually go."

"Sir Hugh is from Scotland," Guy objected. "We go to my estate."

"You don't even know if your estate is still yours!" Ida scoffed. "It's been what, ten years? What makes you think the villagers still work for you? What makes you think some other lord hasn't taken over your land and manor? You haven't exactly been taking care of it in a decade."

"The only way to find out is to go there."

"That's what this is, isn't it? You just want your lands and title back."

"This isn't selfishness! This is me trying my utmost to protect the people who happen to be under my care at the moment, and that includes you. Middlesborough is sure to be overrun by Sir Hugh, hence, it is not safe. Sir Hugh is from Scotland and knows that area better than we do. We couldn't hide from him there. Hence, not safe. My estate could be safe. It's far from here, it's fortifiable."

"I don't think—"

"We're going!" Guy interrupted. "Whether you like it or not, we're going. And don't even think about staying here or going off to Scotland alone. Robin wouldn't allow that, and you know it. We stick together until this storm has passed."

"I hate you."

"I am aware of that fact."

Silence followed this exchange, and Andrew lifted his head. Guy had sunk into a wooden chair by the bed that seemed too small for his lanky form, looking haggard and distraught; Ida was standing by the window, her clenched fists and set jaw the only evidence of her anger.

Andrew was concerned about Guy. He hated to see his lifelong friend in distress. Guy's brow appeared to be permanently furrowed, his eyes constantly dark with worry. He was relapsing into the brooding nature he'd had back when he worked for Prince John and the previous Sheriff of Nottingham.

Andrew was also worried about the rest of the gang; were they alright? Had any of them been injured? Caught?

And he was petrified when it came to his wife and young son. Where were they? Were they safe? Had they been hurt? Captured? Worse?

Just thinking about Jane and Richard made Andrew's throat constrict. He closed his eyes to stop the flow of tears that was just beginning.

"We leave in the morning," Guy said quietly.

Andrew opened his eyes. Faith had scooted along the bed closer to where her husband's chair was and had draped an arm around him, leaning forward to rest her head against his shoulder.

Ida still stood by the window, watching darkness descend over the town.

Andrew got to his feet. "In that case, I'm going to bed."

He moved across the room to the door that led to an adjoining chamber where he was staying. Ida had a room across the hall. They were all similarly furnished with a bed, covered in a wool blanket or two, a small table, and two or three wooden chairs scattered about.

Once in his own room, Andrew fell into bed and kicked off his boots. He let the canopy fall closed and shroud him in darkness. He tried to picture Jane and Richard safely tucked away in some corner of Sherwood. He recalled Jane's sweet smile, and Richard's bright blue eyes.

Andrew stopped fighting the liquid that escaped from his eyes and simply let himself cry.

***

As soon as the sun was up, Andrew and his friends ate the food Guy had ordered be brought to their rooms—bread, cheese, fruit—fetched their horses from the tavern's stable, and started on their journey. It was a cool morning. Guy led the small group, and Ida took up the rear. Andrew half wondered if she'd desert them at some point on their journey. The trees dotting the landscape were turning various shades of yellow and red. Andrew tried to enjoy the scenery and not think too much about his wife, his son, or the other missing members of the gang.

It was impossible not to think of them, but he did try, if only for his own sanity.

The road to Gisbourne, Guy's estate, was a long one. It had been a very long time since Andrew had followed Guy from the estate, across England, and eventually to Nottingham. The lives they had lived on that old estate were distant, but vivid. Oh, so vivid.

Andrew could still remember Lady Gisbourne's gentle smile, the feel of her arms around him and how it felt to be loved, to have a mother. He couldn't remember his life before being bought by Lord Gisbourne to be Guy's manservant. He didn't know if he even had a mother; but he had Lady Gisbourne. He could still remember how it felt to be cared for by her.

As they plodded along, Andrew became less and less aware of the greenery surrounding the road.

He heard the crack of the whip as Lord Gisbourne punished Lady Gisbourne for intervening when he would beat Guy as a child. He recalled huddling with Guy in his dark room, holding each other tightly and hoping Lord Gisbourne wouldn't come for them again. He could still hear Lady Gisbourne's soft footsteps as she came to comfort them without her husband's knowledge.

He could still feel the horror at discovering Lord Gisbourne had murdered Lady Gisbourne, remember watching Guy's goodness fade away after his mother's death. Giving way to his despair and his darkness, and eventually, his cruelty.

And now they were going back to that memory-filled estate, both of them changed men.

Middlesborough disappeared behind them, and Andrew focused on the road ahead. Guy would be facing old demons when they reached the Gisbourne estate, and he would need support.

JANE

Jane focused on her son's breathing, even and slow, in the hopes of bringing a sense of calm to herself. He was sleeping so peacefully, as if the world wasn't a terrible place.

It was their second night in the woods. Jane wasn't sure how her life had come to this. She'd lived a relatively normal life, her childhood mostly uneventful. Of course Prince John's rebellion and the cruelty of the previous Sheriff of Nottingham had led to some upheaval as she reached adulthood, but very little of her personal life had been upended. And then King Richard returned and all was put to rights. She'd met Andrew, and they'd fallen in love in peace. Nothing very interesting had ever happened to her.

And now she was a fugitive, living in the woods, with no idea what had become of her husband.

"How are you doing?" Dusty had come to sit beside her.

"With which part?" Jane sighed. She brushed her fingers through Richard's hair as he slept, the ache in her chest making it hard to breathe.

"You miss Andrew, and you're worried about him."

"Very."

Dusty took her hand and squeezed it. "He will go to Middlesborough as soon as it is safe, we'll meet him there, and then travel to Scotland. All will be well."

"I hope you're right."

"And the ambush...how are you dealing with that?"

"You mean, how do I feel now that I've taken someone else's life and ended it mercilessly? Not great." Jane shuddered.

"When I think about it, I can still feel the crunch of bone and the squelch of flesh as I drove my sword into…"

"It isn't pleasant," Dusty said. "But I don't think he was dead, if that's a comfort to you. From what I saw, his wound was treatable. I would have stopped and treated it myself if I hadn't been in charge of making sure the rest of you got away safely."

"You would have healed Sir Hugh's soldier?" It shouldn't have surprised Jane; Dusty was a healer, after all. She firmly believed everyone deserving of her skills.

"I would."

"And you are sure I didn't kill him?"

"He wasn't dead when you struck him, and if he received the medical attention required, no. He's not dead."

Jane sighed in relief. "Well…I still hurt someone, rather grievously…and I want to believe he deserved it for trying to kill my family. But I'm strangely glad he's not dead."

"I don't relish the idea of any of Sir Hugh's soldiers dying in that fight," Dusty said. "I'm sure some did, and I don't blame any of our friends for doing what was necessary to survive. But I don't relish it…"

"What are we going to do now?"

"Follow the plan. If no one is in Middlesborough, then we go to Scotland as discussed. Don't worry, Jane. We'll find everyone again; I know we will."

***

Will and Much had left the new camp first, surveying the woods and ascertaining if Sir Hugh's soldiers were anywhere nearby. There was no sign of the soldiers or the rest of the gang—thankfully there were no bodies of the latter discovered in the old camp—so Dusty and Will decided it was time to take the group to Middlesborough.

Richard was sleeping in her arms, and Jane pulled him close. His small head was resting on her shoulder, his dark hair that so resembled his father's falling over his face, covering his sweet face. Richard was going to look exactly like his father Andrew, Jane was sure of it. But where was Andrew right now? She could only hope and pray that he was alright.

Mary, Much, and Elinor were packing what little of their belongings had come unpacked in the last few days. Will and Dusty were discussing the safest path to Middlesborough. That's where they were headed today, to wait for the rest of the gang. And if no one showed, they'd go to Scotland. Six adults and as many children traipsing around England hoping not to be caught by mercenaries and killed. When did her life become this?

She knew the stories; she was intimately connected with Robin Hood himself and his family since she'd married into it. Yet she hadn't lived the adventures they had, and she wasn't used to living on the run.

She and her family had suffered under Prince John and the Sheriff as any resident of Nottingham had, and had been saved so many times by Robin or Lucy or Will or any of the other members of the gang. They'd been her heroes. She knew they'd been outlaws, been hunted. She had simply never imagined herself in their shoes one day.

As soon as everything was packed, they mounted their horses and set off. Jane was riding one of Robin's many horses, a gentle brown horse named Jack. She and Andrew only owned one horse, Quest, and she was hopeful her husband was riding the bay to safety right now. Or perhaps Quest was safely stabled at an inn in Middlesborough and Jane would see her husband in a few short hours.

Even though he wasn't hers, Jane knew Jack fairly well. Robin was very free with his stable, a stable that was overflowing with horses he'd collected over the years. He owned some because he was the Earl of Locksley and needed horses both for himself and to run the farms on his estate. Then he'd acquired more horses after becoming the Sheriff of Nottingham. Yet he wasn't selfish with them and let any of the gang, and often many others in Nottingham and the surrounding area as well, borrow his horses without any thought of being paid. Jane had taken Jack on many a ride, and she felt a kinship with the gentle horse.

Richard had woken up a bit when Jane first mounted Jack, but the cadence of the trotting that followed seemed to lull him back to sleep.

It wasn't long before they exited Sherwood and set out across the open plain in the direction of Middlesborough. Jane hoped Andrew was there, and the rest of the extended family as well. She doubted she'd ever get a good night's rest again until they were all together once more.

***

The arrival in Middlesborough was met with disappointment. No one was there yet. Will procured them several rooms at the tavern on the edge of town Robin had told everyone to go to, and they settled in for the night. The journey had been several hours long, and they were tired and emotionally-wrought.

They'd taken a meal together in Will and Dusty's room, and were about to retire to adjoining rooms to get some much needed sleep. Although Jane was still under the impression she'd never sleep again.

Darkness had fallen on the world outside, but Dusty's room was bathed in a soft orange glow from the fire crackling cheerfully in the corner.

Jane had gone to her room, the one adjoining, to check that the fire was lit and the bed turned down, and was just returning to Dusty's room to collect her son and put him to bed.

There was a sharp knock on the door and then the tavern keeper immediately entered. Jane paused in the doorway between her room and Dusty's, waiting to see what he wanted.

"I'm sorry to bother you," the man said softly. "It's just that, well, I thought you'd want to know, Will."

"What do I need to know, David?"

"Sir Guy of Gisbourne was here, and several others with him."

"They were here?" Jane asked, coming back into the room.

"Who was?" Much asked.

"How many?" Elinor demanded.

"Where did they go?" Mary asked.

David held up his hands to slow the onslaught of questions. "It was Sir Guy and three others, plus a little girl."

134

"Do you know who, David?" Will asked.

"Other than you, Will, who grew up here in our town and still live with us, and Little John who was our own outlaw many years ago—and Robin Hood himself, of course—I don't know your gang by sight. Just the names that are becoming legend."

"What did they look like?" Jane asked.

David scrunched up his nose in thought, his green eyes wandering up toward the ceiling. "Well I think one was Sir Guy's little wife, and I presume the child was his as well."

"Ida and Andrew broke off when we were escaping to go help Guy," Dusty offered. "It could be them, with Faith and little Lucy as David said."

"That would be the right number and gender of people," David agreed.

"Where did they go?" Will asked.

Jane's breath caught in her throat. Where was her husband?

"They didn't say. But they left early this morning, almost as soon as the sun was up."

"This morning!" Jane gasped. She had missed her husband by only a few hours? At least she knew he was alright. A weight lifted from her shoulders, and she felt free. She also felt like she would burst into tears at any moment.

Elinor still didn't have any word of Little John.

"Mama?" Edward asked. The children had been gathered in one corner of the room, with bread and cheese set out before them. William had a piece of bread hanging from his mouth, Daniyah was laying down with her head in her brother John's lap, seemingly sleeping. Mary and Richard were both watching the adults with wide round eyes. Obviously they'd also been listening to the conversation, as Edward had, though they likely understood very little of it.

"Your mama is safe," Jane said in answer to Edward's question, moving toward the group of children. She gave Edward a gentle hug and then scooped up Richard.

"And so is papa." She kissed her son's cheek. Edward and William gazed up at her expectantly. "We'll see your mama soon, I promise."

The children just watched her with their big, scared eyes.

"If they follow the plan," Much said, "they'll be headed for Scotland next."

"We'll leave in the morning and see if we can overtake them," Will said. "If we don't catch them, we'll meet up in Edinburgh."

Dusty moved to sit with the children, as did Elinor, softly speaking comfort to them.

Jane took Richard to her room and put him to bed on a small straw mattress near the fire to keep him warm, tucking a wool blanket around him. Then she lay in the larger bed herself, contemplating this new development. She'd see Andrew again very soon. It was all going to be okay.

***

As soon as the sun was up, they set out for Scotland. Or, more accurately, as soon as they managed to wrangle six toddlers into clothes, feed them, and get them onto the horses, they set out for Scotland.

Jane's heart felt much lighter than it had in the past few days. Andrew was alright, and they would be together again soon. If one group of the gang was alright, then the rest likely were as well. The only one that they needed to be worried about was little Marian, who was likely still in Sir Hugh's clutches.

Dusty had estimated it would take about two weeks to reach Edinburgh, so if they didn't catch up to Andrew and the others, then it would be a fortnight before Jane saw her husband. Though that thought pained her, she felt that it was bearable; he was safe. That was more than enough. She could wait a few days to see him.

As they continued their ride—no longer worried about her family—Jane began to think of other things. Being hunted as they were was a strange experience. Jane felt she wasn't quite as prepared as the others had been when they joined the gang. And her training with Ida had been cut short due to Sir Hugh's untimely arrival.

"Will?" Jane moved her horse closer to Will's at the front of their group.

"Yes, Jane?"

"Would you train me when we make camp each night? Ida and Mark were teaching me to use a sword, but as they are not with us at the moment, I could use a new instructor."

"What weapons? The sword only?"

"Just a sword."

"I can do that. I heard their training was put to good use in our escape."

Jane grimaced. "I did fight one soldier and disarm him. A nasty business. I don't like it. But I'm afraid given our circumstances being able to defend myself and have my comrades' backs is vitally important."

"I agree," Will said. "I'll gladly teach you."

"I'd say I could use instruction," Elinor jumped into the conversation. "But considering my circumstances, it might be best not to try."

It had been over a month since Elinor had told them all she was expecting Little John's first child. In that month, she had already begun showing. She was probably right, learning to use a sword in her condition might not be a feasible task.

Jane hoped the journey to Scotland wasn't going to harm either Elinor or the child, as well. Pregnancies were a dangerous business, and traveling while with child only added to the danger.

FAITH

Faith watched the clouds drifting across the sky as she and Promise trotted along behind Guy. Ida was to her left and Andrew brought up the rear. Little Lucy was currently riding with her father, sitting in front of him and tangling her hair in Shadow's mane.

They had been traveling for several days. Ida had rarely stopped talking, berating Guy the entire journey. She thought this plan was stupid to begin with; she was also furious that Guy was not following the plan laid out by Robin; and at the heart of the matter, she was devastated to be traveling a different direction than perhaps her husband and children were. Assuming Allen and the twins had even made it out of the ambush alive at all.

Faith was sure that they had, but it was impossible to convince Ida that they were alive. She needed to see them to have any peace of mind, and as they were now traveling in the opposite direction than any other survivors might be, it was impossible to give her that peace of mind.

Faith understood where her frustrations stemmed from and she felt compassion for Ida. For the last hour Ida had been silent. Andrew had quietly commented to Faith at one point that it was a nice reprieve. But Faith thought the silence was worse than the shouting.

What pain was Ida harboring? She would need to talk it out at some point; keeping it buried would not be healthy.

Faith glanced toward Ida. She was staring straight ahead, following Guy's lead, but her eyes were unfocused and her brow furrowed. What was she thinking about?

Faith nudged Promise closer to Ida's mount. "Are you okay?"

"I'm fine!" Ida snapped, glaring at Faith. "If we all die because Sir Hugh tracks us down to your husband's meager estate and we have no way to defend ourselves, I'm never going to forgive him."

Faith didn't point out that Ida had never forgiven him for his past mistakes anyway. Her current attitude was not a new one.

"If you need to talk about anything, I'm here. I know we've been through a lot the last few days—I know you've left your heart in Sherwood. But you have to trust that they made it out and are on their way to safety somewhere."

"Not *somewhere*, Faith. Scotland. That's where everyone is supposed to be going. And we're not…"

"You know why Guy believes this to be safer—"

"I don't need it to be explained again." Ida urged her horse forward and trotted past Faith and Guy.

Faith sighed. There was little she could do to help someone who didn't want her help.

Chapter 9

ROBIN

They had come to Nottingham only two days after running away from Sherwood. Sir Henry didn't own enough horses to accommodate all of them, so they'd walked. It was not the pleasantest walk, considering they were all still sore from the desperate run they'd just endured. Robin ignored the ache in his bones and the blisters on his feet. What did he care? He had more important things to worry about!

The minute they'd set foot in Nottingham Robin had run off before anyone could stop him. Robin discovered later that Sir Henry had insisted the rest of the group follow him to the tavern and stay there while he sorted out the mess Robin had likely gotten into.

Robin had picked a secret entrance at random and gone straight into Nottingham castle. He'd made his way through the dark passages, listening in every room and corridor, desperately hoping that amid the political talk, gossip of servant girls, clumping of boots, and clanging of pots and pans that he'd hear his daughter...or at the very least learn where she was being kept.

The darkness he'd been enveloped in had begun to seep into his heart and mind until he was thoroughly depressed. He'd traversed those dark, tight spaces several times and found nothing. What if he never found her? What if she wasn't even alive to be found?

Eventually, disheartened, he'd left the castle. Sir Henry found him wandering aimlessly through the streets of Nottingham, unaware of his surroundings, and brought him back to the tavern.

Sir Henry had procured several rooms for them at one of the many taverns in Nottingham, and they'd spent a week trying to decide how to get Marian safely out of Sir Hugh's clutches. It was a week filled with wild ideas and plans from every person involved. Somehow, someway, they had to infiltrate the castle, get Marian, and get out.

"It's hard to make an efficient plan when we don't know where she is," Allen sighed. "It makes it hard to gauge how long we'll have to be in the castle when we can't go straight to her."

Robin leaned over the table, his hands curled into fists and resting on the edge of the chart spread out across it. It was a drawing of the layout of Nottingham castle that Robin had created so they could make a plan to rescue Marian. Scribbled across it were charcoal lines going every which way, various attempts at rescue and escape routes being drawn over and across each other. It was no longer a useful piece of parchment with all the scribbles, but they were all staring at it anyway. They were all gathered around the table in the common room that connected the rooms Sir Henry had procured for them.

"Perhaps I can simply pay a visit to the Sheriff," Sir Henry suggested. "As a baron, it would not be out of the realm of reasonable possibilities for me to pay him a visit."

"And then what?" Little John demanded. "Steal Marian back and have all of Sir Hugh's wrath incurred on you, your family, and your town?"

"We can at least find Marian," Gilbert said. "That will make your plans more precise and more likely to succeed when you rescue her."

"If she's even in the castle," Allen said glumly. "Robin couldn't find her."

"Forgive me for my skepticism," Sir Henry responded, "But Robin was in utter darkness and could only traverse in those areas of the castle that have secret passages, which as I understand it is not the entirety of the castle. Marian could be any number of places that he could not go, or merely sitting in a room where he did pass by but did not hear her."

"I hope you're right," Little John said.

"Any other possibility is too painful to entertain," Allen sighed.

Robin lowered his head, momentarily stricken with the idea that Marian had been murdered.

But no, Sir Hugh would want to use this advantage over the outlaws as long as he could. He wouldn't kill Marian.

What else he might do to her though was anybody's guess. Robin sighed and left the group surrounding the table and walked into the room he shared with Lucy. He stood still in the middle of the room, not seeing his surroundings.

He saw Marian. Her sweet young face. And he heard her. He heard that desperate wail that had erupted from her throat when Sir Hugh had snatched her from her mother's arms.

Robin clenched his fists, trying to maintain control of the darkness that threatened to engulf him.

He couldn't protect his own daughter.

And what of his gang, scattered to who knew where? If, indeed, any of them still lived.

He'd failed as a father, as a leader of his gang. He'd made the stupid decision to stay in the old camp, rather than making a new one, or even leaving Nottinghamshire, or for that matter leaving England altogether so that his extended family wouldn't be chased and harassed and kidnapped.

He had failed.

Robin closed his eyes, defeated.

The ache in his chest at the thought of what might happen to Marian—tortured like Marcus, or simply locked in a lonely prison cell, or even starved to death—the intense desire to simply hold his daughter again, the shame at making the decisions that had led them all to this point...

Robin could see Marian, his first wife, with Guy's sword still in her. The blood spurting from her, staining her clothes. The tear that hung in her eye just before she breathed her last. He hadn't been able to save her.

What if he couldn't save little Marian either?

Robin gave up on holding it together and simply let the darkness take him. He collapsed to the floor, ignoring the sharp pain as his face smacked into the hard wood of the floor.

It wasn't long before Robin felt gentle hands on his shoulders pulling him into a sitting position. Lucy was kneeling behind him, and she wrapped one arm around him—the broken one still in a splint—resting her face on his shoulder, her cheek against his.

"Robin..."

144

Robin leaned into her embrace, trying to draw strength and comfort from her.

"We will rescue Marian."

"Will we? I feel more helpless now than when Marian died. Our daughter is with that monster...and the gang is lost...and I failed..."

Lucy was silent for a long time. When she did speak, there was a calm assurance and confidence in her voice. "You see an obstacle in our path. Marian taken, the gang scattered. Obstacles to overcome, and you think you can't do it."

"I can't."

"How could you have forgotten, husband of mine, that our God is greater than any paltry human? We *will* get our daughter back. Then we'll find the gang, and then we will decide what is best to do next. Whether that is fighting King John, or finding a new home somewhere else. Have faith, Robin. We will win."

They stayed in each other's arms, supplying to each other the support they needed without saying a word, for a long time. Allen eventually interrupted their peaceful reveries by poking his head in the door to say that Sir Henry and Gilbert were leaving for the castle to see if Sir Ralf would take the bait.

"They'll be back for supper," Allen said. "Hopefully with news of Marian."

GILBERT

Gilbert followed Henry across the cobblestoned courtyard of the castle, eyeing the soldiers stationed by the gate they'd passed as well as those standing guard by the door they were now approaching. As they went up the steps, Gilbert rested his hand lightly on the hilt of one of his swords. Four soldiers was hardly a fight, in his estimation, but regardless of whether he'd win such a fight the important thing was to always be prepared. Even if the enemy was four sorry looking soldiers employed to a Sheriff of a shire that Gilbert had no interest in.

Robin Hood he was interested in, and therefore rescuing the child was of the utmost importance. Nottingham, though? The people here, the politics, any of it, mattered not a whit to him. Even the people and politics of Ilkeston hardly mattered to Gilbert. Henry cared for the people and dealt with the politics, and Gilbert killed the men he was paid to kill.

It was a pleasant arrangement.

It wasn't that he disliked people, it was simply that compassion was not his strong suit. He could get angry at the people responsible for hurting others, kill them if at all possible. Avenging the hurt he could do, and enjoyed, but comforting the hurt was not a skill he had mastered, or cared to cultivate.

The soldiers made no move to stop them when they opened the great oak doors and strode into the castle. Neither of them ever having occasion to come to Nottingham, they weren't entirely sure how to proceed from there. Yet they knew the layout of the castle very well from studying those maps with Robin Hood and his gang.

"The Great Hall perhaps?" Gilbert suggested as they stood, hesitating, unsure where they ought to go.

A page soon approached them. "Your business in the castle, sirs?"

"We're here to see Sir Ralf, the Sheriff of Nottingham," Henry answered.

"Follow me." The page turned and walked down the corridor so Henry and Gilbert followed.

"Your name?" the page asked when they stopped by two large doors that led to the Great Hall.

"Sir Henry, Baron of Ilkeston," Henry said. "And a knight in my employ, Gilbert."

The page nodded and then opened the doors, leading them into the Great Hall. A man, presumably the Sheriff, was standing by a table across the spacious room with a parchment in his hand. He looked up as they came in. Gilbert thought the crimson cloak he was wearing was a tad ostentatious and definitely impractical.

Gilbert couldn't count the number of men he'd managed to strangle with their own cloaks in a fight. Henry frowned on that of course, thought Gilbert fought a little too dirty, but if it was Gilbert or the opponent then Gilbert had no qualms doing what was necessary to survive.

"Sir Henry, Baron of Ilkeston here to see you, Sheriff," the page said.

"Baron of Ilkeston?" Sir Ralf eyed Henry. "What can I do for you?"

"I was merely in the neighborhood and came out of courtesy," Henry replied.

"Ah, well…" before Sir Ralf could say more, a door to the left of them opened and a man with fiery red hair came in.

"Sheriff."

"Sir Hugh. How is your daughter today?"

"Cheerful. She's enjoying having a friend. Said friend even stopped crying today, so I do believe we're making progress."

Gilbert's ears perked up. Not only was this Sir Hugh, but he may have just been speaking of Marian.

"You have a daughter?" Henry asked casually.

"I do," Sir Hugh said, turning toward them. "A sweet child. And I recently acquired another child as a playmate for her. I do hope that they'll be good friends as they grow up together."

Gilbert was surprised at how sincere Sir Hugh looked and sounded as he spoke, unlike most men made of cruelty that Gilbert had known.

"Who are you?" Sir Hugh asked pleasantly.

"Ah," Sir Ralf spoke up, "Sir Hugh, this is Sir Henry, Baron of Ilkeston."

"Ilkeston?" Sir Hugh roared, taking a step back and drawing his sword. "My soldiers chased Robin Hood that far and no further."

"That doesn't mean these gentlemen were involved," Sir Ralf said mildly, as if outbursts from Sir Hugh were a daily, and insignificant, occurrence.

"The only one who made it back from Ilkeston said the others had been killed by a dual-wielding knight." Sir Hugh's gaze dropped to Gilbert's waist where his two swords rested against either hip. "There aren't a lot of those in England."

"We did kill unknown soldiers in Ilkeston," Henry said gently. "However we did not know they were yours, or that they were chasing the outlaws. I merely saw soldiers chasing what I assumed were my own serfs through my town and I ordered Gilbert to deal with them."

148

"Next time," Sir Ralf said with a sharp laugh, "Perhaps you should ascertain the truth before killing soldiers in your town."

"Indeed," Henry bowed. "I will keep that in mind. I meant no offense, Sir Hugh."

"What are you doing in Nottingham?" Sir Hugh demanded, his sword still drawn.

"They are visiting me," Sir Ralf began, but Sir Hugh interrupted.

"And you don't think it's strange that they came here, directly after aiding Robin Hood in his escape? They are allies with the outlaws!"

Sir Ralf seemed to contemplate this for a moment, before a hard glint entered his eyes. "Is that so?"

"We kill allies of Robin Hood," Sir Hugh stated calmly, taking a step forward and brandishing his blade.

"We are not allies of Robin Hood," Henry objected.

"Whether you are or not, if you can kill soldiers without learning the truth of their purpose...so can I," Sir Hugh replied.

Gilbert calmly drew both his swords. "Good luck with that, lad."

In truth, Sir Hugh looked no younger than Gilbert did himself, but that didn't matter. Goading his enemies was one of the best parts of battle.

"May I?" Sir Hugh glanced toward the Sheriff.

"Please. I'll have no spies in my midst."

"Go," Gilbert said to Henry. "I've got it."

Henry didn't question him but turned on his heel and left. Sir Hugh lunged forward at the same moment and Gilbert grinned, preparing to fight the pretentious mercenary.

149

ROBIN

Robin draped his arm over Lucy's shoulders, and she leaned into his embrace. They were sitting in the common room between the chambers they all shared. Mark, Little John, and Allen were with them. Mark sat in a chair on the other side of Lucy, while Allen paced along one wall and Little John waited by the door expectantly.

"What if Marian isn't in Nottingham?" Allen said. "What if Sir Hugh sent her somewhere else? Or what if she's..."

"If you say dead," Little John growled, "I will kill you myself."

It wasn't long before Sir Henry came bursting through the door. "We have to go! Now!"

"Go where?" Allen asked.

"What happened?" Robin demanded, leaping to his feet.

"Sir Hugh suspected us, and now he and Gilbert are dueling. We need to get out of here. They know I'm helping you."

"What of Marian?" Lucy asked.

"Sir Hugh has her, of that I am sure. He says she's the new companion for his daughter."

"He has a daughter?" Allen asked, incredulous.

"That doesn't matter," Sir Henry snapped. "Sir Ralf could have all the soldiers in Nottingham headed this way. We need to *move.*"

"We'll go to Marcus." Robin said.

"He's already being watched!" Lucy objected, but Robin was already heading out the door. The rest of the group grabbed their meager belongings and ran after him.

Robin darted through the streets of Nottingham, trying not to knock over too many people in the street, only remembering to try and keep a low profile halfway to Marcus' home. When he reached the street where Marcus lived, he approached with more caution, scanning the area for any signs of someone watching the house. Seeing no one, he went to the door and knocked.

It was several minutes before anyone answered, by which time the rest of Robin's companions had joined him.

"Robin, is this wise?" Lucy asked quietly.

Before he could answer, the door opened slowly, just a crack. Robin could see Marcus' wife, Lillian, just inside.

"Robin?"

"Can we come in?"

Lillian threw the door open and grabbed Robin's arm, pulling him inside and into a hug. The others followed, and Sir Henry shut the door.

"They took him, Robin!" Lillian wailed. "They took my Marcus!"

"What?" Robin pulled out of her embrace. "Who took Marcus?"

"When you escaped Sir Hugh's attack on your camp, they came for Marcus," Lillian explained with tears in her eyes. Her hair was a mess, as though she hadn't dealt with it in days, and her eyes were red, suggesting she'd been crying quite a lot. "He's locked up in the dungeon. He's going to hang!"

"Not if we can help it," Little John said firmly.

"But we can't do anything, can we?" Allen said. "Sir Hugh has already sent us running once today."

"We're getting into the castle tonight," Robin said. "And we're getting Marian and Marcus out."

Allen and Sir Henry both looked skeptical.

Robin shrugged. "As my dear wife would say, 'when have we ever lost?' We'll save them both. Now let's get planning. We need to be out of Nottingham by morning."

"Where will you go?" Sir Henry asked.

"Middlesborough first," Robin said. "And then to Scotland. But first we save my daughter, and Lillian's husband."

"Thank you, Robin," Lillian said softly.

"Of course. You don't think I'd leave Marcus to hang, do you?"

Lucy moved forward and wrapped her one good arm around Lillian's shoulders. "Let's have some tea while my men formulate a plan."

Lucy gently pulled Lillian off into another part of the house. Robin was glad Lucy was with them; if it had been left up to him, Allen, or Little John to comfort the poor woman, they'd have been lost.

***

When darkness descended on Nottingham, Robin, Mark, Allen, and Little John made their way through the streets of the city toward the castle. Lucy, due to her still recovering broken arm, stayed with Lillian and Sir Henry.

The streets were quiet, except for the occasional stray dog howling. It was also dark, no moon in sight, although the light of fires and candles that leaked into the streets from various houses whose residents hadn't boarded up their windows for the night illuminated the streets enough for them to see without walking into a wall by accident. Every tavern in the city was also shining brightly, with doors and windows open, roaring fires warming their common rooms while unfortunate men drank themselves into oblivion.

The four of them made their way softly toward the castle. Robin led them to a street by the castle with a line of shops that were back to back with the wall that surrounded the castle courtyard on one side. As he slipped into the nearest shop, a bakery, through an open window, he recalled all the times he'd made this same trip into Nottingham castle. There were many memories, both as a child exploring the exciting new secrets of the castle—to the baker's amusement—and as an adult, rescuing the innocent and spying on the evil Sheriff.

Robin moved along the wall at the back of the shop silently, not wanting to wake the baker or his family who were sleeping in the room located above his head. They were friends of his; they'd helped him during Prince John's rebellion, and they would certainly help him now, but he didn't want to bother them by waking them in the middle of the night.

At the back of the bakery, Robin found the loose slab of wood located in the wall of oak, three feet across and six feet tall, that covered the secret entrance. In the light of day, the wood blended with the rest of the wall and no one was the wiser. The only way to figure out which board covered the entrance, as Robin had learned as a child, was to locate a fingernail-sized hole at waist level that the fake wall had in it. Whether it was there by chance or carved out on purpose by whomever had built the secret passages, Robin didn't know. Robin was only grateful the baker had never decided to block the entrance or change the wood that covered it.

He found the hole, and slid the large piece of wood out of the way, revealing the castle courtyard's stone wall. The wall was several feet thick; several *hollow* feet. Whether the original architect of Nottingham castle had created the secret passageways for their own amusement or for such a time as this, Robin could only guess.

Robin moved into the small space between the wall that faced the courtyard and the wall that backed the bakery and other shops. His companions followed him, Little John pulling the slab of wood back into place. Grooves in the floor held it in its spot so that it wouldn't fall down or slide without being moved by human hands.

Robin and his companions moved through the tight space— particularly for Little John—as quietly as they could, never speaking. They'd all done this before; they knew the routine. Every one of them had traversed the secret passages during Prince John's rebellion to spy on the Sheriff, to visit Lady Marian when she was under house arrest, and to release people from the dungeons. The latter being their focus tonight. That, and finding little Marian.

They followed the secret tunnel along the perimeter of the courtyard. Once the wall connected with the castle itself, they found a tunnel running perpendicular to the one they were in. Robin turned to the left and continued on. The tunnels were completely black in the middle of the day, but it felt somehow darker at night. The thought of Marian being hurt somewhere in these walls wasn't helping to ease Robin's sense of dread.

Surrounded by the cold stone, Robin rubbed his hands together to warm up a bit. He stepped lightly, as he'd learned to do long ago, so as not to create echoing footfalls on the stone floor.

Robin led his gang through the secret tunnels all the way down to the dungeons. He located the crack in the smooth stone that would turn outward into the dungeons just beside the wooden door that led to the dungeons when one wasn't traversing through secret passageways.

Robin leaned against the cool stone, listening. He couldn't hear anyone. No guards talking about how long they'd been on duty or what they were going to eat for dinner. No wails of prisoners being tortured. Nothing.

Taking a deep breath, Robin pushed the hidden door open and stepped out into the open. A look to the right revealed the hallway with cells lining either side where common prisoners were held—tax debts, thievery, etc—was empty. A door at the far end of the hallway of cells was closed, and Robin assumed Sir Ralf had stationed guards on the other side of it. To his left was the door that led into the deeper level of the dungeons. Normally this was where murderers and the like were thrown. Although Robin assumed Marcus, and anyone else connected with Robin Hood, would be held down there as well.

"Anything?" Mark asked softly, leaning into the open.

"No one. Marcus is probably in the deeper level."

"Do you think there will be guards down there?" Allen asked.

"We'll find out.

Mark, Allen, and Little John squeezed out of the hidden tunnel and Little John closed the door behind them.

"Let's get Marcus and then find my daughter," Robin said. He took a deep breath and then swung open the door to the lower level.

Twenty soldiers, bows drawn, met his gaze.

"Trap," Mark hissed.

Robin jumped back and slammed the door shut again as the soldiers loosed their arrows. Most of them caught in the heavy wooden door. A few whizzed past Robin's ears.

Allen grunted, and Robin turned to see that he'd taken an arrow to the shoulder.

"Now would be a good time to leave," Little John said, ripping the arrow out of Allen and earning a howl of displeasure for his efforts.

"Not in the passageway," Mark said. "They'll know where it is if we use it now."

"How are we going to escape if we aren't in the passageway?" Little John huffed, leaning against the wooden door to keep it closed as the soldiers on the other side wrestled to get it open.

"We run," Robin sighed.

He took off down the hallway of cells toward the far door, Allen and Mark following.

"I'll hold the door until you're through," Little John called after them.

Robin reached the far door and drew his sword before he swung it open. There were only two guards there, and he and Mark easily dealt with them.

As Robin, Mark, and Allen darted through the door, Little John let go of the one he was holding and ran after them. The soldiers came spewing out of the lower dungeon after him. He was hit by two arrows before he made it through the far door and Robin slammed it shut.

"Now we run," Little John said, ignoring the arrows protruding from his back. Robin wished there was time to deal with the wounds his friends were garnering, but they needed to get out of here.

The four of them took off down the familiar corridors, twenty soldiers in hot pursuit. They were at a disadvantage because the soldiers had bows and arrows and they were only armed with swords. The soldiers could wound or even kill them with their arrows before they ever got close enough to swing their swords. Yet despite this, they managed to keep ahead of them and out of the range of their arrows merely because they knew the terrain better.

Sir Hugh's soldiers, and even Sir Ralf's soldiers, were not native to Nottingham and hadn't lived in this very castle for years. Robin and his friends ducked into bedrooms and libraries and dressing rooms, sending servants and guests scurrying in every direction to get out of the way. The soldiers followed, of course, but they were often caught by surprise when Robin and the rest of his crew would dart through a closet that they hadn't realized had doors on both sides or evade them through other similar means.

When they burst into the kitchens, every servant and cook turned as one to see what the commotion was. Robin had eyes only for the chief cook; the only mother he'd ever known.

"Sarah!"

"Robin?" Sarah had a fistful of chopped carrots that she was holding over a pot of boiling water and must have been about to drop them in. "What?"

"Soldiers!" Robin ran to her side. "Twenty or so of them." Sarah dropped the carrots into the stew and picked up a knife.

"Not if I can help it."

Robin kissed her cheek and kept running, Mark, Allen, and Little John still behind him. He heard Sarah giving orders behind him.

"Pour that bucket of butter by the door, that's it. And get the jars of milk! On the floor, with the butter...there you go."

As he left the kitchen behind, Robin heard the door he'd entered only moments before bang open and then the thud and clank of soldiers slipping and falling to the floor or sliding into the walls or tables nearby, their bows flying from their grip to smack into walls or drop harmlessly to the floor. Cursing filled the air, along with the clatter of arrows falling from quivers and scattering across the buttery, milk-covered floor.

Robin grinned and kept running.

Without soldiers on their tail, Robin slowed their pace somewhat, but they didn't stop running.

As they darted around a corner leading to the more luxurious chambers, where Robin assumed the Sheriff and Sir Hugh would be staying, Robin ran headfirst into a man running in the opposite direction.

Robin took a step back, trying to catch his breath. A glance up told him he'd run into Gilbert.

"Robin."

"What are you doing still in the castle?" Allen demanded.

"Searching for Marian...and being chased by soldiers."

"Did you find Marian?" Robin asked hopefully.

"Not yet. I take it you haven't either."

A handful of soldiers came running down the corridor where Gilbert had come from.

Gilbert grinned. "I let them chase me so they'd think they had me. Make it all the more fun when I beat them in a matter of seconds. The shock and disbelief just before the horrible truth of the danger they're in passes over their face..." Gilbert shrugged, drew his two swords, and trotted forward to meet the group of soldiers. As he'd predicted, he dealt with them in a matter of seconds.

Gilbert turned back to Robin and his companions. "Shall we check these bedrooms for our missing Marian?"

All five of them moved down the hall and began opening door after door. A few of them were empty, a few of them had nobles or their wives who were visiting Nottingham because of the coming Fair. Most of these let out exclamations of surprise but did nothing more, and whoever had opened the door to begin with quietly shut it and moved to the next one. Some, however, reached for a sword or a dagger. Little John usually knocked these brave souls out with a hit to the head; Gilbert killed them.

Robin was losing hope of finding Marian when he kicked open the door to his own apartments, where he and Lucy had been living before John became King. And there was Marian, sitting on the bed, the canopy drawn back, with one of her own dolls in her arms. A little girl who looked a bit older than Marian was sitting beside her, another of Marian's toys in her hands.

"Papa!" Marian leaped off the bed and Robin darted forward and caught her before she hit the stone floor. He sank to his knees, Marian in his arms, and buried his face in her neck. He tried to speak, but his throat seemed sealed shut. His vision blurred with tears. He took several deep breaths trying to gain his composure, but to no avail.

"Who are you?" the little girl on the bed asked.

"We're Robin Hood and his gang," Mark answered. "Marian's family. Who are you, little one?"

"Isla. My papa is Sir Hugh. He doesn't like you." She didn't speak with hatred or disdain, but rather matter of factly.

"Robin," Little John said firmly. "We need to leave. Now."

Robin stood, Marian still in his arms, and stared at the little redhead on the bed. Sir Hugh's own daughter. Robin wished he wasn't thinking what he was thinking….but he was definitely thinking it.

They could take Isla.

"Do you want to come play with Marian?" Robin asked kindly.

"Where?" Isla asked, her eyes bright and cheerful. Trusting.

"On an adventure," Robin said. "To Scotland, maybe."

"Papa talks about Scotland. His home. I want to see it." The girl grinned, and then reached up her arms to be held. Mark scooped her up, eyeing Robin with something like horror.

Robin ignored him and made straight for the entrance to the secret passageways located at the back of the room. Once they were inside, Marian's arms around his neck tightened.

"Dark," Marian whimpered.

"We'll be out of the dark soon, little one," Robin soothed. "Just wait."

"It's funny in here," Isla giggled from Mark's arms behind Robin.

***

As soon as they entered Marcus' home, Lucy stole little Marian from his arms and wrapped her in a hug of her own. Lillian came running with an expectant, hopeful expression.

Robin sighed. "We didn't find Marcus. We were ambushed. Sir Hugh or Sir Ralf, or both of them, must have known we would come to save him."

Lillian's eyes widened, and tears leaked from the corners of them. "Oh no!"

"We'll still save him," Mark said. "We just have to try again."

"Who is this?" Lillian asked, noticing the red-headed girl still in Mark's arms.

"Sir Hugh's daughter," Allen said, sinking into a chair by the table and wincing as he grabbed his shoulder.

"You're wounded!" Lucy exclaimed, passing Marian back to Robin. She set about cleaning and binding Allen's wounds, and then Little John's as well.

"Anyone else have a scratch that needs dealing with?" Lucy asked.

"No one else was harmed in the slightest," Gilbert replied cheerfully.

"In that case, we need an explanation now, Robin." His wife then gave Robin a look that made it quite clear he was in very big trouble.

Robin sat at the table beside Allen and everyone else gathered around. Mark still holding Isla, and Marian in Robin's lap.

"I have no intention of harming Isla."

"You were going to hurt me!" the little girl exclaimed.

"No," Robin said firmly. "No one is getting hurt. I just…" Robin studied the little girl. She wasn't going to understand this. He turned to Lucy. "I couldn't leave an innocent child with those men. Sir Hugh. Sir Ralf...any of them."

"So you weren't trying to get back at Sir Hugh?" Lucy asked softly. "Not trying to make him feel what you felt?"

"The thought may have crossed my mind, but it wasn't my main intention!" Robin insisted.

"It's too late to do anything about it now," Little John said.

Little Isla started crying. Lucy scooped her out of Mark's arms and carried her into another part of the house, giving Robin a look of disgust before she disappeared.

"Friend," Marian said, looking up at her father with her big brown eyes, so like her mother's. "Friend sad."

Robin sighed. "I know your friend is sad. But we'll make her happy again, I promise."

SIR HUGH

She was gone. His perfect daughter, with her red curls and her dimpled cheeks and her trusting, sweet, good nature. Gone. And little Marian, wild thing that she was, was also gone.

Gone.

Sir Hugh had kidnapped the outlaw's daughter, so he could well believe Robin Hood would retaliate in like manner.

And due to the suffering he must have endured while his daughter was gone, Robin Hood might hurt Isla. Kill Isla.

Sir Hugh couldn't breathe. Isla was the only thing in the world that mattered to him. The only bit of goodness he could claim for himself. And she was gone.

He was going to kill the outlaw for this.

Sir Hugh punched the wall, ignoring the immediate pain that followed this action because the wall was made of stone. He could handle a broken hand, what he couldn't handle was the pain in his heart.

He hated outlaws. He hated the one that now had his daughter, the light of his world. He hated the outlaw that had murdered his sister—the first light of his world—when he was fifteen. He hated them all.

And someday...someday he was going to kill every last outlaw in the world. All of them. Everywhere. Dead.

Chapter 10

GUY

Guy's horse kicked up dust along the lonely road as they trotted ever nearer to his childhood home. The closer they came to his old estate, the more Guy regretted this decision.

The rolling green hills around him were more than familiar. Every tree, every farmhouse, every blade of grass, exuded painful memories. This was where he'd grown up, where he'd been abused by his father, loved by his mother. This is where he'd relied on Andrew to survive his childhood, met the late Sheriff of Nottingham and joined him to escape his past.

It was the memories of his mother, more than anything else, that was causing Guy to wish he hadn't come back here. They were nearing the grounds of the manor now, and every dry leaf that flitted across the ground seemed to ooze with memories of Lady Gisbourne.

Her gentle smile.

Her sparkling eyes.

Her tears…most especially the tears she'd cry when Lord Gisbourne would beat Guy.

The ache in Guy's chest only intensified when he realized he couldn't remember what his mother looked like, couldn't recall the sound of her voice. Oh, he knew she had bright eyes, and the most beautiful smile imaginable. And he knew she always told him the same thing: 'Don't ever lose your heart, my little Guy.' But he couldn't recall the actual sound of her voice. Was it high? Or deep? Or melodic?

He didn't know.

And that hurt almost more than the memories.

The only thing that hurt worse was recalling the day he'd discovered that his father had murdered his mother.

Guy slowed his mount, Shadow, until he was almost walking. Faith and Andrew matched his pace without comment, but he heard Ida's loud sigh from somewhere behind him.

Guy was dreading reaching the manor. Every brick of that house, every hallway, every room, was going to scream of his mother.

This was the worst idea he'd ever had. Why hadn't he just taken his little group to Scotland?

"I know there are so many memories" Faith said softly, moving her mount closer to his. "Will you be alright, Guy?"

"I'm fine."

"You know you can't lie to me," Faith smiled gently.

Guy sighed. "If I'm honest, Faith...I'm overwhelmed with the weight of these memories."

"Tell me about them."

"Not yet. Once we're there and are safely settled...I'll tell you everything."

He'd shared much of his past with his wife before, beginning to tell that long tale before they were wed and continuing to let her see into his heart and his past as the years went by. But there was so much he still had buried.

The manor came into view, standing tall and proud and reminding Guy of his father. Before they reached the house, however, they came to the open gates in the wall that surrounded the manor, stables, and a bit of the woods behind the house. Two guards were standing there and they gestured for Guy and his party to stop.

"Who are you? And what business do you have here?" the shorter of the two soldiers asked.

"My name is Sir Guy of Gisbourne," Guy said, summoning up the sort of authority he had been wont to speak with when he was lord of this manner, and also when he was right hand to the late Sheriff—in other words, the sort of voice he never used anymore, one that invoked fear. Faith jumped slightly when he spoke.

The two soldiers stared at him and then the tall one shrugged. "I'd better go get Lord Ancel."

The tall soldier turned on his heel and sauntered off toward the manor. The short one studied Guy for a moment before saying,

"You look a bit like Sir Guy...I mean, I were only seven when you left with Sir John to who knows where...and then reports started coming back from Nottingham about you...that was nigh on ten years ago. I was just a kid...but I'd believe you was him."

Guy studied the youth, wanting to laugh at his little speech but doing his best to maintain his appearance of sternness.

"Who is Lord Ancel?" Ida asked.

The young soldier turned to her. "Oh, he's a lord from somewhere or other...I'm not sure where. The younger son of a Baron or an Earl maybe? Who knows. He showed up when I was ten. Decided to rule Gisbourne estate since the Gisbournes themselves had all gone away. What with Lord and Lady

Gisbourne being dead, and Sir Guy gone off on some adventure with that Sir John fellow."

"He took over the estate?" Guy asked.

"Yeah. He's been our lord for a good seven years now."

"Well that's going to end now," Guy said. "You all swore your allegiance to me."

"But you haven't been here, have you?" the youth retorted. "So, we couldn't very well be your serfs and servants because you weren't here."

"I'm back now," Guy replied. "And I intend to reclaim exactly what was mine previously. Lands, title, serfs, and all."

The tall soldier was approaching again, followed by a short, fat, red-faced man wearing a purple cape.

Guy was concerned that his steward had never mentioned that another lord was running his estate. In all the years he'd been in Nottingham he had been receiving regular updates and occasionally payments of the revenue his estate collected, keeping up a consistent correspondence with his steward. But he had somehow neglected to mention Lord Ancel?

When the soldier and the fat little lord reached the group, the man huffed a few times to catch his breath. And then looked up, so far up, to where Guy was sitting proudly on his black horse, Shadow. It gave Guy more than a little satisfaction that the poor man had to tilt his neck back so far just to see his face.

"Who do you think you are?" the man asked in what he must have thought was an intimidating voice. Guy refused to smirk, but that high pitched squeak was making it difficult.

"I am Sir Guy of Gisbourne. This is my estate. I thank you for looking after it in my absence, but I will be taking it back now."

"But you haven't been here!" Lord Ancel squeaked. "You can hardly expect...well...things have changed. When I got here, things were in a bit of disarray because the peasants hadn't had a lord for three years. Your estate was falling into disrepair and I built it up again."

"And I thank you for that," Guy said. "I'd offer to repay you for such service, but I am going to hazard a guess that you've enjoyed my prestige, power, wine, luxurious meals, and so forth long enough to make up for any discomfort suffered in rebuilding the estate."

Lord Ancel stared up at Guy and Guy stared down at him. "Well...well…"

"Well...I am willing to let you remain as a guest under *my* roof until you find suitable lodgings for yourself elsewhere. However, I will be taking over responsibilities for my estate from here. I have no more need of your service. You can hardly be shocked at my claim to authority here; after all, I assume you are the one who has been making sure I continued to receive revenue and reports of my estate while I was in Nottingham."

"Well, with rumors that Prince John himself was your friend I couldn't run the chance of...er, that is to say…"

"You are no longer needed here," Guy said sternly.

"The peasants—"

"Swore oaths of loyalty to me. They work for me, their allegiance is to me. Did you have them swear any oaths to you when you stole my estate?"

"Stole!"

"Did you?"

"Well...no…"

168

"Did the King appoint these lands to you as King Henry did to my father?"

"Er...no..."

"Then this discussion is over. The estate, the serfs, all of it is mine. If you'll excuse me." Guy trotted his horse past a sputtering Lord Ancel and straight to the stables. Ida, Faith, and Andrew followed.

They dismounted and Guy saw to it that a nearby stable boy took care of their horses before he led his little group to the house itself.

Guy paused before the great oak door that would lead him into the home he hadn't seen in almost ten years. He closed his eyes, sweating, his heart in his throat; overwhelmed with more emotions than he could count.

He felt a tiny hand grasp his, and glanced to his side where Faith stood. Little Lucy was in her arms and they were both smiling at him.

He could face these memories...the demons in this place that still haunted him. He could face it all, with his wife and daughter by his side.

Guy opened the door and stepped into the front hall. It was large, with stone walls and floor that echoed with every footstep. Guy stood still in the middle of the room; Faith continued to hold his hand. Andrew came and stood on his other side, either offering support or hoping to receive some himself.

Guy took a deep breath.

To his left was the wall he'd often lean into, cowering, when his father whipped him. And there in front of him the doorway to the library where his mother would peek out to offer

169

silent encouragement. And there, hanging over the fireplace by the stairs, was the whip. Guy had never touched it, after his father had died. He'd just left it there, hanging where it always hung. That horrible reminder of how weak he was and how his father hated him for it.

"Can we burn it?" Andrew asked, following his gaze.

"It's a good whip," Guy responded. "We can probably find a better use for it."

"What's wrong with the whip?" Ida asked, coming up behind them.

"It was my father's preferred weapon when he would beat me as a child," Guy responded, trying not to sound too depressed when he said it.

Ida didn't respond.

Guy glanced over his shoulder and saw something he had never seen before. Ida was looking at him without disgust or hatred. The expression on her face resembled pity, or perhaps even compassion, and that shocked Guy.

"Let's get settled," Guy said. "I'll give you a short tour, show you where bed chambers are located. I need to deal with Lord Ancel. Just walking over him will probably have repercussions...I'll need to deal with actual politics and legalities this afternoon." Guy sighed. "You can all get settled in and get some rest. We've had a long journey."

IDA

Ida plopped onto the soft bed, staring up at the wooden ceiling above her. She'd had a bath, a scrumptious meal, and was now attempting to sleep.

Which was a bit difficult for multiple reasons. Number one being, she desperately wanted to know what had become of her sons and her husband. Number two, and this was surprisingly pressing on her mind much more than the former at the moment, Guy had apparently been abused as a child.

It made sense, now that she knew. The hard man that he had been in Nottingham, before becoming friends with Lucy and marrying Faith. His cruelty and hatred, the tortured look he'd always worn on his face. It all fit. And somehow, despite everything he'd ever done, she felt sorry for him.

And that was the most terrifying thing Ida had ever encountered. She felt sorry for Sir Guy of Gisbourne.

Her mother and baby brother had been murdered because of the Sheriff and Sir Guy. She didn't know which had given the order and didn't care. Everyone had always tried to assure her that it must have been the Sheriff, and maybe it was. But it didn't matter, Guy had killed other people's mothers and brothers, so it was all the same.

But he'd been abused as a helpless child.

That didn't excuse his behavior in Ida's opinion, not at all. But at the very least it made him human, gave some plausible reason for the monster he used to be. For a monster he certainly had been; he'd even murdered Robin's first wife!

Ida didn't know what to do with these feelings she was experiencing. She hated Guy. She'd clung to that dislike and disgust even after he became their ally against the Sheriff, and after King Richard came home and pardoned him. Even during the years of peace, when everyone was getting married and the extended family kept growing, Ida never could forgive Guy, or Andrew for that matter.

They had both been good men for many years, but she couldn't let go of the past. The things Guy had done!

Ida sighed, considering new possibilities.

Her own husband, Allen of the Dale, had worked for Guy, for the Sheriff. It had been brief, but it had happened. She certainly didn't hate him. And why not? Because losing his mother, father, wife, and infant son had made him paranoid beyond anything rational. He was always afraid he would lose people that he loved and was desperate to do anything to save them. He'd actually believed helping Guy and the Sheriff would protect people that he loved. It had been stupid, but he'd had a reason.

Guy's cruelty had been stupid, but he'd also had a reason. Ida didn't want to forgive him, and certainly didn't want to be his friend. But she had to at least stop hating him. That much, she was certain about. She had to stop.

LUCY

"What the hell were you thinking, Robin?" Lucy stood, one hand on her hip—the broken one still in its sling—glaring at her husband. "Kidnapping an innocent child? Are you completely insane?"

They had moved from Marcus' house to Sherwood, making camp deep in the woods. They'd discussed various ways of rescuing Marcus, before everyone fell asleep. Lucy had managed to calm Isla and get her to sleep, but the child refused to go anywhere near Robin or anyone else for that matter. But now that everyone was sleeping, Isla included, Lucy thought it was time to tell her husband exactly what she thought of his actions.

She'd dragged him off some distance from the camp so as not to wake anyone.

Robin leaned against a tree in front of her, arms crossed, his head lowered in dejection.

"Robin?"

"I wasn't thinking, alright? I made an error of judgment, I'm sorry for it. What do you want me to say?"

"I can't believe you, Robin...I just...how could you do that?" It was hard to make out Robin's expression in the dark woods. The moon was up, but not much light was filtering through the branches above them.

Lucy took a step closer and Robin flinched.

Lucy paused. She had no intention of physically harming her husband, as he ought to be well aware.

Lucy slowly walked to the tree and leaned against the rough bark beside her husband, studying his downcast face. He was genuinely ashamed, she could see that.

"You shouldn't have done it, Robin."

"You're right, I shouldn't have. And I'm sorry. What do you want me to do? Take her back?"

"Yes.."

"That would be dangerous."

"If we're going to attempt rescuing Marcus again, then we could give Isla back at the same time."

"Maybe."

They were silent for a moment. It was the most tense silence Lucy could remember sharing with Robin, although the day she forced him to go and speak to Guy during the evil Sheriff's reign was a close second. Robin and Guy had not exactly been on speaking terms after Guy had murdered Robin's first wife Marian.

"Don't ever do something like that again, Robin."

"I won't. I promise."

"You'd better not."

Robin looked up at her then, his face stricken. "What more do you want me to say? I shouldn't have kidnapped Isla. I know. I'm sorry! Don't hate me for it..."

"Robin…" Lucy dropped her head to his shoulder. "I don't hate you."

Robin sighed.

"I could never do that. I just wished you hadn't kidnapped that little girl. That's not what heroes do, Robin. And certainly not what followers of Jesus do, for goodness sake."

"I'm sorry."

"So am I. We can't change it now, but hopefully you can find a way to make it right."

"I'll certainly try."

"Make an exchange. Marcus for Isla."

"That is one idea…I'll consider it."

ALLEN

Allen couldn't sleep. Lucy and Robin had returned to camp after their little confrontation. Allen hadn't been able to make out what was being said, but he could hear the sound of their voices while they were arguing. That had been hours ago. Since then everyone had been sleeping soundly, save for Robin who was on watch. But Allen couldn't sleep.

His heart ached with worry for Ida. He knew his wife could take care of herself—she was a capable warrior, after all—but he still worried. And his sons...what had become of them? His breath quickened, and his palms became increasingly more sweaty. He didn't know where his family was, and that was slowly killing him inside. The ache in his heart grew sharper with every passing day.

The hours passed slowly as Allen fretted over his missing loved ones. Light began creeping into the forest. Dawn had arrived.

Allen reluctantly rolled to his feet. Lucy and Robin were both awake, sitting a few feet away from Allen. Marian and Isla slept by their feet.

Allen was horrified that Robin had kidnapped the little girl. In many ways it felt very unlike Robin to commit such a criminal act. And yet Robin had always been impulsive, acting on emotion more often than reason.

Little John sat up a moment after Allen did, but Mark, Sir Henry, Gilbert, and Lillian were all still snoring.

"We save Marcus today," Little John said emphatically.

"Yes, we do," Robin replied, glancing toward Marcus' wife.

As soon as everyone was awake and had eaten a bite, they set out. Lucy stayed in their make-shift camp with Marian and Lillian. Isla, however, was taken with them.

Isla was in near hysteria, crying and flailing her limbs. "Leave me alone! I want to go home!"

Robin and Little John attempted to soothe her, and Gilbert just watched with an amused expression.

Eventually, Mark knelt beside her, shooing Robin off.

"You'll only scare her, you're the reason she's here."

Isla stared at Mark, tears still rolling down her cheeks.

"It's okay, little one. We're taking you to see your father today."

She was perfectly content after that, perched on Mark's shoulders and watching the world with fascination as the group walked through the forest toward Nottingham.

As they walked, Robin reiterated the plans that they had all discussed the night before, trying to decide which to implement.

Getting Marcus safely away from Sir Hugh was the main objective, and giving Isla back to her father the second.

Getting into Nottingham was as easy as it ever was. It was certainly beneficial to them that nearly every single resident of that city adored Robin.

They gathered in the common room of a tavern near the edge of Nottingham and Robin glanced at each of them.

"I've decided which plan to use."

"That's good," Allen rolled his eyes. "It would be a pity to come all this way and not choose."

"What are we doing, Robin?" Mark asked.

"You are all staying here. I'm going to the castle and explaining to Sir Hugh that we wish to trade Isla for Marcus."

"And if he captures you?" Allen asked. This didn't sound like a good plan, and was, in fact, Allen's least favorite of the ideas they'd come up with the night before.

"I'll let him know if any harm comes to me he won't get Isla back."

"You won't let me go back to Papa!" Isla shrieked.

Robin sighed. "I will, of course I will. You don't understand...I just need to be sure he won't kill me before he gets you back."

Isla stared at him from atop Mark's shoulders, her eyes wide, not comprehending. Allen felt sorry for her, but he wasn't concerned. Robin would never harm that little girl, he merely needed leverage.

"I'll come with you, Robin," Gilbert suggested. "I can handle anything Sir Hugh sends at you."

"Are you sure?" Robin asked.

"Very."

Robin turned to the rest of the group. "Stay here and don't get into any trouble." With that he walked straight out of the tavern.

"Anything happens to him, and we're all dead," Allen said.

"We can handle Sir Hugh's soldiers," Little John replied.

"And Gilbert won't let anything happen to Robin," Sir Henry said.

"I meant Lucy," Allen said, half-laughing, but there was little mirth in his voice. "Anything happens to Robin and Lucy will kill us all."

"She doesn't seem like the killing type," Sir Henry commented.

"She isn't," Mark said.

"When do I see Papa?" Isla asked, kicking her legs against Mark's chest and pulling on his hair. Not with any malice, but simply because she was so excited.

"Soon, Isla," Mark said. "Very soon."

They waited there, in the corner of the tavern, for over an hour. People came and went, ale was drunk, laughter filled the air.

At one point a small brawl broke out across the room, but was quickly broken up by two of Sir Ralf's soldiers that had entered the tavern. The group watched those two soldiers closely, Little John shifting in front of the others and preparing to take them down. But the soldiers had simply gotten a drink, sat for five minutes, and left again.

Eventually, Gilbert entered the tavern and walked toward their corner. Mark, Allen, and Little John were on their feet immediately.

"Robin?" Allen asked, not wanting to know the answer.

"Is headed this way. Let's get out of Nottingham." Gilbert turned on his heel and marched from the tavern. Allen and the others hurried to keep up with him.

"What happened?" Mark asked.

"Sir Hugh is coming," Gilbert said.

"Papa!"

"He's bringing Marcus and Robin," Gilbert continued, ignoring Isla's outburst. "We're making the trade outside of Nottingham so we can make a quick escape should Sir Hugh double cross us."

The group stopped a few hundred yards from Nottingham's gate. The road leading into Nottingham was not entirely empty, as visitors waiting for the Fair, merchants coming to sell goods, and weary travelers were on the road. Yet it was not busy yet. It was too early in the morning for there to be a steady stream of folks entering Nottingham.

It wasn't long before Sir Hugh, Robin, Marcus, and ten of Sir Hugh's soldiers exited Nottingham and came towards them. They stopped ten feet from Allen and the others. The few travelers headed into Nottingham sent curious glances toward the stand-off, but no one stopped to gawk or ask questions.

"I want my daughter," Sir Hugh said icily.

"Papa!" Isla wiggled on Mark's shoulders and he struggled to keep her from jumping, moving his hands from her ankles to her waist and back to avoid that very thing.

"Let Robin and Marcus go first," Little John said.

Sir Hugh didn't respond. The two groups glared at each other for a full minute. Robin appeared concerned but unharmed. Allen was horrified to note that he couldn't say the same about Marcus. He was bare chested, wearing only trousers. No shirt, no shoes. Across his chest were several long, red, festering gashes. His arms bore a number of similar cuts, as well as bruises of every size and varying in color—black, blue, green. His face also had a number of these variously colored bruises. His expression was grim, though that wasn't entirely out of character for Marcus.

The silence was broken when Mark moved forward.

"What are you doing?" Allen hissed.

Mark took two steps in front of the rest of them, and set Isla on the ground, keeping his arms around her waist so she wouldn't bolt. "You let Robin and Marcus go, I let go of Isla."

Sir Hugh studied Mark for a moment, and then nodded. Robin and Marcus ran toward Allen and the others, and Mark let go of Isla who darted into her father's embrace.

"Let's go!" Robin shouted. He ran for Sherwood Forest and the others took off after him.

Allen heard Sir Hugh shout behind them, "Take them! Don't let a single one escape!"

A glance over his shoulder showed the ten soldiers charging forward and Gilbert drawing his two swords and preparing to fight them. Allen was considering telling Robin to offer to pay Gilbert double what Sir Henry did just so they'd have his expertise whenever a crisis arose. He was a useful man to have around.

They ran through the forest to the make-shift camp where Lucy and Lillian were waiting with Marian.

When they arrived, panting and breathless, Allen leaned over with his hands on his knees to catch his breath. At least his lungs weren't burning yet. If they had to do another days long run, he was going to resign from the gang, find a hole in some mountain somewhere, and bury himself there...never coming out again.

Lucy embraced her husband and kissed him as soon as they entered the camp, leaving Allen longing for his wife again. Lillian also leaped into her husband's embrace.

"We need to be ready to run again," Robin said. "Gilbert may not be able to handle all those soldiers, and Sir Hugh certainly has more. He had no intention of actually letting us go, he wanted his daughter back but he wanted all of us, too. Assuming Gilbert can't hold back his wrath, we need to keep moving."

"You underestimate Gilbert," Sir Henry laughed.

"Indeed he does," Gilbert declared, marching into the camp. "Ten soldiers dealt with, Sir Hugh running for Nottingham with little Isla in his arms."

"Then we head for Middlesborough," Robin said. "To see if anyone is there. If not, we go to Scotland."

"Will you come with us?" Allen asked Sir Henry and Gilbert collectively, though he was mostly hoping for Gilbert to say yes.

"We have openly helped you now," Sir Henry replied. "You're stuck with us, I'm afraid."

"I'm coming, too," Marcus said, Lillian still clinging to him. "We're not safe here in Nottingham."

Chapter 11

WILL

They were approaching Edinburgh. The lights of candles in windows and lanterns hanging by doors made the hillside look as though it was made of stars. Night had fallen, but Will chose not to make camp. They were this close to the city, they might as well finish the journey.

They had not overtaken Guy and his small group along the road to Edinburgh, but Will wasn't surprised as their friends had a full day's head start and they didn't have six children under foot. What did give him pause was the fact that none of the towns they had passed through had seen hide nor hair of any travelers matching their descriptions. Will had subtly asked various innkeepers along the road, and no one knew of such a traveling party as the one he described. It was possible, of course, that Guy had decided to stay outside of any towns to avoid being detected and followed by Sir Hugh.

It wasn't long before they reached the city. The streets were nearly deserted, everyone having already retired to their homes for the night. The city was sleeping, aside from a stray dog or two, and silent, apart from the noises of drunk men singing and arguing floating down the street from a distant tavern.

Will led them down one street after another in search of the abbey Allen had told them to find when they came to Edinburgh. It took a bit longer than he'd expected, but eventually they spotted it.

As they made their way up the front steps of the old church building, Will glanced over his shoulder, past his comrades, half-paranoid someone could be following them. There was no one to be seen, however.

Will reached his free hand up—the other holding a sleeping John—and knocked on the old wooden door. There was no response. So he knocked again.

"Do you think anyone is actually in the abbey?" Elinor asked. Little Edward was asleep in her arms, resting atop her bulging belly.

"There should be a friar or two, shouldn't there?" Much asked, a sleeping William in his arms.

"Maybe they don't live at the abbey," Jane suggested, shifting her sleeping son in her arms.

Mary had her sweet namesake child in her arms, and Dusty had Daniyah. Will was glad none of them had to carry more than one child. Even with just John, his arm was aching. His legs were sore as well. He was used to riding a horse on a fairly regular basis, but not for the extended periods of time that he had in the last month. He was sore, raw, tired, and wanted his extended family out of the cold and safely tucked into bed. They all needed rest, and the security of knowing they were safe, at least for one more night.

Will knocked again.

This time they could hear someone shuffling toward the door. It soon creaked open, and a hunched little man stood before them. He was wrinkled and his hair was grey and Will thought he might possibly be the oldest person he'd ever met in his life.

"What can I do for ye?" the old friar croaked. He was dressed in a simple grey tunic, tied with a rope that had three knots in it, and he wore a pair of very sorry looking sandals that had certainly seen better days.

"We seek shelter," Will said.

"Of course," the man smiled kindly. "There are plenty of inns in Edinburgh. Shall I show you where the best ones are?"

"We'd prefer to stay with you," Dusty said. "We are being hunted. Allen said we could come here."

"Hunted?" the little friar asked. "By whom?"

"A man called Sir Hugh," Will replied.

"Sir Hugh! He's a well-known mercenary. He has vowed to kill all outlaws," the friar said. "Are ye outlaws?"

"We are members of Robin Hood's gang," Will replied.

The friar's eyes widened, and he studied them all for a moment.

"Well...well..." Suddenly he grinned. "Ye said an Allen told ye to come 'ere...would that be my Allen? Allen of the Dale?"

"That's the one," Dusty said.

The friar moved back from the door. "Come in, come in. I've got a few spare beds, though perhaps not enough for all of ye."

"The floor works just as well," Will said.

They all moved inside and the friar led them through the church to the private rooms at the back, behind the altar. There was a decent sized common room, with a table and chairs, along with some extra chairs dotted about the room and a large fireplace along the back wall. Opening off of that room was a small kitchen and three small bedrooms.

184

"This one is mine, but ye are welcome to all three rooms," the friar said. "How about ye put the bairns to rest and then we can talk."

Once the children were settled in one of the rooms, all six of them snuggled into the bed, the adults gathered in the common room. Will was pleasantly surprised that none of the children fussed when transferred from their arms to the bed. That was an unusual, but very welcome occurrence. Will was worried, however, that there was no sign of Guy and his companions.

"I'm Friar Roderick," the little old man said. "It seems an age ago now, but I can still remember when little Allen was born...or when I married him to young Eri."

"Married!" Much gasped. "He was married?"

Friar Roderick's old eyes grew dark and sad. "Aye. But she and the bairn and all his kin save himself were killed in a tragic fire. So long ago...did he never tell ye?"

"I've never heard the story," Jane said.

"Me neither," Much said.

"Well then I will nae be the one to tell ye. That's his story to tell."

"Friar Roderick," Will said. "Have you not had anyone else come seeking shelter?"

"Oh I get travelers all the time," Friar Roderick replied.

"I am looking for a specific group of people," Will said. "They were headed this way. They are part of our band. We got separated when Sir Hugh attacked."

"I haven't had any others from Robin Hood," Friar Roderick said. "If that's what yer asking."

"Where could they have gone?" Elinor wondered. She was leaning back in her chair, her hands resting on her swelling belly.

"Maybe they got lost," Mary suggested.

"Do you think they're alright?" Jane asked, her voice wavering.

"I'm sure they'll be fine, wherever they are," Dusty said, wrapping her arm around Jane. "Think about it, Jane. Who is in that group? Your husband, perfectly able to take care of himself. Guy, also perfectly able. Ida. She won't let anything happen to them for sure."

"How long are ye meaning to stay 'ere?" Friar Roderick asked.

"We hadn't made plans beyond arriving here," Dusty said.

"Once the rest of the gang arrives we'll be able to decide our next course of action," Will added.

"Well ye are welcome 'ere as long as ye need a place to stay. Though it may get crowded as the rest of ye arrive," Friar Roderick chuckled. His laugh was rather raspy and grated on Will's ears, but he couldn't help but smile, too, at the twinkle in the little Friar's eyes.

"Thank you, Friar Roderick," Dusty said. "We really do appreciate this."

"I could nae leave weary travelers in the cold, nor could I turn away the very people Allen now calls his family. But I will warn ye, I can nae fight. Should Sir Hugh come calling 'ere, ye will be on yer own."

"Should Sir Hugh come calling, we'll lead him away from your abbey," Will said. "We don't want to bring any trouble upon you."

GUY

Rain splattered the ground, causing tiny splashes of mud to dance into the air before plopping back down to the earth. Guy marched through the mud and rain into his house, pulling off his cloak and tossing it over the back of the first chair he came to as he strode toward the large hearth. The whip still hung in its rightful place.

He was going to take it down eventually.

Guy glared at the whip, remembering how he used to wince at the mere sound of it cracking, even when his father was only taunting him and no physical pain was incurred. Though he had felt the sting of it often enough as well. He hadn't been afraid for no reason.

Guy pulled off his boots and moved closer to the fire. The weather outside suited his mood perfectly. He'd been right to fear the memories this place would awaken. He should have taken his small group to Scotland. There were no memories for him there.

Faith soon appeared, humming to herself as she glided into the room.

"Guy! I thought you were visiting the villages today."

"I was."

Faith came to stand beside him, wrapping her arms around his waist. But she jerked back immediately. "You're soaked!"

"It is raining, dear."

"You need to get out of those wet things," Faith tugged on his arm. "Come on."

Guy pulled away from her. "I'm fine."

"You're going to get sick." Faith studied him, arms crossed. "What's wrong? Why do you look so miserable?"

Faith moved to his side and once more wrapped her arms around him. "Did someone say something? You're not the man you were the last time you were here, ruling this estate. It will take them time to see that, but they *will* see it."

Guy smiled. "It isn't that. I was thinking about my father." "Oh."

They stood in silence for a time, wrapped in each other's embrace, watching the fire crackling before them.

"Do you want to talk about it?"

"No." Guy let go of his wife. "I need to change, as you said. I wouldn't want to catch a sickness because of my carelessness."

Guy didn't know why he had so little desire to talk to Faith about the memories resurfacing; she already knew so much of what he was remembering. Yet he couldn't bring himself to speak those memories aloud.

He couldn't face the past. It was everywhere, unavoidable, but he couldn't face it. That was why he had yet to visit his mother's grave, and why he couldn't talk to Faith.

ROBIN

After rescuing Marcus and giving little Isla back to her father, they had gone straight to Middlesborough. The entire journey to Middlesborough all Robin could think about was that he had kidnapped a child.

Kidnapped her.

What was happening to him? His fear for his own daughter was hardly an excuse.

To be fair, he had given her back the next day, yet the mere fact that he'd kidnapped her in the first place was abhorrent. Robin was also disturbed that his friends were so willing to follow him, in anything, that none of them stopped him. Mark had listened to Robin and carried the child out of the castle despite looking horrified and Little John hadn't done anything to stop it despite being perfectly able to physically restrain Robin.

He could remember the days when his friends would tell him when he was being an idiot, and he wished they had done so that day as well. His wife had, of course, as soon as she knew what he'd done. He was blessed to have her around to keep him in line.

Robin made up his mind to talk to Mark, Allen, and Little John later and insist they stop him next time he tried to impulsively do something as loathsome as kidnap a child.

In Middlesborough, Lucy had set to work dealing with Marcus' many wounds. Little John had gone to speak to various people he knew from his days as an outlaw in the area, before joining Robin Hood's gang in Nottinghamshire, to see if he could find out anything about their missing friends. He'd discovered that everyone had been through Middlesborough about a week before and had then set off for other places, though no one knew where.

Realizing the rest of the gang was already headed for Edinburgh, Robin had given the order and they'd set off for Scotland on foot that very day.

Traveling along the dusty roads towards Allen's old home, Robin was still lost in thought.

"What are you thinking?" Mark asked, falling into step beside him. "You look troubled."

"I was thinking about the rest of our family. I am impatient to be in Scotland where I can watch over them all. Being at a distance is difficult; I can't do anything for them."

"They're likely already safe in Scotland," Mark said. "They're fine."

"I was also thinking it is unfortunate no one had the courage to stop me from kidnapping Isla. Are you all so afraid to cross me?"

"We're not afraid of you," Mark chuckled.

"Then why didn't you stop me?"

"You're our leader, Robin. We follow your lead."

"You shouldn't follow blindly. I make mistakes. Clearly."

"Well next time I'll be sure to tell you you're an idiot."

"Thanks."

***

A few days later, they were seated around a table in the back corner of an inn, enjoying a meal before they retired to bed. Lucy had Marian on her lap and was trying to keep her from causing chaos. The small girl had already broken two plates and dumped a platter of meat pies onto the floor.

Robin wondered what Little John and Elinor's own child would be like when it arrived in the world. Rambunctious like Marian, Edward, and William? Quiet and gentle like little Lucy? Or something in between, like John and Daniyah? Robin knew his friend was concerned for his wife and anxious to arrive in Scotland and find her well.

"We should arrive in Edinburgh in three or four more days," Allen said over the din of the noisy room. The room was filled with tables, and most of them were filled with various travelers enjoying a meal as well as locals enjoying an ale or two before retiring to their homes and beds.

"Is it strange coming back to your old home?" Lucy asked.

"Not yet," Allen replied. "I suppose once we reach Edinburgh I might be overwhelmed with memories." Allen's eyes darkened for a moment, but then he shook his head and shrugged. "Have you ever been back to your childhood home, Lucy?"

"No."

"Do you miss it?"

"Hardly."

Allen nodded. "Me neither."

Robin considered Allen for a moment. What was it like, returning to his past?

Robin had felt something of the feeling after returning from the Crusades. But aside from that adventure, he'd never left Nottingham for very long. He'd never needed or wanted to be far from his childhood home.

After the adventures in Sherwood had come to a close, Will had gone back to his childhood home in Middlesborough; he and Dusty had been living there still when John became King.

Robin wondered if now, being hunted, they'd go back to Nottingham at some point, or if they were forever going to be living on the run. Would they have to leave England and Scotland altogether and travel across the rest of Europe to find a safe haven? It wasn't a pleasant thought.

Gilbert came sauntering over to the table from where he'd been conversing with various knaves across the room.

"A lot of interesting folk here," Gilbert said, sitting down between Sir Henry and Allen. He was very drunk.

"Learn anything of interest?" Sir Henry asked.

"Well some princess died recently," Gilbert said, leaning his head against the back of his chair. "John...Jane...no, Joan. Joan was her name."

"Joan!" Allen gasped.

"Joan of Sicily?" Robin asked, leaning forward. "Richard and John's sister?"

"Yeah...that's the one," Gilbert replied, eyes closed.

Allen and Robin stared at each other wide eyed.

"What's wrong?" Little John asked.

"We knew her," Allen said. "On the Crusades."

"She was a friend," Robin said softly.

Joan was dead.

Robin had met her on the Crusades. Richard had stopped in Sicily to rescue his sister from imprisonment before traveling to the Holy land. The rest of their travels had been far more entertaining with spirited young Joan accompanying them.

"She was in love with Robin," Allen grinned. "But he, of course, only had eyes for Marian back then. Poor Joan."

Robin shook his head, but he knew it was true. Joan had loved him, and he had spurned that love for his darling Marian.

"How'd she die?" he asked Gilbert.

Gilbert did not respond.

192

Sir Henry poked Gilbert in the ribs. He made no response. "I do believe our friend has passed out."

ANDREW

Andrew heard the muffled sound as he was headed down to the library. He had just been passing by the room where Guy had spent his days as a child when he heard what sounded like a sob, muffled by a pillow. It was a familiar sound. Andrew had heard it more times than he could count as a child. Usually after Lord Gisbourne had beaten Guy for some imagined fault. Andrew would then sneak into Guy's room and the two boys would sit on Guy's bed and simply cry in silence until Lady Gisbourne came to comfort Guy.

Andrew pushed open the door to the room slowly. As he had expected, Guy was there. He appeared to have gained some measure of composure since the moment that Andrew had heard the muffled sob. He was seated on the floor by his old small bed, arms crossed, staring at the ceiling.

Andrew moved across the room and sat beside him. They remained silent for a long time.

Andrew didn't know which memory from the past had brought Guy into this old room, or what had broken his heart enough that he would cry in this place where so many tears had already been spent. But it didn't matter. Andrew was well aware of the hurt that had been inflicted on Guy, had witnessed every wound, and didn't need words to empathize.

After a while, Guy turned to him. "How are you?"

"Me?" Andrew stared at his friend.

"I know you don't have pleasant memories here, either."

"I'm coping. And you?"

"Falling apart."

"You should talk to Faith."

"Ah. You've noticed my avoidance, have you?"

"I always notice."

"True."

"You should talk to her. When I am in pain, I talk to Jane and somehow or other she always assuages my turmoil." Andrew sighed, suddenly overwhelmed with a longing for his wife.

"I'm sorry. I should have waited in Middlesborough a day or two longer, if only for news of the rest of the gang. I still would have brought us here, but I could have waited to know if your wife and son were safe. They could have come with us."

"It's too late now," Andrew shrugged. "I will simply continue to pray for their safety and that we will have word of them before too long. But you, my friend, are lucky enough to have your wife with you. So talk to her."

Guy sighed. "I intend to...eventually."

ALLEN

It was still early in the morning, the sun had risen but was not yet high in the sky. It was a cool morning, the air crisp. Birds were singing in trees along the road. Edinburgh had come into view ahead of them. Allen couldn't keep his eyes off of that city.

Along the road to Scotland, Allen had been wondering what he would feel when he returned to his childhood home. He assumed memories would come flooding back. But how potent would they be? It had been years since he had been plagued by them. The trip to Scotland hadn't seen the memories giving him nightmares or invading his peace of mind. He'd thought about his childhood a great deal, but he hadn't been overwhelmed.

Now, however, as Edinburgh came into view, the memories were more vivid than they had ever been before.

His wife Eri's gentle smile. His sister Alice's dimpled grin, green eyes, and curly red hair.

The fire. Mostly the fire.

Allen could see the flames licking over his house, feel the heat on his skin. He was choking on the smoke once more, tripping over Florie's dead body as he desperately tried to reach his family.

A rotting branch fell from a nearby tree, hitting the ground with a crash and startling Allen out of his reverie.

They were close to Edinburgh now. Allen swallowed hard as he studied the buildings that were coming into view. He knew every house, every shop, every tavern.

"Allen, you take the lead," Robin said suddenly. "As you know where the abbey is."

Allen nodded dumbly, unable to speak.

He hadn't been here in more than ten years. Yet so much appeared unchanged.

Allen grimaced as he walked down the familiar path leading to the abbey. He remembered making this walk on the day of his wedding. Waiting at the top of the steps for Eri and her procession to arrive. Saying his vows…

The abbey came into view. The first thing Allen noticed was that it looked exactly the same. The second thing he noticed were William and Edward arguing in the little garden patch beside the abbey. William picked up a stick and hit his brother and Allen took off running.

He ran to his sons and he fell to the ground beside them, opening his arms.

"Papa!"

Edward and William tackled him and the three of them rolled in the dirt, hugging and crying.

As Allen sat up, he noticed Dusty leaning against the side of the abbey, grinning. "I'm glad you made it to Scotland finally. We've been worried."

Little Marian soon jumped into Allen's lap to hug Edward and William and then the three of them rolled off his lap and began tussling in the dirt.

"Where is everyone?" Robin asked, briefly hugging Dusty.

"Inside," Dusty said. "These two little ones needed to lose some energy," Dusty gestured toward Edward and William."

"Elinor?" Little John asked, joining the group.

"She's safe, very pregnant, and inside. You'll have a little one before you know it," Dusty smiled.

Little John immediately entered the abbey. Slowly the others began to follow, Allen and Lucy collecting their children before going inside. Allen also paused to say hello to his horse tethered to the fence at the back of the small garden. There were six of them there, but Allen only paid attention to his own horse, Outlaw. He hadn't realized he missed Outlaw until he saw him tethered there. He rubbed his forehead against Outlaw's nose, causing William and Edward to giggle from where they sat on his hips.

Once inside the abbey, there were hugs to be had, and tears shed among the group. Allen shook hands with Will, received a tearful kiss on the cheek from Mary, a hug from Jane, a wave from Elinor—who remained sitting in her chair but was quite happy to see everyone, especially her husband—and a hug from Much.

Most of the children latched onto his legs for a moment or two before darting off to hug someone else. Allen noticed that Mary and Much's little Mary was quite a bit bigger than last he'd seen her. She was supporting her own weight in her mother's arms and she watched everything around her with wide eyes and a grin.

Robin introduced Sir Henry and Gilbert to the group, and explained how they'd helped to rescue both Marian and Marcus. Marcus himself, along with his wife Lillian, got many hugs and kisses from the children before Dusty sat Marcus down so she could examine Lucy's handiwork and see if she might improve upon it. The poor fellow was still covered in cuts and bruises, some of which were healing and some not so much.

"Who runs the abbey now?" Allen asked during the ruckus of greetings.

"Friar Roderick," Jane said. "He talks about you a lot."

"Friar Roderick," Allen sighed, closing his eyes briefly. "I wasn't sure he'd even be alive still."

"He is," Jane replied. "Though only just. I swear he's as old as anyone I've ever seen."

"Where is he?" Allen asked.

"Getting some food at the market. We devour quite a lot what with the six of us plus the children. It's a good thing he's getting more food, now that you've all arrived." Jane paused, a look of vulnerability and pain crossing her face. "You haven't seen Guy and his companions have you? Andrew? We don't know what happened to them."

"We haven't seen them," Allen replied. "Although the innkeeper in Middlesborough said they'd been there and then left. We thought they came here." Allen could feel his heart constricting. He had his sons once more, but his wife was still missing!

"We thought so, too," Jane sighed. "But they aren't here and they haven't showed up since we arrived."

Allen sighed. He knew his wife could care for herself better than almost anyone in the gang but he wanted more than anything to be able to see her, hold her, know she was safe.

The whole gang was almost reunited. There were only four missing, plus one child. The world almost felt right again. But not quite. And Allen knew it wouldn't feel right until he was with Ida again.

The exuberance of the group didn't die down. They were still chattering and noisy when Friar Roderick came back, two large baskets overflowing with fruit, vegetables, meat, cheese, and bread hung over his arms. He was bent nearly double trying to carry the laden baskets and Lucy and Dusty ran forward to take them from him, carrying them to the small kitchen.

Friar Roderick straightened and studied the group.

"There's more of ye than when I left," he said simply.

Robin stepped forward. "Friar Roderick, I'm Robin of Locksley."

"Robin Hood," Friar Roderick said, smiling

"Yes," Robin smiled. He then proceeded to make introductions.

Allen stared at the wrinkled little friar, overwhelmed. His breath caught in his throat, and his palms grew sweaty.

That ancient friar had been a friend to him in his youth. He'd wed him to Eri. Allen hadn't expected to ever see him again.

As Robin's introductions came to a close, Friar Roderick turned his old eyes on Allen. He smiled and opened his arms.

"Come 'ere, Allen!"

Allen stepped into his feeble embrace and trembled slightly at the onslaught of emotions that overtook him.

Friar Roderick stepped back and studied him. "Ye look like yer father, that's for sure."

Allen brushed a stray tear from his eye. "It's good to see you, Friar."

"Och, what's this? Are ye still pretending ye talk like old William? Like an Englishman? What nonsense! Ye should ne'er have lost yer good Scots voice like that. 'Tis a pity."

Allen laughed. "I've been speaking without my accent for more than ten years. I am not sure I could go back to it, now."

"Pity," Friar Roderick croaked. "Ye sounded better before."

Allen laughed again.

"Have ye seen William yet?" Friar Roderick asked.

"What?" Allen gasped. "He died on the Crusades."

Friar Roderick grinned. "Did he now? Well then I guess I've been having chats with his ghost every day at the market."

"William's alive!" Allen stared at Friar Roderick. William had been his friend, his uncle, his second father, when he was a child. He'd gone on the Crusades as Allen had, though not with Allen specifically, and Allen had never heard from him again.

"Ye will have to go and find him. He's been living in a tavern for five years, since he returned. He's been saving up money and trying to rebuild yer old home, Allen. I think he wanted to finish it and then come find ye and tell ye about it. So ye could bring yer family 'ere."

"He's rebuilding the manor?"

"Aye. 'Twas hard the first few years. He'd come 'ere and talk with me after each day of work, broken and crying, overwhelmed with the memories and emotions. He's gotten better though, and has almost finished rebuilding it."

"I can't believe he's alive, much less rebuilding my home," Allen said. "But I can't come back here to Scotland. My family is in Nottingham."

"Right now it appears yer family is in my abbey."

"Well yes, but we want to go home eventually."

"Do ye think it will ever be safe with that John as King of England? Nae, it will nae be safe for ye. Let yer family live 'ere, Allen. All of them," Friar Roderick gestured to the gathered group of people around them. "Ye will be safe 'ere."

"I suppose we can consider it," Allen said slowly. He wasn't sure he liked the idea. He'd left this place behind for a reason.

Chapter 12

FAITH

From where Faith was sitting on a low couch, under a large open window, she could see the stables, several fields, and a part of the woods that surrounded the back of the manor from here. Guy had been busy with business since the day they had arrived. Dealing with Lord Ancel, traveling to the many villages under his lordship to speak with the peasants who worked for him. Letting them know he was back, that he expected their fealty, but also that he was a different man. He wouldn't be cruel this time. There had been a few uprisings of various farmers who thought he had no business coming back and taking over from Lord Ancel, but Guy had easily dealt with them. He was good at ruling, and now he was actually a good ruler too, not like he had been before.

He'd been troubled though, ever since they arrived. He hadn't talked to her about it very much; he kept putting her off with promises to explain everything later. She knew most of his history already, he'd told her about his father and his mother before they got married. But here in his childhood home, there seemed to be more history and more painful memories than he'd shared before. Or at the very least, the emotions from his past were simply more raw. She wanted to help him, to ease his suffering.

Andrew had been more forthcoming, talking about the hardships of growing up under Lord Gisbourne. He himself hadn't been beaten as much as Guy, but he had still been mistreated. And Lady Gisbourne had been his savior. Andrew and Faith had talked a lot since coming to the Gisbourne estate. Both about Andrew's experiences and also about their shared worry over Guy.

Little Lucy sighed behind her, and Faith glanced back at the large bed in the center of the room. Her daughter was sleeping in that bed, swallowed up in the middle of it with blankets, pillows, and so much space surrounding her. Faith had drawn back the canopy so that she could see her sweet child. Little Lucy rolled over and sighed again, but appeared to still be sleeping.

Faith turned back to the window, studying the goings on outside. There were several servants down by the stables dealing with horses, and she could see a young man and a girl near the edge of the forest. From the distance she couldn't make out who it was.

Faith had been trying to get to know all the staff on the estate. She was, whether she wished it or not, Lady Gisbourne now, and the running of the household ought to fall on her. She wanted to know everyone that worked there so she could encourage them both in their work and in the Lord.

At any rate, whoever the young couple was, they appeared to be kissing under the cover of the trees at the edge of the woods.

Faith grinned, and turned away from them, studying the servants trying to catch one of the horses. It had escaped from the rope one of them had been leading it with and was running through the pasture now, looking beautiful and strong and free. Faith realized that it was Shadow, Guy's own mount. His black coat was sleek and shiny and his mane flew behind him as he ran. Faith laughed softly at the spectacle.

The door creaked open behind her and Faith turned around. Guy entered the room and strode toward her.

He stopped by the bed to kiss Lucy's forehead and then came to Faith and leaned down to kiss her.

He noticed Shadow and grinned a little, though his eyes were dark.

"What is it, Guy?"

"I promised you, and keep promising you, that I will tell you everything that has been on my mind and heart since we arrived. All the memories that make my knees week and my hands tremble. Every moment of my childhood that left me crying, or trembling with fear, or overflowing with love for my sweet mother..."

"You can tell me anything, Guy."

"I know. And I intend to." Guy grabbed her hands and pulled her over to a small table along the wall. He sat her down, and then put a parchment in front of her and handed her a quill.

"I'm going to tell you the entirety of my story, and I want you to write it down."

"Why? Not that I mind," Faith quickly added after her initial question. "I am simply curious."

"I think it will help me put the past to rest," Guy replied.

Faith brushed a lock of black hair out of his face, studying his dark eyes. "I'm willing to do anything that will help you have peace of mind, my husband."

Guy smiled. "I know. Just listen, that's what I need. Listen and write it down."

GUY

Guy had spent several hours talking to his wife, spilling out everything that was weighing on his heart. All the horrifying, painful memories, every ounce of grief and horror, every detail that pervaded his mind.

He'd cried. Faith had cried. She had written everything down as he told his long tale, emptying his heart of its ragged emotions.

Evening had come. And now, as the sun was setting on the horizon and painting the sky in orange, pink, and gold, Guy was walking slowly toward the one spot on his manor that he hadn't visited since his return.

His mother's grave.

Faith was beside him, her hand in his, offering him silent support.

The grave wasn't far from the house and they arrived much faster than Guy was prepared for. He hadn't been here in so many years, and all the memories he'd just dealt with over the last few hours rushed back to the surface for a moment.

The earth covering the grave had sunk over the years. It was no longer a mound, but the grave was still obvious. The freshly-turned earth had given way over the years to grass and was now overgrown with bright purple flowers. His mother's favorite blossom.

Guy knelt next to the grave, and reached out to pluck one of the flowers. The fact that they were growing here was almost unearthly. Guy was not a superstitious man, however. He believed in a God of miracles and this...this was a miracle. A small one, perhaps, but it was monumental to Guy.

Faith wrapped her arms around him and they cried softly for a few minutes. When their tears dried, Guy felt better than he had in all his life. A darkness that had been hiding in the back of his heart and mind since his youth had finally lifted. He felt clean and new.

Guy heard a nicker behind him and turned toward the stables and pasture, some distance away. Shadow was standing by the fence, watching him. Guy couldn't see him clearly from the distance and the darkness of twilight, but as he watched, Shadow pranced and tossed his head, looking beautiful, proud, and strong. Guy grinned.

He still carried the scars of his childhood, and they would perhaps cause him pain until he died, but he could face that pain now without cowering beneath the weight of it.

WILLIAM

He'd given his workers a rest. They were gathered some distance from the newly built house, eating and drinking, some of them taking a short nap. They had been working hard all week to put the finishing touches to the house and William was glad to see them getting a break. They deserved it. William himself was standing before the house, studying it.

He'd designed it to be as exact to the previous house that had stood here, before the fire, as he could recall it. And now, staring at this familiar house, his heart ached. Other than the new wood, the outside looked just as it had before. William took a deep breath and entered the house.

The front room looked similar to what it used to be. The door to the kitchen to the right, the lord's chambers straight ahead, the door to the stairs leading to the upper level just left of that room. The fireplace on the left wall.

The room was empty. It didn't have the furnishings it used to have, no stools, no tables, no tapestries on the walls depicting the great acts of the Logan clan. William hadn't decided on how to furnish this home he was building for Allen. Did he try to recreate the home that used to be here, with all the same chairs and have the same tapestries spun for the walls? Or was it a new home that deserved new furnishings and new memories?

William avoided going into the kitchen, Florie's kitchen, and went upstairs instead. The study, the sleeping chambers— including Allen's old room. It was all as it used to be. The only thing that remained was furnishing the new house, and then he could go and find Allen, wherever he was now, and bring him home.

There were rumors that Allen of the Dale had been an outlaw with the great Robin Hood of England and lived in Nottingham even still. That was where William would go first when he went to find his old friend. The boy he'd known since he was born.

William could still vividly recall trying to keep Duncan calm the day Allen was born; Duncan had been convinced that a family curse would kill both his son and his wife.

William smiled to himself, remembering Allen as a wild toddler, throwing tantrums or playfully dragging his mother all about the house.

William absent-mindedly rubbed his thumb, recalling the time Allen had nearly bit it clean off.

In a flash, Allen was all grown up and marrying Eri, then having a son of his own.

And then the fire.

William shuddered. He'd been devastated to lose his family and had joined the Third Crusade to get away from the memories.

He'd never expected to come back to this place, and he was sure Allen would have similar objections. There were too many memories here, as evidenced by the fact that William still hadn't inspected the kitchen since it had been built the year before.

Florie's kitchen.

The woman he'd loved.

The woman he'd refused to pursue due to societal constraints.

Oh how he regretted that decision.

A servant and a knight; it just wasn't done. Yet it should have been. He should have married her. But he hadn't, and then she'd died in that fire and he was left with nothing but regrets.

William made his way downstairs but stopped abruptly when he entered the front room because a man was standing by the door. William wasn't sure if he was looking at a young Duncan or an old Allen, though he knew the latter was obviously the case as Duncan was both older than that young man in the doorway and also very dead.

"William?"

"Allen!"

William's heart leaped to his throat and he moved forward and embraced Allen. He hadn't seen the boy since before the Crusades. He wasn't a boy now.

"What brought you to Scotland?" William asked, stepping back and studying Allen. He looked remarkably like his father Duncan. That, in itself, made William tear up, but the memories shared with Allen himself and the joy at seeing him once more were what really had his eyes watering and his throat constricting.

"My family is being hunted by a mercenary hired by King John so we fled to Scotland."

"Your family?" William asked, surprised.

"Robin Hood and his gang, and my wife and two sons."

"You have a new wife?" William asked, surprised but also delighted. "I thought you might, but I have heard no clear reports, only rumors. And you never wrote."

"*You* never wrote!" Allen responded. "I thought you were dead!"

"I am sorry about that," William said. He hadn't realized his silence would lead Allen to believe he had died, though looking back, that seemed a rather obvious conclusion for Allen to come to.

"After the Crusades ended I wandered through various countries looking for purpose. I had intended to be killed on the Crusades, much as you had. It didn't work out that way, of course, and I wasn't about to kill myself so I tried to find another purpose. Eventually, almost before I realized what was happening, I found myself back here. I decided to rebuild your father's estate for you, if you'd have it. That has been the purpose that's been driving me for the last five or so years."

"I don't think I can live here," Allen replied, looking around the room. There were tears shimmering just behind his eyes.

"Your new family could give you good memories of this place," William suggested.

"I have good memories," Allen responded, his voice hoarse. "I have good memories of my parents, and Alice, and Eri, and baby Duncan…" Allen cleared his throat and turned away for a moment. "I have good memories. That's half the problem. Because they're gone."

"I know. It's overwhelming being here." William sighed heavily. "I half wish I had decided to build a different house on this spot, rather than the exact same one. At any rate, I will understand if you choose not to dwell here. But I do have something for you. It's back at the tavern now, where I've been living."

"What is it?"

"Your father's claymore. I had to get a new handle for it, but the sword itself wasn't destroyed in the fire."

Allen didn't respond, but tears sprang to his eyes once more.

"I found it when we were clearing away the rubble before we started building," William said. What he didn't say was how he had wept when he found it. He'd simply curled into a ball right there in the pile of rubble, hugging the giant sword to himself, and cried like he never had before, even more than when the fire had killed everyone.

He'd known Duncan's father and mother. He'd been a second father to Duncan himself, and then again to Duncan's son Allen. He'd been with Duncan from his birth to his death. Watched him grow up, watched him fall in love, marry, worry himself sick that he would never have healthy children because of the supposed Logan curse. Finding that sword had been like finding a piece of Duncan again. William had even been there when Duncan had his claymore commissioned, the first day he held it, the first time he wielded it.

"Thank you, William."

"You deserve to have it, Allen."

The claymore belonged to Duncan Logan's family. It was a Logan family heirloom now. It hadn't always been considered thus, as Duncan was the one who'd had it made. It wasn't a claymore that had been in the family for generations upon generations. But now it would be passed down through the years and be the inheritance of every Logan after Allen. That was, at least, Duncan's intention when he had it made, and certainly William's intention now.

William shook himself to rid himself of gravity. "Now, where is this new family of yours?"

"At the Holyrood Abbey," Allen said. "We've been staying there since we fled England."

"Who did you say was after you?"

"King John, to be honest. His hatred is at least understandable considering all we did to undermine his rebellion during Richard's reign. He hired a mercenary, Sir Hugh, to hunt us down and kill us."

"I've heard of Sir Hugh," William said thoughtfully. The man was renown in Scotland and England both. "He has made it a personal ambition to kill every outlaw in existence."

"So we've been told."

"He's from Scotland," William said. "You might not be safe here."

"We've thought of that, but so far he hasn't appeared to come looking for us. It's possible he doesn't know where we went."

"I hope that's true. At any rate, I want to meet your family. Let's go to Edinburgh, get your father's claymore, and then head to the abbey. The men I hired to build the house know what they're doing far better than I do. They don't need my supervision."

ALLEN

Allen watched his old friend walk over to the bed and kneel down, reaching under it. Old was an apt description. William looked ancient, though not quite as withered as Friar Roderick. The silver hair, the wrinkles, the translucent skin were all there. But he wasn't frail like Friar Roderick. He was still very much the William that Allen remembered from his youth.

William pulled the impressive sword out from under the bed. It had a new pommel as William had said it would, but it still had the Logan crest etched into it as the previous handle had. The blade was much longer than the broadsword that Allen currently carried, and he knew from past experience that it was much heavier. The claymore was very much a two handed sword. Allen had experimented with it as a child, usually without permission, but he had never wielded it in combat and wasn't sure he would be able to.

William stood and turned to him. "Allen…"

Allen reached for the sword of his father, taking it from William. As his hand closed around the leather pommel etched with the Logan crest, the memories of this sword—of his father using it, of stealing it to practice his own skills, of it hanging above the fireplace in their house for so many years—washed over Allen.

And more than the memories of the sword itself, the memories of his father enveloped him. His twinkling eyes, his superstitions, his laughter, his kindness, his fierceness in protecting his family, his fear of the Logan clan curse. This sword was Duncan Logan.

"Bear it well, Allen of the Dale."

William sounded so incredibly serious as he spoke that Allen looked up at his friend and actually laughed.

"And on that note," Allen shook his head. "Let me go introduce you to everyone at the abbey. Five of the gang are still missing, my wife among them."

The levity of the moment before vanished.

Ida was still missing. Allen's heart felt heavy. Where had his wife gone? Was she alright?

"I'm more than eager to meet your family, Allen," William said.

Allen nodded, strapping the massive claymore onto his back and leading William out of the tavern and in the direction of the Holyrood Abbey.

The only member of the gang who knew his story was his own wife, Ida. Therefore there was going to be some explanation needed when he introduced William to the rest of them.

Chapter 13

FAITH

Faith had gone for a walk in the woods behind the manor. It was a beautiful place, though perhaps would be more beautiful in spring or summer. It was autumn now, and many of the trees were either barren of their leaves or else a sad brown color. Still, several creeks bubbled cheerfully through the woods, and there were still birds and other small furry animals scurrying about the place to make it a pleasant afternoon walk. The air was crisp and cool, the chilly breeze hinting of the winter storms to come.

It was restful, and Faith felt content. Guy had been healing from his childhood trauma over the last weeks. He was happier than Faith had ever seen him, more relaxed, more content.

Faith followed one of the gurgling streams, enjoying the peaceful afternoon. It had been nearly two months since Sir Hugh had found the camp and sent them running. After the initial threat that first day, nothing had happened. They'd come to the Gisbourne estate, Guy had easily assumed control, and now they spent their days leisurely. Waiting for news either of Sir Hugh's movements, of King John's return to England from his war in France, or of the rest of the gang and their whereabouts.

That was the hardest part. Not knowing what had happened to all of their friends. Faith was worried about all of them, yet she knew her Lord would care for them. Her worry was for naught; God was in control.

Faith also knew she was more fortunate than others. She had her husband and her daughter. Ida had no news of her husband and her sons, and that must be tormenting her. Andrew as well had no idea what had become of his wife and son. Andrew, at least, had faith in God. Ida was not a believer. She was one of very few among the gang who did not know the Lord personally, and that must only be making her suffering all the worse. She had no Comforter such as Faith had.

In the months since they had come to Gisbourne estate, Guy had been working to gain his tenants trust, visiting every farm and village in his estate to greet them; taking them food, assuring them of his just leadership. He had also been working with Andrew to find ways to fortify the estate in the event that King John or Sir Hugh came calling.

Faith suddenly stopped walking. Ida was sitting on a fallen log near the stream only a few yards in front of her. She seemed lost in thought.

Faith slowly approached her.

"It's alright, Faith," Ida sighed, not looking at her. "You don't have to be afraid of me."

"I wasn't afraid," Faith laughed, sitting down beside Ida. "I didn't want to disturb you."

"Because you thought the lion might bite your head off."

"Not at all."

"Whatever."

Faith tried not to sigh audibly. Ida's disdain for her had been evident from the day that they met, and all these years hadn't erased it. Sometimes Faith thought they had gained a deeper level of friendship, but more often than not, Ida showed that Faith's mere existence was a nuisance to her.

It had been a new experience for Faith, being so despised. She was generally liked wherever she went, and even when she wasn't, it wasn't hard for her to win people over. But Ida had held onto her dislike for so many years now that it worried Faith. It also didn't make sense to Faith. She knew Ida looked at her as weak and afraid because she wasn't a fighter like the rest of the gang and that was the only thing Ida would admire. Yet the same could be said of Much, and Ida and Much shared a rich and meaningful friendship while Ida despised Faith. She didn't understand why Ida disliked her so and wondered if Ida even knew the reason herself.

"What were you thinking about before I interrupted your reverie?"

"Nothing."

"That's obviously not true," Faith said softly.

"I was thinking about my husband and my sons, and other things you wouldn't possibly understand because your family is right here. Safe."

"I can understand being worried, Ida," Faith said. "Most of our family is missing. We have no idea where they are or what happened to them. Did they make it to Scotland? Were they captured? Was anyone killed? My imagination can run as wild as yours when it comes to worrying about our family. And yes, I do have my husband and my daughter. I do realize I am not in quite the same position that you and Andrew are in. But I don't have perfect peace of mind, Ida."

To Faith's surprise, Ida smiled. She looked over at Faith for the first time since Faith had joined her, a light in her eyes.

215

"I didn't know little Faith had so much spirit," Ida grinned. "If you were like this more often, I might like you better."

"I'm not naturally vivacious."

"It isn't talking a lot that I want from you; just that you'd have backbone, like you just did."

Faith chuckled. "I do have a backbone. I have simply learned to be meek and peace-loving. To give over my own way in favor of someone else's. Unless what people want is wrong, sinful, I have learned not to put my own desires first but rather theirs."

"Lucy is that way too, but she isn't timid and afraid," Ida pointed out. "And Jane can be very generous to other people in that manner, but again...backbone."

"I'm not afraid, Ida. I don't know what has given you that impression over the years, but I'm not afraid. I will admit I can be shy or timid. But never afraid."

"If you say so."

"I do say so," Faith said gently. "I have no reason to fear anything. Whatever may come my way, I have a God who is so much bigger."

"Can I please not get a god-lecture from you? Lucy and Dusty preach enough as it is. And it doesn't help that everyone else in the gang seems to be falling under that spell."

"It isn't a spell," Faith laughed. "It's truth. Beautiful, remarkable, crazy, truth."

"That's nice for you, and the others…"

"But not for you?"

"First of all, my whole family was murdered. Why didn't your god stop that? Secondly, you preach of a savior...well why do I need one? I'm a good person."

Faith thought about that for a moment. "To your first question, I am sorry. Tragedy happens, and it happens because of the sin in the world. That was never how God intended the world to be. But He loved us enough to give us a beautiful, terrible, thing called free will. And because of that, men abuse each other and tragedy happens. It's sin, it isn't God."

"Couldn't he stop it?" Ida demanded.

"Technically speaking, is my God powerful enough to intervene? Yes. Why doesn't He? For a multitude of reasons, some of which I will never understand. For one thing, if He always dictated how our lives went, we wouldn't have free will. Is that what you would prefer? You seem pretty stuck on the idea of everyone having a backbone and making their own way in the world."

"Fair enough."

"And for another thing, sometimes the things in our lives can be used in wonderful ways to teach us, to grow us, or to reach other people, help other people in similar circumstances. We don't always understand His ways, but the one thing I can hold onto with certainty is that my God is good and He loves me. No matter what I go through, or if the world looks so bleak I can't see a way out of the mess. If I can't hear His voice or I feel abandoned or question why He isn't helping me the way I think He ought to, I can hold onto the fact that He is a good God. I might not be able to see how He works sometimes, but even when it looks like He isn't there I know for a fact that He is. He's good. He loves me. I can trust Him, regardless of my circumstances."

"I can't put that kind of faith in someone. It would be opening myself up to too much heartache. I am not that vulnerable; I refuse to be."

"But He won't break your heart, Ida. He's trustworthy."

"Maybe."

"Do you trust Allen?"

"Of course I do. What kind of a question is that?"

"You trust your husband, your human husband who makes mistakes and wrong choices. But you won't trust a God of perfection who never does wrong?"

"You make a compelling argument, Faith. But it's just not for me, okay. Leave it at that."

"I'll pray for you."

"Faith!"

"I will! Whether you like it or not," Faith smiled.

Ida shrugged. "Whatever. Can you just leave me in peace for now? Go do your praying somewhere else."

Faith squeezed Ida's hand and then stood. "I'll continue my walk, but I won't stop being your friend, Ida."

Ida rolled her eyes, and Faith continued on her way.

SIR HUGH

Robin and his gang had disappeared. When Sir Hugh's soldiers had left Nottingham in search of the outlaws after he'd arrived back at the castle with Isla, they'd found no trace of them. Not in Nottingham. Not in Sherwood Forest. They were gone.

That had been frustrating enough, but now it had been over a month and there had been no news of them.

Sir Hugh had been executing his soldiers left and right for their incompetence. The outlaws couldn't have simply disappeared. There was a trail to follow and until his men found that trail, Sir Hugh would continue to kill them. Not all of them, of course, or he'd have no one to go looking for the outlaws.

Sir Hugh had been sending letters to every person he knew in England asking them to be on the look-out and to send him word if they had any news of the whereabouts of Robin Hood and his gang. He'd expected to have an immediate reply. If not Robin's group, then one of the other groups of outlaws that had scattered after the initial attack on the outlaws' camp. How could so many people, with so many children, travel the world unseen? It shouldn't be possible! Someone should have seen something.

Sir Hugh was sitting at the desk in his room, his elbow on the table, head resting in the palm of his hand. On the desk before him were various responses from his contacts. No word. Haven't seen the outlaws. Try the North of England. Try the South of England. Try anywhere but here because we haven't seen them. All of the letters were some variation of that and it was making Sir Hugh's blood boil.

"Papa!"

Sir Hugh shook himself out of his gloom as Isla came bounding across the room.

"Lookie!" Isla held up a little doll made of strips of cloth, with beads for eyes.

"Where'd you get that?" Sir Hugh asked, pulling his sweet child into his lap.

219

"Bithiah."

The servant girl who watched Isla all day. Sir Hugh stroked his daughter's hair. He'd have to find a way to thank the girl...without actually thanking her. Maybe some extra payment, without explanation. That would work.

The Nottingham Fair had come and gone with no word on the whereabouts of Robin Hood and his outlaws. It was aggravating. The outlaws themselves needed to die because they were outlaws. And Robin Hood...well, Sir Hugh had special plans for that weasel for kidnapping Isla.

There was a knock on the door. Sir Hugh set Isla down and went to answer it. A servant stood before him, a letter in his hand.

Sir Hugh took the letter with a sigh, shutting the door in the servant's face. It was just going to be one more excuse as to why no one had seen the outlaws. Sir Hugh might just start murdering the men who sent him these useless letters if someone didn't have an answer for him soon.

Sir Hugh sank into his chair and sighed heavily. He turned over the letter to break the seal and paused. The seal was of Gordon, a nobleman who lived in Edinburgh. It was the first response from Scotland that Sir Hugh had received.

Sir Hugh broke the seal and quickly read the contents of the letter. A slow grin spread across his face.

Sir Hugh got to his feet, leaving the letter on the desk, and went and kissed his daughter. Then he marched out of the room in search of Sir Ralf. They had work to do. His army was depleted, so he'd have to borrow some of Sir Ralf's soldiers or round up men of his own. The latter seemed the better option because what he'd seen of Sir Ralf's soldiers wasn't anything to boast about. They were drunk and incompetent more often than not. If Sir Hugh's soldiers acted the way Sir Ralf's did, he'd probably kill them. Which was honestly the likeliest reason as to why his men didn't act that way.

GUY

Guy strapped on his boots, with some difficulty as little Lucy was pulling on the straps and trying to eat them. Once his boots were on, Guy pulled his daughter into his lap.

"What do you think you are doing, young lady?"

It was still relatively dark outside, as the sun was not quite risen. Faith was still slumbering in the bed in the middle of the room. Guy was sitting on a small bench at the end of the bed getting ready to leave. He was planning on visiting several of the villages within his estate today. He'd forgotten how much work went into running an estate this size. He hadn't realized it at the time, but he'd been incredibly lazy living in Nottingham all these years, doing very little of anything that would qualify as productive.

Lucy grabbed a lock of his black hair and tugged on it. "'Air!"

"Yes, that's my hair." Guy kissed her cheek. "You need to stay here, and behave yourself."

That wasn't asking a lot. Lucy rarely didn't behave. Guy was quite proud to have the most well behaved child in the gang...although how she'd turned out that way with him as a father, he had no idea.

Faith rolled over, sighed softly, and then sat up. "Bring her here, Guy."

Guy brought his daughter to his wife and then bent down and softly kissed them each on the cheek.

"I'll be gone most of the day."

"I know. I'll make sure there's a warm plate of food for you when you return this evening."

"What are you planning on doing today?" Guy asked.

"I am not sure. Although I might talk to Ida."

"Ida?"

"We had a lovely conversation the other day, about God. I think she might be ready to believe, Guy."

"That's good."

"Yes it is. We had such a good conversation...I think we're moving past the disdain and toward a real friendship."

"I'm glad, Faith."

"Go on, Guy. You've got work to do. I'll see you later."

"I love you."

"I love you, too."

Guy left his wife and daughter and traversed the many passages of his home until he came to the kitchen. He grabbed a bit of bread and cheese from the cook and then headed for the stables. As the sun was only just beginning to appear, the world was wrapped in the cold greyness of a winter's dawn.

Andrew was sitting on the fence of the pasture beside the barn waiting for him. He hopped down when Guy got close to him.

"Where to first?"

"I'm not sure, but we'll probably be heading west today."

The two of them entered the barn together and Andrew moved toward a stall to saddle a proud bay Guy had given him a few years back named Quest. Guy headed toward Shadow's stall and noticed that Ida was also in the barn.

"Good morning, Ida."

Ida ignored him and continued saddling her horse, Midnight.

But a moment later, as Guy was hefting his own saddle onto Shadow's back, Ida peeked her head into the stall with an amused grin on her face. "I had the strangest conversation with your wife the other day."

"Did you?"

Guy wondered if she was about to talk about God and wasn't sure he could handle it. Of all the people to lead someone to Christ, he was the last member of the gang who ought to be given that responsibility.

"She has very odd ideas, as most of you do, about many things. I think the strangest part of the whole encounter was that she seemed very satisfied with the way our conversation went."

Ida mounted her horse and sat, looking down at Guy, still with that amused expression on her face. "She seemed to be imagining we were actually friends by the time we were done talking. To be honest, Guy, you have the oddest little wife in all of England."

And with that, Ida trotted out of the stable.

Guy finished saddling his horse and he and Andrew set out toward one of the many villages on the Gisbourne estate. The sky was a mixture of oranges and pinks as the sun made its slow climb over the horizon.

"What on earth did Ida and Faith talk about?" Andrew asked as they trotted along.

"I have no idea, but they certainly came away from it with very different ideas of how it happened," Guy replied. "Faith was telling me this morning how wonderful her talk with Ida had been."

"One can only wonder what they discussed."

"I'm not sure, but I'm afraid it may have been about God."

"Afraid?"

"Ida is one of a very few of us left who doesn't believe. And Faith can be a little pushy with her...faith."

"I don't believe it. Faith is as quiet and gentle as they come."

"True. Yet even so, she doesn't listen well. She hears what she wants to hear and forces her own idea of how people should be responding to God onto them. Her direct approach was actually helpful in the strengthening of my own belief, but I am afraid that it would only push Ida further away."

IDA

Ida let Midnight have his way for the most part; she didn't have a destination, merely needed some space to think. She rode around Guy's great estate, following small dirt roads that led to little villages or lonely farms much like the one she and Allen lived on outside of Nottingham. Then she wound her way back around to the vast woods on the edge of Guys's estate. The entirety of those woods did not belong to Guy, but enough of it did that Ida felt safe getting lost in the trees.

She missed her husband. She was desperate to know that he was safe.

And she longed for her sons. She needed to feel them in her arms, hold them close.

Hot tears splashed down Ida's cheeks and Midnight shifted uncomfortably underneath her.

As much as she hated to admit it, and despite what she had told Guy, Ida wanted what Faith had. She was quietly confident in a way that Ida, in all her brashness, couldn't boast. And she was comforted, which Ida needed right now and couldn't have. She wanted to have the calming assurance that everything would be fine that Faith and most of the rest of the gang shared.

She didn't know where her husband was. Had he gone to Scotland? Had he died in the skirmish in Sherwood Forest?

Ida could feel her heart constricting, her hands beginning to tremble.

Her sons...were they dead, too?

Ida lost track of her surroundings as her vision blurred and she cried. The tears seemed never ending. Tears for her husband, her sons, her extended family that was out there somewhere, her own pain and loneliness.

Ida's vision was completely clouded by her tears; she was no longer directing Midnight. He didn't seem too troubled about it.

Ida angrily wiped the tears from her face after having wept for what felt like an eternity. She realized with a start that Midnight had led her back home; the stables were only a few yards in front of them and Midnight was plodding toward them slowly. Evening had fallen and Guy was just exiting the stable with Andrew, the two of them laughing over a shared joke as they made their way toward the house.

Ida slowed Midnight until she could enter the stable without Guy and Andrew witnessing her lack of composure.

Ida dismounted and got Midnight settled in his stall. Then she sat on a bale of hay and stared at her horse, not really seeing him. She was losing her confidence, her determination and she didn't have her family. She felt like everything that defined her had been stripped away and what was left was a sad little woman without purpose.

Ida took a few minutes to regain her composure, or at least a facade of it, before she entered the house. The last thing she needed was her three least favorite people of the gang asking her questions about tear-stained cheeks.

Chapter 14

ROBIN

Robin crossed his arms, unable to keep a grin from stretching across his face. He was sitting on top of the roughly-hewn table in Friar Roderick's common room. Much was sitting on the bench just behind him, his head in his hands.

Elinor was in labor in the room next door.

Another child for the gang to spoil.

Robin's grin stretched farther across his face.

He only had one child of his own; Marian. But he claimed all of his followers children as his own. He felt responsible for them because he was responsible for their parents' safety. Even during the years of peace between Richard's return and his death Robin had felt the need to look after his gang as they married and started families of their own, some of them going so far as to move away from Nottingham altogether.

Robin was aware of Will pacing the far wall, Allen leaning against another wall to his left. A glance at Much showed that his fingernails were cutting into his cheek, he was so tense.

Mary and Jane were entertaining the children in one of the sleeping chambers. Gilbert was standing in the doorway to the chapel just watching the goings on with an amused expression on his face. He was not invested in this new birth, and the way every member of the gang seemed to think the child was theirs amused him greatly.

Sir Henry was sitting at the table across from Much, conversing amiably with William—Allen's old friend—and Marcus. The three of them were also less concerned for the appearance of the child as the gang, although they cared a bit more than Gilbert did, Robin was sure.

Robin turned his focus to the most amusing part of the room. Mark, who was struggling to keep Little John from barging into another of the sleeping chambers.

The one where Lucy, Dusty, and Friar Roderick were assisting Elinor in her childbirth.

Mark was holding both of Little John's arms, standing in front of him and using the door behind him as leverage to push Little John backwards. It was an impressive feat for anyone to hold back Little John's mountainous girth and strength.

Will paused in pacing along the wall to chuckle at the sight. "Mark, I'd be careful. He'll break you before too long."

Robin glanced down to where Much was sitting again.

"Much!" Robin tapped his forehead. Much looked up surprised. "Elinor's going to be fine. Stop looking like that."

"Do you think we'll get a boy or girl?" Much asked.

"Yours was a girl," Mark panted, still holding Little John back from Elinor's door. "So this one will probably be a boy."

"Are you always like this?" Sir Henry laughed. "All of you acting like expectant fathers even when only one of you is having a baby?"

"Yes," Allen laughed. "We can't help it."

"I think we need another girl," Will said.

"We're exactly even on boys and girls right now," Robin commented. "So I don't have a preference either way."

Little John stepped back, giving Mark a rest, and turned to the group, grinning. "Don't forget this is *my* baby."

"Well if he or she turns out like my twins," Allen laughed, "you won't have to worry about anyone claiming your child. They won't want anything to do with them."

Much chuckled. "The twins aren't so bad, just...rambunctious."

"Insane," Will said. "Insane is a better word to describe the twins."

"We can't forget about Marian," Mark laughed. "She's as bad as the twins, or worse."

"In short," Robin said, "Just hope your son or daughter is more like little Lucy."

Shrieks of laughter came bursting out of the room where the children were being kept busy by Mary and Jane. Much grinned.

Robin felt content. Despite the fact that they had been chased from their homes, life was still good. They had so much to be thankful for.

The laughter of the children from one room was interrupted by moans from the other. Much sighed and put his head back into his hands.

Marcus gave Much a sympathetic look. Robin knew Marcus had lost all three children Lillian had given birth to. None of Robin Hood's gang had lost a child, but it was a common enough occurrence. Robin's grin faltered for a moment.

The moaning ceased and a sharp wail filled the air. Little John made another dash for the door and Mark, Will, and Gilbert darted forward and dragged him back again.

The wailing quieted a moment later.

Robin could tell Much was holding his breath.

There was a lot of bustling to be heard in that room with the new baby, and several voices crooning softly. The most distinct voice was that of Friar Roderick, raspy and creaky as he cooed at the new baby.

A minute later Lucy opened the door, her sleeves rolled up past her elbow and glistening with a thin layer of sweat, and waved at Little John, "Come on in! You've got a little girl!"

Little John disappeared into the room, Lucy closing the door behind him. A collective sigh of relief echoed in the common room, which then led to most of the men bursting into laughter.

Mary opened the door where the children were playing, little Mary in her arms. Edward and Marian darted out the minute the door opened and tackled each other, rolling under the table.

Mary moved toward the table. "We heard the baby...boy or girl?"

"Girl," Much replied.

Mary bent and kissed his forehead. "You can stop fretting now, dear husband."

Much grinned. "Fretting is my job, just as much as pacing is Will's role during birth. It wouldn't be a family birth if I didn't fret at least a little."

"That is very true," Mark laughed.

Robin hopped off the table and crept over to the door behind which Little John and Elinor were getting to know their new daughter. He put his ear close to the door and waited, grinning.

230

"Have they named her?" Will whispered, taking Robin's spot atop the table.

Robin shook his head, motioning for Will to be quiet, which made Sir Henry burst out laughing. Much chuckled along, watching Robin grimace in Sir Henry's direction.

Robin suddenly winked at the group waiting with bated breath and barely restrained laughter to hear what he had learned.

"Her name is Rachel...and Little John is *adorable*." Robin wrinkled his nose and rolled his eyes, laughing. "You all need to come hear this. I've never heard him sound so...*sweet*. In fact, I've never heard him say that many words at one time. He's quite vivacious at the moment."

There was a scramble as Will leaped off the table, and Allen and Mark sprinted for the door. There was a distinct thud as the three of them collided into the door as Robin dove for the table to stay out of their way.

Little John's voice came growling from within the room beyond, "If you don't mind your own business out there, I'm coming out!"

His threat, far from discouraging the animated group, sent them into howls of laughter. Mark rubbed a sore elbow that had been injured in the charge for the door and Allen mockingly bent to kiss it the way he might kiss his sons' minor injuries.

Robin grinned. "Alright, everyone. Behave. We'll get our chance to meet little Rachel soon enough."

GUY

It was a cold day. Guy had spent the morning walking the grounds with his steward and his head of militia, making plans. Now that he finally had the business of running his estate back under control, it was time to prepare for the possibility that King John or his cronies would eventually come calling. The estate needed to be fortified so it was easily defendable, the farmers and villagers needed to be prepared to stock food within the manor in case of siege and also be ready to fight at a moment's notice. Training for the serfs needed to begin so they would be capable of fighting off professional soldiers. There was so much to get done.

Now, however, Guy was taking a break. He'd come inside, his ears, nose, fingers, and toes completely numb from the cold, and found a fire to sit beside and warm himself. He had a mug of ale in his hand and he was watching the flames crackling in front of him with fascination. Fire was a curious thing. Always changing, shifting, and leaving destruction in its wake. And yet it was beautiful, and it also provided comfort on freezing days like today.

Andrew came and sat in a chair near Guy, reaching his hands toward the fire and shivering.

"What have you been up to?" Guy asked.

"Working with your blacksmith to get a supply of weapons created and ready in case of any war we might have to fight. I wish we were in Nottingham. That castle was defendable! This manor...we'll see."

"I know...but it is what it is…"

"It might be my imagination, but I also think it was warmer in Nottingham."

Guy laughed. "That is definitely just your imagination."

"Do you think we can make this place defensible...last out a siege or fight off an army?"

"I think we can, Andrew."

Andrew nodded. "And how likely do you think it is that King John will even come calling?"

"It would more likely be Sir Hugh who comes calling…"

"My question still applies," Andrew chuckled.

"I don't know, Andrew. I like to think it isn't that probable, considering how long we've been here already and nothing has happened. I believe we should prepare in case, either way."

"Better safe than sorry."

"Exactly."

"We have our work cut out for us, Guy, getting this place defendable and getting the villagers prepared for a fight. Most of them have never seen combat."

"Most of them can use a sword though," Guy said. "And besides, there is no fury like that of a man defending his own home and family."

Andrew nodded.

Guy truly hoped that such a sentiment proved true should Sir Hugh or King John come for them. He'd said it confidently enough, but even so, one could never be sure.

MARCUS

Tiny little Rachel was nearly a week old. She was constantly being passed around the group, everyone demanding a chance to hold her every few hours. Marcus would have thought she would be the most loved and spoiled child in all of England—and Scotland—except that every other child in the gang was also fighting for that position.

They were eating dinner—bread, cheese, and meat pies—and little Rachel was currently in frail Friar Roderick's arms. Marcus smiled at the tender expression on the old man's face.

"She's a perfect bairn," the old man crooned. "A bonnie wee lass."

"You aren't going to get an argument from me," Elinor laughed.

"I don't think anyone could deny her perfectness," Allen said around a mouthful of pie.

Marcus couldn't disagree with them. Yet his heart ached for his own child. To have a little bundle of perfectness to call his own, and hold close to his heart. The three he'd lost; a new one...any child to call his own.

Marcus glanced at his wife, seated beside him and calmly eating her food. She seemed undisturbed. But Lillian had been broken after they lost the first one. By the third she had resigned herself to never having a child live. Marcus hated that she had to resign herself to such a fate.

The sound of the abbey door slamming, and then footsteps hurrying through the chapel, had everyone crowded around the table looking up to see who it might be.

William came bursting through the door, breathing heavily. He leaned against the table for a moment to catch his breath before he straightened and exclaimed, "There's an army!"

"An army?" Robin asked. "What army? Where?"

"I was out at Allen's estate...er...the Logan estate...and I saw Sir Hugh and his army. They're headed this way. They've found you!"

"Robin?" Much turned to him, wide-eyed.

"We have to run," Robin said firmly.

"But where?" Mark asked. "Where do we go?"

"We need to leave," Dusty said. "We need to go abroad where he can't track us down."

"France?" Will suggested.

"The King is in France!" Jane objected.

"We'll head for Dover," Robin said. "And then figure it out. Go get whatever belongings you have with you. We leave immediately."

"Are you coming, William?" Allen asked.

"No, Allen. They don't know our connection, I won't be in danger. And the more of you there are, the slower you'll travel. Plus, I am getting too old for adventures. I am not sure I could handle the hardships."

"Let's get going," Robin interrupted before Allen could object. "Pack, and grab your children, and meet me outside the abbey."

Marcus followed Robin outside. The sun was low on the western horizon, pale and dull in the wintry sky. There was a sharp chill in the air, and Marcus crossed his arms to keep out the cold. "Robin…"

"We'll be alright, Marcus. We might have to keep running, but we'll be alright."

"I'm not going to the continent."

Robin studied him, his blue eyes concerned and confused.

"You're not coming? What do you mean?"

"If Sir Hugh follows you, as he likely will, I'll be safe going back to Nottingham. Lillian and I can return to our home. Don't argue with me, old friend. I'm going home."

Robin slowly nodded. "Hide in Edinburgh until Sir Hugh has passed through before heading for Nottingham. And be safe, Marcus."

Marcus clasped Robin's hand in an affectionate farewell. He truly wished he could fight injustice by his side as he used to, but he needed to keep Lillian out of this fight. "Good luck, Robin. God be with you."

"And you as well, my friend."

Marcus nodded. He waited for Lillian to exit the abbey and then led her down the street in search of a tavern to hole up in until the army had gone through the city. They hadn't gone far when William fell into step beside them.

"Come with me. I know Edinburgh better than you do, and the locals know me. They won't be as concerned with an Englishman hiding in their city if you're with me. We can hide together until it's safe to come out."

ROBIN

Robin had brought the horses from the stable up the street down to the abbey, and now he was counting heads. There weren't enough horses to go around, as one party had made their way to Scotland on foot. Robin glanced around at the group gathering outside the abbey, packs over shoulders, weapons strapped on, children being scooped up.

"We'll have to ride double," Robin said, swinging into the saddle of Hero, a roan from his own stables that Mary had been riding since the gang had left Nottingham.

"Double, plus children," Elinor commented.

"Which is more like triple," Allen added. "Or quadruple…"

"You get my point," Robin rolled his eyes, reaching a hand down to his wife. Lucy passed Marian to him and then mounted the horse behind him, wrapping her arms around his waist. Robin wished Arrow hadn't bolted back when the camp had first been attacked, or that he'd had the time to go looking for him. He missed his horse. None of the others he owned compared.

Unfortunately, even riding double with a child between them, there weren't quite enough horses to go around.

"I'll run," Gilbert said, shrugging. Then he scooped up little Edward and placed the small boy on his shoulders. "Are we ready?"

Robin checked over the group again, making sure everyone was there. Friar Roderick stood in the doorway of the abbey, leaning against the doorframe. "I'll be praying for ye."

"Thank you, Friar," Allen replied.

Robin took a deep breath. It was cold. He could just faintly see his own breath on the air. This was going to be a rough ride to Dover.

"Elinor, keep Rachel well covered," Robin instructed.

"Already on it, Robin," Elinor smiled over at him.

Robin nodded. "Alright. Let's do this."

"Where we go?" Marian asked as Robin urged his mount forward. She wrapped her tiny arms around his neck and peered up at him with those big brown eyes that looked just like her mother's.

"We're going on a trip."

Robin glanced behind to see the group falling into line, Gilbert jogging alongside with Edward giggling on his shoulders.

"Little John, Will, take up the rear," Robin ordered. They had children with them, but someone needed to guard their back if Sir Hugh's army caught up with them, children in their arms or not.

Lucy's arms around his waist tightened. "We'll be alright, Robin. God is still watching over us."

"I know. I'm just tired of running. And I'm still worried about the missing five members of our family."

"Guy, Andrew, and Ida are all perfectly capable of looking out for themselves and for the others in their care. Wherever they are, I'm sure they're fine."

"I hope you're right."

Chapter 15

SIR HUGH

He'd arrived with his army in Edinburgh, and following the directions given in the letter Gordon had sent him, he'd marched his men straight to the Holyrood Abbey. As Sir Hugh trotted forward on his grey stallion, Night, he took note of the trampled ground in front of the abbey. Maybe a dozen horses? Less?

"There's no need to stop," Sir Hugh said to his second in command. "They've already fled, and not too long ago. We follow their tracks. Find them. Kill them."

The number of tracks he could discern was worrisome. It wasn't enough to be the whole group of outlaws as Gordon had suggested it would be.

"Yes, sir," the rugged soldier responded to his order. His name was Torin and he was the best that Sir Hugh could find in both Scotland and England. They'd only been working together for a year or so. Sir Hugh usually worked alone, but there were times, like now, when he required a great number of followers. When he'd gotten the letter from King John asking for his aid in tracking down outlaws, he'd come straight to Torin's door asking for his expertise and his army.

Sir Hugh had almost sent him packing after the failed attempt at capturing Robin Hood and his gang in their own camp back in August. But he needed Torin and the army that followed him, at least until Robin Hood was dead. Most of his own men had been killed, of course, both by the outlaws and by Sir Hugh himself in his frustration. Yet Torin and Sir Hugh had managed to wrangle up enough men to replenish their army before setting out on this particular hunt.

It was a cold evening. The sun, pale and useless, was falling to the horizon to the west. The closer it got to that horizon, the more visible Sir Hugh's breathing became in the air in front of him. The same was true of the soldiers around him.

Sir Hugh pulled his velvet lined fur coat close about his arms and shoulders, sealing out the cold. He didn't care if he had to live in this weather for an eternity, as long as Robin Hood died before it was all said and done.

SIR HENRY

"Robin!" Little John was yelling from the back of the train of horses. Sir Henry glanced over his shoulder, trying not to drop young William whom he had in his arms. The little boy was facing forward, his hands clinging to the fabric of Allen's shirt in front of him, as much for warmth as for stability. His tiny hands were on either side of the giant claymore that was slung over Allen's back. The boy was fascinated with his father's sword and would sometimes loosen his tight grip on his father's shirt to caress the sheath and the pommel, though the latter was a stretch for his small arms to reach as it was high over Allen's shoulder.

"What is it, Little John?" Robin called back, not turning around.

"The army is closing in!"

"How many?" Robin asked, this time turning around in his saddle.

Sir Henry did the same, keeping his grip on William as he did so. From his peripheral he caught sight of Allen doing the same. There was a cloud of dust in the distance behind them.

"They're too far to tell," Will called to Robin.

"But likely hundreds," Little John finished for him.

Gilbert, running alongside the horses, moved closer to Allen's mount. "Can you carry another?"

Allen slowed his horse's steps and reached down to get his son Edward from Gilbert's shoulders. He kept his son in front of him, transferring the reins to one hand and wrapping his other arm around Edward's waist.

"What are you doing?" Sir Henry asked his friend after Gilbert had relieved himself of Edward.

"Someone has to hold them off," Gilbert grinned.

"An entire army?" Sir Henry stared at his friend in disbelief. Still...it was Gilbert.

Sir Henry sighed. "Allen, can you hold two?"

"What?"

Sir Henry leaned down to whisper in William's ear. "Don't let go of your father." Then he slipped off the back of the horse, hitting the ground and falling to his knees.

"That was graceful," Gilbert commented, holding out his hand to help him up.

"Thanks," Sir Henry rolled his eyes. "Now how do we hold off an army?"

"Very carefully."

The rest of the group had nearly passed by. Will slowed down as he passed the pair of them, giving them a concerned look.

"We'll be fine," Gilbert grinned. "We will meet you in Dover."

"It's an army," Will said, as if that should be reason enough to turn around.

Sir Henry knew Gilbert would never rationalize in that manner, and he couldn't leave his dual-wielding friend to do battle alone. Not on a scale this big. For the first time since he'd known Gilbert, it looked like his friend was going to bite off more than he could chew and Sir Henry couldn't let him do that alone.

"Go on," Gilbert waved Will off. "We're fine. We'll see you at Dover."

Will reluctantly galloped after the rest of the gang, after both he and Dusty gave them very concerned looks.

"Will we be fine?" Sir Henry asked, drawing his sword and watching the approaching army with some trepidation.

"I take a hundred, you take a hundred," Gilbert shrugged. "I've needed a real challenge for a while now."

"We're going to get caught, thrown in prison, and tortured for information."

"Probably. But we'll kill a lot of them before that, giving Robin and the rest of them a decent chance of getting away."

"I have known you my whole life; I have called you friend for many years. And I have never pegged you as a self-sacrificing type."

Gilbert laughed. "I have my moments. This is one of them."

The dust the army was kicking up was becoming more defined. Sir Henry could see helmets and shields now, and could definitely make out the fiery red hair of Sir Hugh at the front of the line.

The sun was dipping into the horizon to the west and the air was bitterly cold. Sir Henry took a deep breath and slowly released it, watching his breath materialize in front of him.

"How well do you suppose those soldiers fight in the dark?" Gilbert asked, drawing his two swords and swinging them around lazily as he watched the sun setting.

"We're about to find out."

The army was drawing even closer now. Sir Henry glanced behind him. Robin Hood and the rest of the gang were nowhere in sight. That much was good. If he and Gilbert could distract the army long enough, the gang might just get away.

Two men. An entire army.

This was not at all a good idea. But Gilbert could not be dissuaded, that much Sir Henry knew. And that was why he found himself preparing to almost single-handedly fight off an entire army on a bitterly cold winter's night in a lonely field in Scotland.

The army was close enough to make out the face of Sir Hugh and the soldiers surrounding him at the front of the line. They were slowing now, no longer galloping but still moving toward Sir Henry and Gilbert at a fast pace. Faster than Sir Henry was prepared for. He wasn't a fighter like Gilbert. Oh, he could use a sword as well as the next man, but he didn't relish a fight the way his friend did. And the odds they were now facing were seeping any remaining joy from the prospect of fighting, that may have been hiding in his heart and mind, out of him.

This was not going to end well.

The army had just about reached them. The setting sun was casting a strange light on the scene that was unfolding. Sir Henry took one last deep breath. Sir Hugh had motioned for his soldiers to surround them, and now the horses were moving to both sides of them. Gilbert took a cocky step to his left so that he and Sir Henry were back to back.

"Just kill as many as you can and I'll take the rest," Gilbert said cheerfully.

Sir Henry knew his friend well enough to know he was faking his confidence right now. There was no way to win this fight. Sir Henry resigned himself to a life in prison...at least until Robin Hood and the rest of them got free of Sir Hugh and found a way to come back and rescue him and Gilbert.

And being stuck in a cell with Gilbert wouldn't be the worst thing in the world. At the very least Gilbert would be entertaining enough that he wouldn't be bored.

Sir Hugh and his cavalry stopped a few feet from Sir Henry and Gilbert on all sides. Sir Hugh smirked, studying them. "Brave, but stupid. Kill them."

The soldiers came trotting forward, weapons drawn.

Sir Henry ducked under a spear and simultaneously sidestepped a sword, all the while swinging his sword forward and slicing off the forelegs of the two horses in front of him. The horses both crashed forward with screams, sending the soldiers toppling to the ground at Sir Henry's feet. He stomped on one of the soldier's hands to keep him from picking up his sword, and cut off the head of the other. Then he killed the soldier whose hand was pinned under his foot.

Two swords came swinging towards his head from opposite sides and he ducked under them, only to get a spear thrust into his shoulder. Pain shot through him, but Sir Henry tried to ignore it.

He swung his sword in quick succession, right, left, right, chopping off as many arms, legs, and heads of men and horses as he could. Whatever was in reach. Horses and men began to pile up around him, forcing him and Gilbert a few feet apart simply because there wasn't enough space to stand side by side among the corpses.

A stray soldier's sword found Sir Henry's thigh, and he fell to his knees. Three swords came for his head but he fell to the ground and then rolled in a tight circle, knocking the legs out from under the three soldiers. He jumped up as quickly as he could, wincing from the pain in his thigh and trying to ignore the feeling of blood trickling down his leg.

It may have been a freezing winter night, but Sir Henry was sweating profusely, his blood pumping vigorously. Half of him felt hot from exertion and the other half was on fire with pain.

He killed the three soldiers he'd knocked over, but then there was another, and another, and another.

A stab to his back had him doubling over. The searing agony from the wound in his back, the one in his leg, and the one on his shoulder was almost more than he could take. The exhaustion from the prolonged fight had his legs wobbling and the sword in his hand feeling so heavy the tip of it dipped toward the ground.

It would be worth it, if Robin Hood and the rest of them got away.

That was the last thought Sir Henry had as cold steel sliced through his neck.

GILBERT

His arms ached and he was struggling to keep his swords steady as he fought off four of Sir Hugh's soldiers. He had a small cut on his cheek that was bleeding more than a small cut had a right to bleed. There was another cut on his arm that wasn't helping his cause of keeping his arms steady. As much as he hated to admit it, his legs were noodles, his arms were two giant boulders, and his movements were that of an old drunk man.

And then he saw Henry's head be chopped off by one of Sir Hugh's soldiers and his world went black.

He'd lost his vision for a moment but that didn't mean his brain wasn't working. He could still plan, even if he couldn't see.

First of all, every one of these soldiers was going to die slowly and painfully.

Secondly, that revenge was going to have to wait because Gilbert's head would be next if he didn't do something drastic.

He felt a sharp prick in his ribs and his vision cleared. The sun had gone down. The moon was shining on the cold night, highlighting the tight circle of horses and soldiers that surrounded the pile of corpses and Gilbert himself. The moon was casting strange shadows on his surroundings, but Gilbert ignored them. The soldier was pulling the sword that had pierced him back out of his chest and Gilbert made his decision.

He dropped limply to the ground.

Dead.

Except not really. That's just what the soldiers needed to believe.

Another excruciating stab wound blossomed on his back and Gilbert tried not to react.

"They're dead," someone said.

"Are you certain that Gilbert fellow is?" Sir Hugh asked sharply.

Gilbert held his breath. If they saw him breathing now, he'd be dead for sure. His lungs were already feeling a lack of air from the exertion of fighting combined with the cold, thin air of the winter night. Now as he tried not to breathe, his lungs burned like fire in protest.

Another sharp prick in his shoulder, though not deep.

"He's dead," the soldier said again.

"Then get back on a horse and let's follow Robin Hood," Sir Hugh said.

"What about the bodies?"

"Leave them."

The jingle of bits and reins, the creak of leather, the pounding of hooves, and similar sounds surrounded Gilbert. One horse stepped on his wrist, cracking a few bones and causing Gilbert to bite his lip so hard it split and began to bleed.

Soon enough, however, the sounds died away and Gilbert was left in silence.

Henry was dead.

Gilbert lay there, face in the dirt, body throbbing in so many different places, his blood staining the ground, wondering if there was any reason to get up and find help. He needed a physician, the sooner the better. But did he actually care? That was the question Gilbert tried to answer as he lay there in that corpse infested field. Did he care to live?

IDA

Ida had buried herself in the library. She didn't often spend her time reading, certainly didn't pursue that particular pastime the way Much or Lucy would. But it was freezing outside, so she couldn't take a ride on Midnight without great discomfort and she needed some way to distract her brain from the fact that she was impossibly lonely, scared, and desperately longing for her husband and her sons.

Ida was curled up in a large wooden chair with a sizable pillow to lessen its discomfort; the sort of chair that would never be found in Ida's little farmhouse. Not that she begrudged Guy his wealth. Robin was certainly the wealthiest of them all, and they all lived in comfort because of it. Robin would never let them live in poverty, and if he had his way they would all live in Nottingham castle with him. But none of them had yet taken him up on that offer. And anyway, it was entirely out of the question now.

Ida focused on the book in her lap, trying to pretend she was reading and not actually thinking about her family again. She pulled the wool blanket she had brought from her room closer about her. Even with the fire roaring in its grate not far away, this room was cold. That was the problem with stone buildings. Ida preferred her little wooden farmhouse in that regard. Not that it was particularly warm in winter months either, but at least it didn't trap the cold the way this stone manor did.

Faith entered the library and paused when she noticed Ida.

"I don't bite," Ida offered kindly.

Faith grinned. "We've been over this. I'm not afraid of you."

Ida was surprised by the tiny smile that tugged at her mouth. She was actually growing a bit fond of Faith, if truth be told. Which was strange, to be honest. All those years of living together in Sherwood Forest during Prince John's rebellion and the reign of the evil Sheriff who had murdered her mother and little brother, and Ida had never been able to get past her disgust of the sweet girl. Yet in the few short months they had been here at the Gisbourne estate, she was slowly growing to like her. Ida couldn't explain why. Though the fact that she had learned of Guy's history and was feeling enough compassion for him that she was almost ready to forgive him for his past mistakes might be aiding in her congenial feelings toward his wife, who had never harmed a soul and whose greatest crime was being too nice.

"What are you up to?" Faith asked, bringing a chair over to where Ida was sitting.

"What does it look like I'm up to?"

Faith rolled her eyes. "What I meant is that you aren't usually holed up in the library."

"Do you come here often?"

"Nearly every day."

"Hmm."

"You're unhappy, Ida."

"Not another god-talk, please!" Ida threw her hands into the air. She couldn't hear about Faith's contentment and reassurances one more time, not when her own heart was in such anguish.

Faith was quiet for a moment. "Alright. No talking about God...I'll try. Why are you unhappy?"

"Why?! My family is gone, who knows where? Allen could be dead. My sons could be dead..." Ida stopped, her throat tightening. She wasn't sure she could say another word without breaking down, which was the last thing she wanted to do in front of Faith.

Faith smiled gently. "It's alright."

"I'm...fine."

"I'll make a deal with you," Faith said softly. "I won't talk about God if you'll just let it out. Crying will be good for you, I promise."

Ida shook her head, but a tear slid down her cheek anyway. She angrily brushed it away.

"It will help to feel the emotions rather than burying them," Faith said gently. "Just embrace it, Ida. You're in pain, and that's acceptable. You have every reason to be feeling pain, so *feel* it."

Ida sighed. "Okay..."

Ida closed her eyes for a moment and let the despair of not knowing what had become of her family wash over her. The tears came fast and hard, splashing hotly down her cheek. Faith moved closer and wrapped her arms around her shoulders. Ida let herself rest in Faith's arms and simply wept.

Allen was gone. Her sons were gone. She didn't know if they were alive or dead; didn't know if they were safe or still being hunted. She didn't know if she would ever see them again.

Ida's heart ached. Her eyes burned as the tears poured, and her hands were shaking in her lap.

"That's it," Faith tightened her embrace. Ida leaned into her, drawing comfort from Faith's calm presence.

When her tears stopped, she took a deep breath, surprised to find that she actually did feel remarkably better. Still worried about her family, but not overwhelmed with despair or crushed by the darkness of what may have happened to them.

Ida took a deep breath. "Thank you, Faith."

"You're welcome."

Chapter 16

GILBERT

Gilbert had laid in the dirt for a while, letting the cold air seep into his bones. The air was cold. The ground was cold. Gilbert was cold. Whether he died from his wounds or from the cold itself, Gilbert wouldn't care. He simply didn't care at all, that was the problem. In the end, though, he had to get up. Robin Hood still needed saving. Henry would have gotten up, so Gilbert got up.

He had no choice. Henry had stayed for him, died for him; it was his fault. And more than that, Henry had died to save Robin Hood and his family. They still needed saving, so Gilbert had to finish what Henry started, he simply had to.

He struggled to his feet, and then was overwhelmed with excruciating pain, doubled over, and threw up. After that he dragged himself toward Edinburgh.

He was on his hands and knees, dragging himself forward. Every inch was excruciatingly painful. The rocks and twigs along the ground cut into his flesh, the wounds he'd received during the fighting had numbed with the cold but now that he was moving again they were burning with unquenchable fire.

He struggled to his feet, gasping for breath, and stumbled two or three steps forward before collapsing to the ground again, his face smacking into the frozen ground with a crack.

Gilbert grimaced. He'd never been brought this low before.

Of course, he'd never attempted to take down an entire army before either.

If Robin Hood survived it might, maybe, be worth it. His own wounds, at least. Henry dying was something he couldn't reconcile himself to, even if he did end up saving Robin Hood and his family in the end.

Gilbert dragged himself all the way to Edinburgh, half crawling, half walking, stumbling every time he stood up.

He made his way to the tavern where William had been staying, in pain, out of breath, and bleeding.

As he stumbled through the door, every head in the common room turned towards him. He ignored them and struggled across the room to the stairs, leaving a muddy, bloody, trail behind him.

As he started up the stairs, he felt hands on his shoulders, pulling him back and he struggled against them. He had to get to William.

"Gilbert."

Gilbert turned to see William and Marcus, both wide-eyed, standing behind him. Somehow he hadn't seen them when he entered, but then, he had been ignoring the people gathered in the common room.

"You need a physician," William said, looking over Gilbert's many wounds with a look of horror.

"What happened?" Marcus asked

"We killed...a few...I don't know..." Gilbert tried to clear his brain. "Sir Henry is dead. Robin Hood and the others got away."

"Come on, you need medical attention," William said. "You can tell us the story later."

William took him to a physician he knew and Gilbert spent a day there.

Only a day.

Then he limped out of the physician's house, insisting he was fine, and went back to that corpse infested field. William and Marcus went with him, worried he wasn't as fine as he insisted.

"I need to bury Henry."

"Let us help," William said.

William fetched a wagon from Edinburgh and they loaded Sir Henry onto it, and then took him to the Logan home that William was rebuilding and buried him there.

"What's next?" William asked, leaning on a shovel over the fresh mound of dirt. It hadn't been easy digging a hole in that frozen solid ground.

"I have to find Robin Hood," Gilbert said firmly.

"Then I guess this is farewell," William said. "You're welcome to stay as long as you need, Gilbert—you need rest. And I can provide any provision you need for your journey."

"And I don't need rest," Gilbert said, ignoring the pain in every corner of his body that said otherwise. "I am going to find Robin Hood before Sir Hugh does."

"Well, I'll help you pack," William said.

"Lillian can probably help prepare provisions for your journey," Marcus said.

William studied Gilbert a moment longer, "I'm not sure you should be going anywhere."

"Don't even try to stop me," Gilbert growled.

"I won't," William said quietly. "But you are in no state to travel, much less fight Sir Hugh. You must know that."

"I know nothing of the sort. If I never come back this way, it was nice meeting you, William. If you don't mind, I'm going to prepare for my journey now. I'll be out of here before nightfall. I have a mercenary to catch and kill."

JANE

They'd galloped across Scotland and England all the way to Dover. They'd had to stop a few times over the last week, spending their nights in various inns along the way. There hadn't been any sign of Sir Hugh and his army, but Robin was sure they were right behind them so the gang had hurried to get to Dover. Jane hadn't slept well at all during their trip due to worry, and she was sure the rest of the gang was equally sleepless.

They were in Dover now, staying at an inn right on the harbor. Jane could see the docks from her window. Robin had left that morning with the intent of finding them berths on a ship to take them across the channel. Where they went after they made it across was anyone's guess.

Robin had gone alone so as not to attract attention. Jane could see him from her window; he was quite a ways down the dock, somewhat obscured by distance, sailors doing various tasks, bystanders milling about, and of course the stacks of barrels and crates scattered across the docks, but she could see him.

The man Robin was talking to was the fourth captain Jane had seen him converse with that morning. This one was tall, broad-chested, very muscular—at least from what she could tell from this distance—and had yellow hair.

Hearing a giggle behind her, Jane turned from the window and surveyed the room. It was a small room, with a bench under the window—where she was sitting—a small bed and one little table. The wooden walls were bare of any decoration, though there was a small fireplace in one wall. Jane was glad of it, for the winter days were cold and the nights even more so. Richard was playing with a small wooden toy Mark had carved for him some time ago.

He seemed content, so Jane turned back to the window to watch Robin. She knew most of the group had gathered down in the common room to await his return but he wasn't visible from downstairs, so she remained where she was in order to watch.

He had been talking to this yellow-haired captain longer than he had with the other three captains, so it was possible he was making progress.

As she watched, the captain shook hands with Robin and then Robin came heading back in the direction of the inn.

Jane moved from the window to scoop up Richard. "Come on, little one. Let's go join the others and see what Robin has to say."

She found Will, Dusty, Little John, and Elinor, with their respective children, in the common room along with Mark and Allen.

"Where are the twins?" Jane asked, sitting down beside Allen at the table where the group was gathered. Most of the rest of the tables in the room were empty, though there were two or three other people at various places around the room eating breakfast.

"The twins and Marian need to get some of their energy out," Allen said. "Mary and Lucy took the children up to Lucy and Robin's room and Much chose to go with them."

Jane laughed. The twins and Marian always needed to get more energy out.

"Robin is headed back this way," Jane said. "I think he may have found a ship."

It wasn't long before Robin entered the inn and headed for their table. "Where's my wife? And Mary and Much?"

"In your room," Mark said. "Do we have a ship?"

"We have a ship to cross the channel. *The Rose*. Is everyone packed?"

"We don't exactly have a lot to pack," Jane said.

"If everyone is ready, we can board the boat now. It'll leave in a few hours."

The group soon dispersed to collect their meager belongings and make sure they had their children. Soon the whole group was walking down the docks toward *The Rose*.

"The last time I crossed the channel was on *The Barbara*," Jane heard Much say softly behind her. She glanced back and saw he was talking to his wife Mary. "At least, leaving England. We weren't on *The Barbara* when we came home again."

"That was during the Crusades, right?" Mary asked.

"Yes. That seems an age ago now."

"I wish I had been allowed to go on the Crusades but...being a girl..." Mary shrugged. 'I should have taken my cue from Dusty and pretended to be a boy."

Jane kept walking, following Robin toward *The Rose*, but she listened with interest to the conversation behind her.

"Dusty didn't have a choice. Saladin and his army ransacked her city. It was become a boy and fight in the army or be a girl and be raped and killed."

"That's a pleasant picture you just painted, husband dear."

"Sorry."

Jane smiled. She could almost hear Much's blush in the tone of his voice, but she didn't turn back around to see it.

The wind picked up a little, and Jane pulled Richard closer to her. "We're almost to the boat, little one."

"Robin!" Mark's sharp cry cut through the air. Jane turned toward him, as did most of the gang.

"What is it?" Robin asked from the head of the group.

Mark was pointing down the docks, behind them.

Jane scanned the area, wondering what had caught his attention. And then she saw it.

Fiery red hair.

For a moment her heart stopped beating, and then it began to pound furiously, as though it wanted to break right out of her chest.

Sir Hugh was on the docks, with a contingent of soldiers. He was looking for something, which was evident by the way he looked around the docks, leaning around every stack of crates or barrels to see clearer. Jane knew exactly what he was looking for: them. As she watched, he stopped a passing sailor and speaking to him, presumably asking if he'd seen Robin Hood and his gang of outlaws.

"When did you say the boat was leaving?" Lucy asked her husband, holding Marian close to her chest.

"Not for a few hours."

"We need to get on board before he spots us," Little John said.

"Don't run," Dusty ordered. "That will draw attention. Just walk."

And so they walked.

Jane tried not to keep glancing over her shoulder, not wanting to look suspicious or draw attention to their group, but it was hard not to know where Sir Hugh was or if he'd spotted them yet. Jane felt like her very breathing alone was loud enough to echo across the docks and draw his attention. Her palms began to sweat and she shifted Richard in her arms repeatedly, afraid she might drop him.

It was an excruciating walk and Jane thought it lasted all day. However, it did eventually end.

They had reached *The Rose*. Robin had a word with the stern-looking captain and then they began their ascent up the gangplank. There was a cold breeze that whipped the sail about above them, along with the sails of the other boats in the harbor, and caused the water below the gangplank to churn.

Jane did her best to ignore the water as she boarded the boat. She wasn't afraid of water, but it was crashing against the docks and the boats in the harbor in such a rough fashion it concerned her. She might have spared a moment to worry about how that water was going to affect their journey across the channel but all her worrying energies were focused on Sir Hugh at the moment. Had he seen them yet? What would they do once he did find them? She ought to say 'if' he found them, but considering how many places he'd tracked them down so far, Jane had little doubt he was going to find them now when he was only a few yards away.

Once they were on board, the captain addressed them as a group. "Stay low. You don't want to be seen. Maybe you should go below deck until we set sail. I'll try to keep Sir Hugh away. And while I'm at it, I'll see if we can't speed things up and set sail sooner than planned."

The captain left the ship then, and the group stared at Robin, wide eyed and terrified.

"You heard the man, we go below deck," Robin said.

Jane followed the rest of the group as they made their way toward the ladder that would lead them below deck and out of view of prying eyes such as Sir Hugh's. Jane looked out across the docks to see where Sir Hugh was at that moment, but couldn't find his red head.

She had to focus intently on going down each rung of the ladder without slipping because of her sweaty hands, not to mention she was still holding Richard.

Once they were all below deck, Jane looked around. Underneath the deck was a long, open room with benches and stowed oars that weren't currently in use. At the far end of the open space was a room, the door of which stood open. Mary could see crates and barrels in that room and assumed it was full of supplies. Robin led them in the opposite direction, toward the stern of the boat, where three doors led into rooms of similar size and all similarly accommodated. Robin took them into one of the rooms which had a dozen or more hammocks hanging from the ceiling.

Robin glanced around, sighing. "Welcome home, my friends. Everyone stay in this room and don't leave it unless I tell you to. Mark, Lucy, you're coming with me and we'll keep an eye on Sir Hugh from the deck."

"Be safe!" Elinor said, throwing her arms around Lucy for a moment.

Robin, Mark, and Lucy all three made sure they had their weapons on them—swords, daggers, bows and arrows—before they went above deck.

As they were preparing to leave, Robin paused, studying the group around him with a concerned expression, one that seemed very fatherly to Jane.

"Just wait here. We'll be back."

Little John, with little Rachel in one arm, put his other arm around Elinor's waist and pulled her close to his side. "Go on, Robin. We'll be fine here. And if anyone comes for us, we'll deal with them."

As Robin, Lucy, and Mark headed back on deck, Will closed the door to their room. "Little John, Dusty, you're with me. Here by the door. Anyone tries to get in, we stop them. The rest of you, scoot back there to the back of the room. And try to keep the little ones as quiet as possible."

"What is it?" John asked, staring at his father.

Will dropped to his knees and hugged his small son. "It's alright, John. We're going to be fine. You go sit with Allen, okay?"

Jane moved to the back of the room, against the wall, with Mary, Much, Elinor, and Allen. Allen had his boys in his lap, his arms wrapped protectively around them. Elinor took tiny Rachel from her husband and sank into a hammock on the back wall. Mary hugged little Daniyah, and her husband had their little daughter still in his arms. Most of the children were whimpering, confused about what was happening but knowing that their parents were very worried.

Jane tugged John to sit down beside her, and held Richard close. She watched Will draw his sword and lean against the wall by the door, ready for anything.

Little John simply stood directly in front of the door. If anyone even tried to open it, he'd just hold it shut. They'd be safe as long as Little John had strength or the enemy didn't have an axe.

Dusty sat by the door, her sword in her lap, her head lowered. Jane knew she was probably praying. Something they should all be doing.

The boat was creaky, and rocked gently in the harbor. Jane leaned her head against the wall and closed her eyes. She could hear voices above deck; sailors calling to one another, giving orders. What she didn't hear were screams, or Sir Hugh shouting. She began to pray for their safety, but was distracted by every little creak of the boat or new voice shouting above deck. Jane had never been so terrified in her life. Even running from the initial attack in Sherwood Forest hadn't scared her this much. It was hard to focus on praying when she was so scared. She knew in her heart of hearts that God would take care of them, she knew He was strong enough and powerful enough to see them through anything. He would protect, comfort, heal. Whatever they needed. She knew that. But somehow, she was still terrified.

"Do you think he'll find us?" Jane asked, her voice wavering slightly.

"Let's hope not," Elinor replied, pulling little Rachel closer to herself.

Jane listened to the whimpering of the children around her and tried not to join in.

MARK

Mark followed Robin and Lucy above deck. They ducked low and crept over to the edge of the boat. The wind felt like it was made of tiny glass needles and Mark's eyes began to water because of it. He hated winter. The three of them crouched against the railing, trying to stay hidden though unsure whether or not they were succeeding, and Mark waited for orders.

They had to get out of this situation. After everything this family had been through, they simply had to survive this. The simple fact that they had been through so much ought to be enough to reassure Mark that they would get through this as well.

Mark's heart was beating loudly in his ears and his breathing was heavy, materializing in the cold air in front of him. Every time he took a breath, he winced at the sound. Not that simple breathing would be enough to attract Sir Hugh, but terrified minds rarely think rationally.

Robin lifted his head just enough to see over the rail to the docks.

"Where is Sir Hugh?" Mark asked.

"Two boats down. He's talking to a sailor who is pointing this way."

Lucy pulled her bow off of her back and fingered an arrow. "Tell me when, and I'll maim Sir Hugh. That will slow him down enough for us to get across the channel."

"He'd chase us even if you shot him full of arrows," Mark said. "Killing him is the only way to stop him."

Lucy shot him a surprised look. "We're not killing anyone."

Normally Mark would agree with her, but their entire family was under threat right now. Their mere survival might depend upon killing Sir Hugh. Besides, they'd been killing a lot of soldiers throughout this journey...although, now that he thought about it, Lucy had probably only been wounding them because that was just how she did things.

The sailors around the deck and up the rigging were moving at a much faster pace than they had been when the group had boarded *The Rose*. Apparently the captain had meant what he said about setting sail as quickly as he could, for which Mark was immensely grateful. Setting sail might be the only thing that saved them from Sir High today.

As the three of them crouched there by the edge of the boat, Mark heard the familiar clip-clop of horses. Their hooves were slapping wood and Mark soon realized that the gang's horses were being led up the gangplank by a servant from the inn they'd stayed at, as well as a few sailors.

Mark glanced toward the sun, pale and cold and not doing much in regard to lighting the world and nothing in regard to heating it.

The desperation in his heart to simply survive, to get out of this mess, was growing.

The sailors were moving to stow the horses down below and they were protesting loudly.

"Where is Sir Hugh now?" Mark asked Robin, unsure if he actually wanted to know the answer to his question.

"Moving this way. The captain is speaking to him now."

"We're doomed," Mark sighed.

"We're not doomed," Lucy said. "Simply in dire straights. But we've survived worse before. We'll be fine. Just you wait and see."

"You have to kill him, Lucy. You have to kill him."

Lucy stared at Mark, but didn't say anything.

"You have to."

Lucy glanced toward her husband.

"You don't have to do anything yet," Robin said. "The captain might be able to get Sir Hugh to leave."

There was a tense moment, where Robin watched the proceedings on the docks and Mark hoped Lucy would give in and shoot Sir Hugh.

"The captain is coming this way!" Robin hissed. "Sir Hugh is following. He looks angry. And the captain looks worried."

Robin's voice was drowned out by the captain bellowing, "Prepare to set sail! Weigh anchor!"

"Sir Hugh isn't buying the innocent act," Robin sighed.

Sailors ran forward to remove the gangplank, and Sir Hugh's voice could be heard shouting at them to stop or be killed.

"Let's move, you sea dogs!" the captain roared.

Lucy rose up and raised her bow. Mark watched, hoping she'd kill Sir Hugh and be done with it.

Sir Hugh caught sight of her. Lucy and Sir Hugh stared at each other for a long moment. Neither speaking. The sounds of sailors working, shouting, throwing ropes, and running along the deck still filled the air. Mark held his breath.

Lucy let her arrow fly.

It pierced Sir Hugh's right side and he winced and doubled over.

"You didn't kill him," Mark hissed.

"No, I didn't."

The ship began to move. *The Rose* was underway.

DUSTY

Dusty felt the ship begin to move and ended her desperate praying with a heart-felt thank you. She looked up, making eye contact with her husband.

"I believe we're safe for now," Dusty said.

Will nodded. "I'll go check."

Will left the room and Dusty glanced around at the rest of her companions. Little John still looked ready for a fight. Most of the children were crying and being comforted by terrified adults.

Dusty got to her feet and collected her daughter from Mary, pulling the weeping girl into a tight hug. "Daniyah...listen to me. It's okay. I'm right here. You're safe, little one. And God is always watching out for us."

Daniyah buried her head in Dusty's shoulder and continued to cry so Dusty simply held her, crooning softly to soothe her. Dusty's shoulder was soon soaked with Daniyah's tears.

"Are we out of danger?" Much asked.

"We probably won't be completely out of danger until King John is dead," Elinor replied. "He'll simply keep sending people to hunt us down and kill us. We'll never be safe while he's alive."

"Where will we go?" Much asked. "Are we simply going to keep running or will we find a place to hide away somewhere?"

"That will be Robin's decision to make," Jane said.

Dusty had little fear. Robin had always led them well. And even more than that, God had never yet let them down. Even when tragedy struck, He watched over them and saw them through. They would be alright, no matter where they ended up.

ROBIN

Robin watched the shore of England fading away on the distant horizon. He thought he could still see the red hair of Sir Hugh, but that was probably just in his head. The air was bitterly cold, the wind biting. If Robin were to describe the weather, he'd say it was a wretched day. Yet they were free, at least for now. Until Sir Hugh followed them, as he was likely to do.

Their journey was far from over.

Lucy leaned against the rail beside him. "Are you alright?"

"Just thinking...I still have a lot of people to protect from monsters," Robin sighed. "At what point are we going to be allowed to live our lives in peace?"

Lucy nodded sympathetically, leaning into him for both warmth and comfort. After a moment she smiled. "Where would be the fun in a peaceful life, Robin?"

Robin chuckled, but there was little mirth in his laughter. "I'm ready to be done with all this...running and fighting and never settling down. I'm done."

Lucy nodded. "Me, too."

"Do you suppose the others are alright? Guy, and Andrew, and Ida?"

Lucy sighed. "I like to think so. They are all capable of taking care of themselves. And I know I don't need to worry because God is watching over them, wherever they are. But where could they have gone, Robin? Why didn't they show up in Edinburgh?"

"I don't know...it worries me."

"It worries me, too. They could be anywhere! What if they showed up after we left?"

"We can't play the 'what-if' game," Robin sighed. "We have too much at stake in the present."

The two of them watched as England faded out of view.

"Where to?"

"I don't know, Lucy. I don't know where we go next. But I do know one thing…"

Lucy studied her husband and nodded slowly. "This isn't over."

SIR HUGH

Sir Hugh sat on a crate at the edge of the docks, watching the ship that held that blasted Robin Hood and his rag-tag crew sail away from England. He'd find them. No matter where in the world they ran, he would find them. King John had paid him to do a job and he would do it. Yet it wasn't for King John or the money that he was now working. It was for himself and for Isla. Robin Hood would die in the end, whether King John paid him or not. Sir Hugh didn't care how far he had to travel to find him, or how many years it took to track him down and kill him, he was going to do it and he would succeed.

One of his soldiers had pulled out the arrow Robin Hood's pathetic wife had shot him with and was now tending to his wound. It was painful but not enough to make him an invalid. He'd gather the bulk of his men, get on a ship, and follow Robin Hood and his sad little group of friends to the continent and beyond. Wherever they went, Sir Hugh would follow.

A servant from the inn where Sir Hugh had put up for the night, a young lad, came running up to him.

"A letter came for you, sir," the boy said. His eyes weren't on Sir Hugh's face as he held out the sealed letter. On the contrary, the boy couldn't take his eyes off of Sir Hugh's wound. He watched the blood trickling down Sir Hugh's side and running over the soldier's hands as he tried to bind it up with wide eyes, unable to pull his gaze away.

Sir Hugh took the letter and cuffed the boy's shoulder. "First wound you've ever seen? Get out of here. Don't you have work to do?"

The boy blushed, ducked his head, and turned back the way he'd come.

Sir Hugh angrily opened the letter as he watched *The Rose* sailing out of the harbor. Robin Hood was getting away. But Sir Hugh intended to find him and kill him. And he'd do it slowly, oh so very slowly. Robin Hood needed to suffer for taking Isla from him, even if it had only been for a day.

Sir Hugh glanced down at the contents of the letter. And a slow grin spread across his face.

Robin Hood could wait. Sir Hugh would hunt him down no matter where he went. There was something closer to home now. Something that would wound Robin Hood even though he was sailing far away, where he thought he was out of reach.

The rest of the gang, numbering no more than three or four people, had been found. Sir Guy of Gisbourne had apparently returned to his childhood home. Well, that's where Sir Hugh was going now. He'd go kill Sir Guy and the few people he had with him, and then he'd chase down Robin Hood.

In the end, all the outlaws would die.

Acknowledgments:

Publishing a book doesn't happen single-handedly, and I'm very grateful for everyone who takes part in this process with me!

Rebekah—writing this book alongside you for NaNoWriMo back in 2017 remains my favorite book writing experience in the history of my time as an author. I could never thank you enough for all of your support and encouragement (and ire over Robin's stupid decisions).

My beta readers—Jonathan, Josiah, Scotland—all of your feedback was greatly appreciated. Also Candace for agreeing last minute to be a part of this process and giving me helpful feedback. Plus agreeing to the livestream cosplay for release day! You are the best!

My editors—Sarah and Elizabeth—I couldn't have published this book without you. Thanks for finding my mistakes.

My cover artist—Mandi Lynn—you are remarkable! I've never been more in love with a cover.

Jesus—you remain the inspiration for my stories and my purpose for writing.

And finally, a note to my readers:

If you made it to the end of the book, thanks! I hope you enjoyed it. And don't worry, book two will be coming soon. If you have any questions, comments, etc, feel free to email me at

mandi@mandigrace.org

If you want to read more books by me you can find them at my website mandigrace.org, and you can find me on Facebook, Instagram, and YouTube.